"I'm not here to comfort you. I'm here to keep you alive."

His breath whispered across her cheek.

"I didn't realize you'd volunteered to be my bodyguard." Erin fought the impulse to turn and touch her lips to his.

"I guess I have, by default." Joseph shifted away. Perhaps he was battling the same urge, she thought. "There's a positive side to my being on leave. Since I won't have to work, there's no danger of leaving you here alone."

"Does that mean I can stay?" Erin asked, elated. Then guiltily, she added, "But I'm putting you out of your bed. Once I meet with Stanley, I should be able to move somewhere else."

"If you like, I can put you in touch with a top-level security service." He fingered a loose strand of her hair. "Or you can stay, if you prefer."

She did prefer. Very much. "Yes. I'd rather be with you."

Dear Harlequin Intrigue Reader,

To chase away those end-of-summer blues, we have an explosive lineup that's guaranteed to please!

Joanna Wayne leaves goosebumps with *A Father's Duty*, the third book in NEW ORLEANS CONFIDENTIAL. In this riveting conclusion, murder, mayhem…and mystique are unleashed in the Big Easy. And that's just the beginning! *Unauthorized Passion*, which marks the beginning of Amanda Stevens' new action-packed miniseries, MATCHMAKERS UNDERGROUND, features a lethally sexy lawman who takes a beautiful imposter into his protective custody. Look for *Just Past Midnight* by Ms. Stevens from Harlequin Books next month at your favorite retail outlet.

Danger and discord sweep through Antelope Flats when B.J. Daniels launches her western series, McCALLS' MONTANA. Will the town ever be the same after a fiery showdown between a man on a mission and *The Cowgirl in Question*? Next up, the second book in ECLIPSE, our new gothic-inspired promotion. *Midnight Island Sanctuary* by Susan Peterson—a spine-tingling "gaslight" mystery set in a remote coastal town—will pull you into a chilling riptide.

To wrap up this month's thrilling lineup, Amy J. Fetzer returns to Harlequin Intrigue to unravel a sinister black-market baby ring mystery in *Undercover Marriage*. And, finally, don't miss *The Stolen Bride* by Jacqueline Diamond— an edge-of-your-seat reunion romance about an amnesiac bride-in-jeopardy who is about to get a crash course in true love.

Enjoy!

Denise O'Sullivan
Senior Editor
Harlequin Intrigue

THE STOLEN BRIDE

JACQUELINE DIAMOND

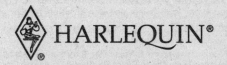

TORONTO • NEW YORK • LONDON
AMSTERDAM • PARIS • SYDNEY • HAMBURG
STOCKHOLM • ATHENS • TOKYO • MILAN • MADRID
PRAGUE • WARSAW • BUDAPEST • AUCKLAND

ISBN 0-373-22800-7

THE STOLEN BRIDE

This edition published by arrangement with Harlequin Books S.A.

® and TM are trademarks of the publisher. Trademarks indicated with ® are registered in the United States Patent and Trademark Office, the Canadian Trade Marks Office and in other countries.

www.eHarlequin.com

Printed in U.S.A.

ABOUT THE AUTHOR

The daughter of a doctor and an artist, Jacqueline Diamond claims to have researched the field of obstetrics primarily by developing a large range of complications during her pregnancies. She's also lucky enough to have a friend and neighbor who's an obstetrical nurse. The author of more than sixty novels, Jackie lives in Southern California with her husband and two sons. She loves to hear from readers. You can write to her at P.O. Box 1315, Brea, CA 92822, or by e-mail at JDiamondfriends@aol.com.

Books by Jacqueline Diamond

*The Babies of Doctors Circle

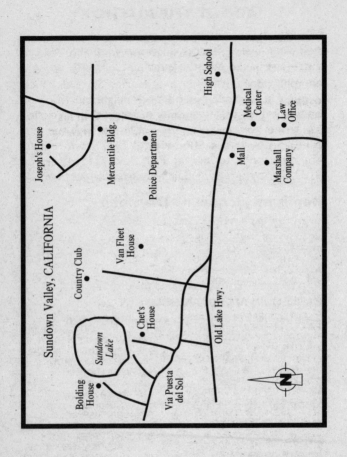

CAST OF CHARACTERS

Erin Marshall—An independent-minded heiress, she's blindsided by attacks, uncertain whom to trust—and has to take the gamble of a lifetime on her wedding day.

Joseph Lowery—A police officer living in the shadow of his father's disgrace, he offers Erin his protection. But he may be unintentionally drawing her into greater danger.

Chet Dever—He lied to Erin about their wedding plans. Was he also driving the van that ran her down?

Lance Bolding—Erin's stepfather may have designs on the Marshall Company, the firm she and her mother, Alice, inherited.

Brandy Schorr—Lance and Alice's new housekeeper is keeping secrets of her own.

Tina Norris—Erin's friend and maid of honor, she's tangled in a web of relationships.

Gene Norris—Tina's brother would do almost anything to realize his ambitions.

Edgar Norris—As chief of police, he blocks Joseph's investigation of Alice's near drowning and may have framed Joseph's father for murder.

Marie Flanders—Erin's missing aunt might be the victim of violence—or a part of it.

Rick Valdez—Is the detective sergeant playing a game of his own?

Stanley Rogers—Longtime accountant at the Marshall Company, he controls Erin's trust fund.

Todd Wilde—Eleven years ago, he may have gotten away with murder. Now he's back, but what does he want?

Chapter One

Erin Marshall first noticed the van a little before 6:00 p.m. She wasn't sure why it caught her eye, since there were still quite a few cars parked in the paved area roped off from the Healthy Children's Fund carnival, which she'd helped organize.

It wasn't just the peeling beige paint or dented bumper that drew her attention. Despite Orange County's reputation for affluence, the daylong carnival in the centrally located city of Tustin had drawn not only late-model cars and SUVs, but also plenty of old clunkers.

Maybe it was the way the van lurked to one side, half-hidden in the shade of an office building that sat empty on a Saturday. And the fact that, despite an obscuring shadow, she could tell there was someone sitting behind the wheel, unmoving as the minutes ticked by.

Was he waiting for someone? Why didn't he come out and enjoy the September sunshine?

"Wanna buy a candy bar?" a girl's voice asked.

Erin tore her gaze away from the van. Before the booth where she'd been handing out pamphlets stood a teenage volunteer with one thick, nutty chocolate bar left on her tray.

"I just have to sell this one and I can go home," the girl said. "You look hungry. How about it?"

It was on the tip of Erin's tongue to say, "I can't eat that stuff." Even though she was only twenty-six, she'd stuck strictly—well, almost strictly—to health food since a heart attack killed her father two years ago.

What was a couple of dollars? And she *had* skipped lunch, and for heaven's sake, it was one chocolate bar.

"Sure." She fished a few crumpled bills from her shoulder bag.

"Thanks!" With a grin, the girl handed it over and hurried toward the cashier's booth. Beyond her, workmen were disassembling the carnival rides on a far section of the asphalt. The scents of popcorn and cotton candy lingered in the air as the vendors closed up shop.

People streamed by, heading home. From the parking area, Erin registered the sound of cars starting. No one seemed the least bit interested in taking a pamphlet describing the fund's free health screening programs.

After tucking away the candy to savor at leisure, she decided to make the rounds to see if anyone needed help closing up shop. Although many tradespeople had decamped, it was her responsibility, as administrative assistant at Conrad Promotions, to keep things running smoothly.

Erin glanced toward the building. The van hadn't gone anywhere.

It probably belonged to one of the craftspeople, she told herself. Any minute, the driver would get out and begin loading unsold wares.

Still, she felt vulnerable. For comfort, she instinctively touched the gold pendant nestled against the front of her blue Healthy Children's Fund T-shirt.

It was hard to say why she'd worn it today. Although she sometimes took it out of the drawer simply to enjoy the precious memories it stirred, Erin couldn't remember the last time she'd worn the jagged half heart design. Maybe it was because, after tomorrow, she'd never be able to wear it again.

It reminded her of someone she'd once loved, someone

who'd probably thrown away the other half of the heart years ago. Erin wished that didn't bother her so much.

A tablecloth flapped in her path, startling her.

"I'm sorry! I didn't see you," called a woman shaking wrinkles from the fabric. She'd already tucked her unsold teddy bears into a box beneath her display table.

"I hope your sales went well," Erin said.

"Terrific!" That was good news, since the fund netted a percentage of everything sold.

Erin moved on through the nearly empty carnival section. She was about to check on the van again when a boy of about four pelted toward her. Behind him lagged his weary mother, pushing a baby stroller.

"Whoa!" Erin held out one arm. "Wait for your mom."

The boy halted in front of her. "I want to go home!"

"Are you planning to drive the car yourself?" she asked.

"Can I?" he asked hopefully.

"Well, no, so I guess you better wait for your mother."

That seemed logical to Erin, but the little boy's face reddened. "I'm hungry!" he wailed.

"I'm sure your mom will feed you as soon as she can," she said.

The woman caught up in time to hear the last remark. "We ate about an hour ago, but he was too excited to finish his sandwich. I promised to split a chocolate bar with him, but I can't find any."

At the thought of the candy tucked into her purse, Erin's stomach growled. Despite her devotion to health food—or perhaps because of it—she could almost taste the chocolate melting on her tongue and the nuts crunching between her teeth.

The little boy whined. His mother's shoulders sagged.

"Here." Erin took out the bar and handed it to the woman. "It's courtesy of Conrad Promotions. We want everyone to go away happy."

"How kind! I'll pay for it, of course." She reached for her wallet.

"It's on the house."

"Are you sure?" Receiving a nod, she said, "That's great! Thank you." The mother broke the candy bar in two and gave a piece to her son.

The smell of chocolate drifted through Erin's senses. Her stomach rumbled again. She hoped nobody heard it over the clamor of workmen dismantling the rides. "Have a good evening."

"You too!"

After the family left, Erin couldn't find a single food stand open. Well, she'd eat a yogurt later at her apartment.

"Erin!" Bea Conrad waved from the cashier's booth. The owner of Conrad Promotions had a friendly face and fluffy honey-colored hair. The T-shirt and slacks she'd worn instead of one of her usual tailored suits made her look younger than her late thirties.

Erin strode in her direction. "Anything I can do?"

"Actually, yes. I have a favor to ask," Bea said.

"Name it." Too late, it occurred to Erin that she might get stuck here without dinner. Well, she'd survive. Maybe.

"What a great attitude! I hope I'm not going to lose you." Bea shook her head apologetically. "Don't mind me. Chet's a real catch. When are you giving him your answer?"

"He's driving down tomorrow." Erin felt an inexplicable urge to touch her heart pendant again. She didn't want to talk about Chet. "How were the receipts?"

"Even better than last year," Bea said. "I don't have the final numbers, but I'm guessing the profit will be around fifteen thousand. That's not counting our mysterious benefactor. I can't believe it! Someone managed to sneak a cashier's check into the donation box again this year."

"Let's not complain about it," Erin teased. "How much was it this time?"

"Twenty thousand," Bea said. "It's from Friend of a Friend Foundation again. I'm surprised you never heard of them. I mean, you *are* from Sundown Valley, and that's where they're located. But I guess you don't pay much attention to what goes on there anymore."

Erin shrugged and said nothing. In fact, she subscribed to the *Sundown Sentinel* and kept close tabs on her hometown.

"I don't know why they're so mysterious." Bea had telephoned the previous year and learned only that the foundation made donations to worthy causes on behalf of an anonymous sponsor. "Well, I'm not going to look a gift horse in the mouth."

"What was the favor?" Erin asked.

"Oh! Thanks for reminding me," said her boss. "I know you made two runs to the bank already, and I was going to make the last trip myself. But my babysitter just called and said Kiki's fussing." That was her two-year-old daughter. "I hope she's not coming down with something. Would you mind making the drop?"

"No problem." Erin ignored a twinge of apprehension when she remembered the van. Tustin was a safe city and it was daylight, although fading fast.

Bea handed over the cash box. The heavy metal container was ridiculously obvious, Erin thought. Well, if someone stole it, she'd send another anonymous check to make good on the loss.

It hadn't been easy keeping her secret while working for Conrad Promotions the past three years, she reflected as Bea turned to accept compliments from an exhibitor. It helped that hardly anyone in Orange County knew her family.

In Sundown Valley, everybody knew about the Marshall Company. The development and management firm owned everything from the local mall to the medical center. Two years ago, Erin had inherited a half interest in it.

She didn't dismiss the advantages of wealth, but it had drawbacks, too. If her mother, Alice, weren't wealthy, would her stepfather, Lance Bolding, have materialized out of nowhere during a cruise last year and charmed the grieving widow into marrying him? And if he hadn't done that, he couldn't have managed to come between Alice and her daughter.

Erin's concerns deepened dramatically four months ago when her mother nearly drowned in the lake near the new home Lance had persuaded her to buy. Although the police had ruled it an accident, she feared for her mother's safety.

But Alice had refused to let her intervene. In fact, they'd quarreled on the phone right after the accident. Since then, her mother had refused to let Erin come to visit. Lance had managed to isolate her almost completely.

Except from Chet Dever. As CEO of the Marshall Company, he'd been her father's right-hand man and, since Alice served as the company's chairman of the board, he often consulted her on business matters. He'd kept an eye on her for Erin these past few months.

After dating her casually in the past, he'd also begun to court her in earnest. Last weekend, he'd asked Erin to marry him. After taking a week to think about it, she'd decided to say yes tomorrow.

Chet was handsome, smart and eloquent. She admired his focus and his ambitious agenda as a leading congressional candidate in next spring's primary. And he was one of the few men she'd met for whom her money was neither an obstacle nor her chief attraction.

Erin's free hand closed over the pendant. The boy who'd given it to her in high school had been her first love, but it made no sense to compare Chet to someone she hadn't seen in nearly ten years. And probably never would again. During their painful breakup, Joseph had made it clear he wanted nothing further to do with Erin.

Yet touching the heart gave her a sense of connection. Why was she thinking about him now? *Why did I wear this today?*

Suddenly she knew the answer, although she hadn't wanted to face it. Because it reminded her of someone with whom she'd felt things she could never feel with Chet: a visceral excitement, an eagerness to touch him, the joy of spontaneity.

Until another man affected her that strongly, she had no business getting married.

"Is it something I said?" Bea asked. "You're off in your own little world."

"I'm sorry." Erin realized she'd been standing there like a zombie.

"I know it isn't the effect of holding so much money, because you handled more than that earlier," her boss pointed out.

"It's Chet," Erin blurted. "It's a mistake."

"What's a mistake?"

"I was going to say yes. I can't marry him." She let out a long breath and was surprised by the intensity of her relief.

"Marriage is a big step, but I thought you really liked him," Bea said. "He made a great impression on my husband and me." Chet had taken them all out for a French dinner.

"I do like him," Erin said. "I just don't love him." *And if I don't love him by now, I never will.*

She realized she'd been hoping all along that she *was* falling in love. Life would be so simple if she could marry Chet.

Her mother would approve, and they might grow close again. And Erin liked Chet's goal of stimulating the economy by shrinking government and encouraging private investment. She'd always wanted to make a difference in the world and with him, she could.

Why had she believed that was enough reason to get married? By now, she ought to know her own mind and have her own purpose in life. Although she'd made a start by working for Conrad Promotions, it wasn't enough.

"You're the only one who can make that decision," Bea told her. "I'm sure you've given it a lot of thought."

"Not nearly enough, or I'd have realized this sooner," Erin answered. "Maybe I should call and save him the drive." Sundown Valley was fifty miles away.

"This is the kind of news he deserves to hear in person," cautioned her boss.

Erin sighed. "You're right. Well, you'd better go make sure Kiki's okay."

Bea gathered her possessions. "See you Monday. And thanks again!"

"Sure thing."

Erin headed for her car. She hoped tomorrow's confrontation wasn't going to be awkward. She knew Chet better than to believe he would accept her refusal without trying to change her mind.

As she ducked beneath the ropes that separated the fair from the parking area, she noticed how quickly twilight was settling in. And how empty the parking lot loomed, isolated in the midst of a huge office park.

To one side, Erin heard a motor spring to life. In her preoccupation with Chet, she'd forgotten the van.

She was disturbed to see it pull away from the building and move slowly toward her. There was nothing between them save a few planters filled with ficus trees and aromatic, flowering bushes.

Erin clutched the cash box tighter. She wondered if she should make a run for it or if she was just being paranoid.

She was quite a ways from her car, which sat forlornly near the rim of the lot. Her legs, weary from a day of standing, protested when she lengthened her stride and the heavy cash box weighed her down.

Surely she was imagining the threat. Yet although there were people not far away—the workmen taking down the rides, a few vendors disassembling their booths—no one paid attention to Erin.

The van speeded up.

Erin reversed course back toward the fair. The van swung toward her.

She hadn't imagined the threat.

"Hey!" she shouted toward the workmen, trying to make herself heard over the racket of their equipment. No one looked up.

A few thousand dollars wasn't worth getting killed for. At least, she hoped the driver was a thief and not some crazed stalker. Although it infuriated her, Erin set the cash box on the pavement and forced her stiff legs into a trot.

The van veered to follow her.

The driver either hadn't noticed that the receipts were sitting on the blacktop or he didn't want them. Disbelief mingled with panic. This couldn't be happening. It was too bizarre. And terrifying.

Erin ducked past the ropes into the carnival area and broke into a run. But with the booths gone, the blacktop here was also nearly bare.

The van tore through the ropes.

Erin put on a burst of speed despite aching lungs. This felt like a nightmare, the kind where she was doomed to fall off a cliff no matter how hard she tried to flee.

She wasn't going to give in easily. If the driver grabbed her, she'd fight and scream for all she was worth. But she prayed it wouldn't come to that.

The ficus sprouting from a nearby planter was too slim to offer protection. There was no time to make a cell phone call, no time to do anything but try to cross a span of pavement that seemed to stretch into infinity.

Even now, none of the workmen had noticed her. The whole incident, which loomed so large in her mind, had to have transpired in a minute or two.

Winded, she turned to face the van. Maybe this was some kind of sick game. Maybe the driver just wanted to scare her.

Glare on the windshield obscured his face. Erin stumbled backward and, at a different angle, the glass cleared.

She saw who it was. And couldn't believe it.

This was no random assault. It was no robbery, either.

The van shot forward. In a burst of desperation, Erin leaped aside, too late. The bumper caught her hip with an agonizing whack.

She flew into the air and through a planter, helpless to stop her flight. Time slowed as branches tore at her arms. The perfume of crushed jasmine blossoms filled her senses.

As if from very far away, she heard one of the workmen shout. Finally, they'd spotted her.

She had to survive. She had to tell someone what she'd seen. The danger was enormous, not only for her but also for her mother.

Erin's shoulder hit the ground and a thousand stars exploded. Then there was only darkness.

Chapter Two

"You're the most beautiful bride I ever saw!" Tina Norris, Erin's maid of honor, gushed as they studied themselves in the full-length mirror.

"Thanks. And you look gorgeous in that shade of green," Erin responded.

"I guess we're just a pair of femmes fatales." Her friend grinned.

Erin had to admit that her mother's ivory heirloom wedding gown fit her five-foot-five-inch figure to perfection. Above the scooped neck glittered a diamond choker, and a matching tiara sparkled in her chestnut hair, which was folded into a French twist. Except for the pallor of her skin, the image was smashingly bridelike and yet it seemed to her that it belonged to a stranger.

A buzzing filled her head and the bridal dressing room at the Sundown Valley Country Club began to spin. With the ceremony less than an hour away, Erin didn't want to get sick.

In the six weeks since the accident, her memory had been a complete blank about that day. She'd also been plagued by confusion, anxieties and nightmares, which the doctor attributed to post-traumatic stress.

Erin pressed her temple. The dizziness ebbed.

"Do you want to sit down?" Tina asked. "You don't look well."

"It's not bad," she said. "Just nerves."

She wished the wedding could have waited until she was stronger, but by next month Chet would be caught up in the full swing of his congressional campaign. Even now, he only had time for a short honeymoon in Lake Tahoe. Erin knew she ought to be excited at the prospect of being alone with her groom, since she'd saved her virginity for her wedding night, but in the past few weeks it had become difficult to summon any emotions at all.

According to Chet, she'd been bubbling with enthusiasm when she called him to accept his proposal. Since her head injury later that day, however, she'd experienced what the doctor called emotional flattening. With her inner compass out of whack, she'd relied on family and friends to guide her.

Thank goodness Chet had proved a rock-steady source of support. No wonder she'd been so eager to marry him, Erin thought. She didn't doubt that the happy emotions would come flooding back in time and, meanwhile, it would be a relief to move forward with their lives.

She was grateful, too, for Tina, her best friend from high school. Tina, now a junior high school life-skills teacher, had come to see Erin after she was transferred to the local hospital. She'd continued to visit during the past month while Erin recuperated at her mother's home.

No one from Tustin had visited or accepted the wedding invitation. Erin had been particularly disappointed when Alice reported that Bea had declined.

Tina broke into her reverie. "How's your leg? Think you can make it down the aisle without limping?"

Between her badly bruised hip and the head injury, Erin had been mostly housebound until now. "Probably. If Chet doesn't step on my feet."

"I'm sure he'll be careful. If he isn't, I'll pound him into dust."

"Spoken like a true friend!"

A loud knock startled both women. "Not the photographer again!" Erin didn't think she could summon one more artificial smile.

"It's probably Chet." He planned to walk Erin down the aisle, since her mother was recovering from yet another bout of bronchitis.

She'd declined to let her stepfather fulfill that function. Although Lance had been pleasant this past month, Erin couldn't bring herself to like him. She hadn't entirely lost touch with her emotions after all, she supposed.

Tina peeked outside. Before Erin could see who was there, her friend stepped into the hall and shut the door behind her.

It had to be Tina's boyfriend, Rick, a detective sergeant who braved her father's disapproval to date her. One might expect more sympathy from a chief of police who'd risen through the ranks, but Edgar Norris had always been a bit of a snob. Now that he'd joined the country club, he preferred that his children move in elite social circles.

Fortunately, Tina didn't share her father's preoccupation with social status. Erin hoped he would come around eventually, because she liked Rick.

Her friend hurried back. "There's a detective here to see you. Can you talk to him?"

"You mean Rick?" she asked.

"No. Someone with a few questions about your accident."

"Now?" Erin could hardly believe the timing, less than an hour before the ceremony. Besides, she'd told the Tustin Police Department everything she remembered—which was a big fat zero. "They drove all this way on a Saturday to talk to me?"

"It's someone local." Tina cleared her throat. "Erin, it's Joseph."

Joseph. It couldn't be him. She knew he'd joined the police force and that he was friends with Rick, but she hadn't expected to meet him. Not unprepared like this. Not in her wedding dress.

Once, she'd been closer to him than to anyone in the world. Then he'd broken her heart, or maybe she'd broken his. Most likely both.

"My accident was in Tustin," she heard herself say. "That's a different jurisdiction."

"I know." Tina picked up her bouquet and fingered the ivory, blue and green flowers. "Joseph investigated your mom's accident. He thinks there might be a connection with what happened to you."

"How could they be connected?" Alice's near drowning and Erin's hit-and-run had occurred four months and fifty miles apart.

"I'd better let him explain it. He promised it won't take long." Tina sounded torn.

"I can't see him."

"He said he tried to talk to you before, but Lance objected and my father ordered him to back off. He seems to think it's important."

The boy she'd adored when she was fifteen was standing right outside in the hallway. Joseph might not belong at her wedding to Chet, but he was already here. How could she send him away? But how could she see him when she already felt so shaky?

The woman Erin had been until six weeks ago could have handled the situation with quiet self-possession. Now, she didn't trust her own reactions. During the past month, she'd found herself doubting everyone around her and getting upset for no reason. How could she maintain her poise with Joseph?

She remembered something that had slipped her mind. At the hospital, she'd learned that, when admitted, she'd been wearing the broken-heart pendant he'd given her in high school.

She wished she knew why she'd put that on, apparently right after calling Chet to accept his proposal. It didn't make sense.

A lot of things didn't make sense, she acknowledged with a start. She didn't know why her friends in Tustin had abandoned her. Also, at her mother's house, she'd imagined that conversations stopped abruptly when she entered a room. That the phone rang and was answered in hushed tones so that she couldn't understand.

In high school, Joseph had been the one she'd turned to with her thoughts. Maybe he could help her sort things out now. In any case, she refused to send him away without saying hello.

"All right," Erin said. "For a minute."

"I'll warn him not to overtire you." Tina went to the door.

Not overtire her? That was going to be hard. She just hoped that, after the interview, she could recover her composure in time to walk down the aisle at Chet's side with an appropriate smile on her face.

Tina ushered in a man. When his eyes met Erin's, emotions pricked and stung like blood flooding through a sleeping limb.

The gray vagueness she'd known since the accident lifted. This was Joseph, her Joseph. She'd missed him terribly, even if she'd refused to acknowledge it.

The years had broadened his shoulders and given him an air of authority, but if she buried her nose in his chest, she knew how he would smell. If she smiled up at him, she knew how his face would glow with warmth. Or perhaps she was imagining it.

His dark blue eyes riveted Erin with their intensity. He hadn't forgotten anything that had passed between them, she was sure of it, yet she saw no sign of tenderness or welcome. This muscular man wearing a navy sports jacket and tan pants had changed in ways she couldn't even imagine.

Joseph glanced toward Tina. "This will only take a few minutes." It was a polite dismissal.

With an apologetic shrug, the bridesmaid left the two of them alone.

"Thank you for seeing me." Remaining where he stood

halfway across the room from her, he took out a notepad. "I need to run over a few details with you."

"Your timing leaves something to be desired." She hoped for a wry smile.

"I'm afraid I had no choice. I wasn't allowed to see you sooner." No smile. No eye contact, either.

"This is awkward. I'm getting married, you know." Realizing what she'd blurted, Erin felt spectacularly foolish. As if the fact that she was standing here in her wedding dress didn't give him a hint! "Is it that urgent?"

"You nearly got killed recently and so did your mother." Although Joseph kept his voice level, she noted his tightly coiled tension. "I'd say that's one heck of a coincidence." The look he slanted her suited his tone: edgy and challenging.

"They were accidents," Erin responded. "I don't know what else I can tell you."

"Were they?"

"Were they what?"

"Accidents." He tapped his pen against the pad and waited.

"I don't know." She gripped the arm of the nearest chair, expecting to get light-headed again. It was the way she'd reacted all month when Chet and Lance and her mother told her things that didn't match her distorted perceptions.

They'd said Alice was fine, even though to Erin she seemed gaunt and nervous. They'd said it made sense to go ahead with the wedding even in her befuddled state.

But her mind stayed clear. This hard-faced policeman wasn't arguing with her perceptions. Instead, he'd implied that someone had deliberately attacked her and her mother.

It was the first thing Erin had heard in the past six weeks that made sense. And it scared the wits out of her.

JOSEPH HAD BEEN prepared to confront a wealthy young woman subtly dismissive of the man she'd once been foolish enough to date. He hadn't expected to care whether she respected him, let alone liked him. No one knew better than he did the uselessness of holding on to the past.

After spending five years among police officers who worked high-stress jobs on rotating shifts, Joseph had seen relationships crumble right and left. People who'd once believed their hearts irretrievably shattered simply picked up the pieces and got over it, and so had he.

Or so he'd believed. Right now, he wasn't sure.

Seeing Erin took him back to the innocent, hope-filled days of high school before his world fell apart. He wanted to cup her heart-shaped face and to smooth those quizzical eyebrows. He wanted her to melt into his arms and help him find the trusting young man he used to be.

Yeah, sure, she'd been pining for him all these years. That was why she was marrying Chet Dever, big-shot candidate for Congress and a superslick operator, judging by the way he came across in television interviews. That was why she sported a diamond necklace and crown that probably cost more than a policeman earned in a year. Or ten.

Still, it bothered Joseph to see her hanging on to a chair for support. What was the darn hurry to get married so soon after a major accident? If he were Chet—well, he'd be in just as big a hurry, he supposed.

"I apologize for the inconvenience, Miss Marshall," he said. "Please bear with me and I'll make this as brief as possible."

"My name's still Erin. And please tell me why you think that van hit me." Despite the pallor of her complexion, she released her grip on the chair and held herself straight. Her late father would have approved.

Joseph forced his attention to the task at hand. He'd better make the best of these few minutes because, after Erin became Mrs. Chet Dever, he'd never get a chance to talk to her again unless this whole case blew wide open. By then, it might be too late.

"I don't know the motive," he said. "I don't even know

for sure that a crime's been committed. Call me naturally suspicious."

"The Tustin police called it an accident," she said.

"The witnesses said they *thought* it might have been accidental. The police aren't so sure." He'd spoken at length with the investigating officer.

Her brown eyes widened. "Chet told me he read the report himself."

"He probably read the cover sheet." Joseph knew better than to call a man a liar without hard evidence. "Basically, no one saw the van hit you, only the aftermath, and there are several unexplained issues."

"What…" Erin broke off, swaying a little.

Joseph caught her arm. "You okay?"

"I get dizzy." She took a couple of deep breaths. In the formfitting gown, the movement made him uncomfortably aware of her bosom, and as soon as she looked steadier, he let go. "What do you mean by unexplained issues?"

Joseph referred to his notebook. "For one thing, the van had been stolen. It was recovered, stripped, twenty-five miles away in Los Angeles."

"If it was a stolen van, that could explain why the driver didn't stop to help me," Erin replied. "What else?"

"Here's the puzzler," Joseph said. "You were carrying two thousand three hundred and forty-seven dollars in a cash box, which you left on the pavement about a hundred feet from where you got hit."

"I did? Why?"

"You got me," he said. "It was sitting there neatly with no sign of damage. It doesn't look as if you dropped it. Why did you set it down?"

"I don't know." Erin's blank expression confirmed that, as she'd told the Tustin detective, she didn't recall the circumstances surrounding the hit-and-run. Crime and accident victims often blacked out the event, even if they didn't suffer from head injuries. Sometimes the memories returned, sometimes not.

"Tustin PD finds that odd and so do I," he said. "It's possible you believed someone was trying to rob you and left it there so he'd leave you alone. But no one took the money. That might indicate some other motive."

"Nobody told me that before."

He had to ask a hard question, even if it upset her further. "Can you think of anyone who might want to kill you?"

Her horrified look went straight through him. "Of course not!"

She was being naïve, of course. The Marshall Company, of which Erin was half owner, wielded tremendous power in this town. It had developed major parcels of property and owned the mall, the hospital and several office complexes. There had to be people with grudges, from competitors to former leaseholders to outright kooks.

Apparently, she'd been sheltered from threats and lawsuits. Although technically Erin held the title of vice-chairman of the board, her position appeared to be largely ceremonial.

As CEO, Dever ran the Marshall Company in conjunction with Alice Marshall Bolding. Erin's mother, who'd become chairman of the board since her husband's death two years earlier, maintained an office at Marshall headquarters and apparently also conducted business from home.

"That brings us to your mother," he said. "I've never been comfortable with the idea that she simply went boating by herself at twilight and fell out."

He knew his report hadn't made a strong enough case to convince his superiors that there'd been a crime. After Erin was nearly killed, however, his concerns had doubled. Although the Tustin police were doing their best to find the driver, he wondered if Erin herself held the key.

"Your mother decided to take out Lance's motorboat even

though it was nearly dark and there was no one around," he continued. "Does that sound like something she would do?"

She shook her head. "I can't imagine my mother sailing in anything less than a yacht."

"She said she'd had a couple of drinks and lost her balance," he went on. "What do you think of that?"

"Even if my mother did get drunk, she'd never admi̇̇" Erin plucked at her lace skirt. "She's always insisted on k̇̇ ing up appearances."

Although he felt uncomfortable talking with his ̇̇ school sweetheart as if they were strangers, at least she ẇ̇ willing to hear him out, Joseph mused. Alice Bolding had become annoyed at his implications and her husband had gone ballistic.

His goal was to resolve his case, and perhaps Tustin's case as well. That was it. Then Erin could marry any darn fellow she pleased.

"Your stepfather claims he went shopping that evening, but he didn't buy anything so there are no receipts," he said. "I haven't found any salesclerks who remember seeing him."

"I've never trusted Lance," she said. "So I can't be objective. But if he tried to kill my Mom, why wouldn't she say so? You must have asked her."

"She denied it," he admitted. "But her body language was extremely tense."

"That doesn't surprise me," Erin said. "I'm sure she didn't like talking to the police."

Alice had always been a proud woman. Joseph hadn't liked her much when he'd dated her daughter, because she'd had a way of making him feel about six inches tall. Even so, he'd been surprised by how coldly she'd behaved when he arrived at the lake, as if she resented his attempt to set the record straight.

Of course, she might have been in shock. Or could she fear that someone would retaliate if she spoke freely? Police dealt with abusive situations all the time, and they weren't necessarily confined to poor homes.

"Did you ask her what happened?" he probed.

"I tried," Erin said. "I phoned her as soon as I heard. I wanted to come up and find out what was really going on, but when I asked whether Lance had anything to do with it, she ordered me to stay away. For months, she would hardly speak to me, and she refused point-blank to let me visit. We didn't reconcile until after I got hurt."

"You've been staying with her. How has she seemed?" He watched her reaction closely.

"Moody," Erin said. "Sometimes she's giddy, then she gets kind of mad at the world."

"Was she always like that?"

"She could be touchy, but I don't think she feels well. The water must have affected her lungs." Concern thickened her voice. "She says she's been fighting off bronchitis, so she rarely goes out and she never invites anyone over except on company business."

Abusive spouses often isolated their victims. "Did you talk to her about this?" Joseph asked. "It sounds like she needs help."

Erin's lost expression tugged at his sympathies. "I didn't dare say anything. My perceptions have been so screwed up, I thought I was getting paranoid. I..." She hesitated.

"What?" he pressed.

"It's silly."

"The things people believe are silly often turn out to be important." Joseph could feel her wondering whether to trust him. He waited, willing her to cooperate. Whatever was going on here, he might never find it out without her help.

"I thought people were whispering behind my back," Erin confessed. "Does that sound crazy?"

"Not at all," Joseph said. "Has your stepfather threatened you in any way?"

She swallowed. "No, actually, he's been rather mellow. That doesn't mean I like him." She twisted her gloved hands together. "After my father died, my mother asked me to move back here, but I refused to leave my job. If I'd been around, maybe she wouldn't have turned to Lance."

"This isn't your fault. Your mother's always had a mind of her own."

"She's changed," Erin said. "I don't think she's in control anymore. Can't you help her?"

Joseph wished he could. He'd become a police officer to help people, and there was nothing more frustrating than when a woman insisted on protecting a man who was abusing her. But there were limits to what the police could do.

"The chief ordered me to close the case," he said. "He puts a lot of stock in making nice with the town's ruling class, and I suspect Mr. Bolding told him to back off."

"You're not supposed to be here today?" Erin said.

"That's right."

"You *are* trying to help." The quaver in her voice hit him in the gut. "You could get into trouble because of me."

"It wouldn't be the first time."

Their gazes met and held, and then she smiled. Just like that, he knew he wasn't over her. He had never been over her. She was the reason every woman he'd dated since high school seemed to lack something vital, only he hadn't understood that until now.

"Why the hell are you marrying Chet Dever?" Joseph braced himself for her to say, "Because I love him."

"I don't know," Erin said.

"What do you mean, you don't know?" Relief mingled with pain as raw as it had been more than ten years ago. "How can you marry a guy if you don't love him?"

"I must love him. I said yes, didn't I?"

"Why are you asking me?"

Erin scrunched her nose the way she used to do when an

idea hit her. Like defying her parents and going to play Mr. and Mrs. Santa Claus at a Christmas party for poor children rather than attending their school's winter formal. Joseph treasured the photo he'd kept from that escapade.

"I don't remember saying yes," she said.

"Excuse me?"

"That whole morning is a big blank," she explained. "He'd proposed the previous weekend. The morning of the accident, I phoned and said I couldn't wait another day to tell him I wanted to be his wife. That's what he told me."

Joseph hadn't expected anything like this when he decided to inject himself into Erin's wedding day. "Whoa. Is it just me or does something smell rotten around here?"

"Smell," she said.

"What?"

"I just remembered. Something smelled sweet. Flowers." She blinked. "I'm sorry. I must be thinking of the hospital."

She was so confused she could hardly follow her own train of thought. "You're in no shape to marry anybody."

Erin gestured at her wedding dress. "I made a commitment, and I always keep my promises." Her voice wavered slightly as she added, "Besides, I'm sure it's what I want."

"You don't sound sure to me."

She hesitated. "I guess I'm wondering why I didn't accept his proposal right away, why I waited. If I could just put my finger on what happened that morning, I'd feel better."

In a little over half an hour, this woman was going to walk down the aisle with a man who, in Joseph's estimation, was both cunning and amoral, and who would dearly love to come into possession of Erin's millions. She had only his word that she'd agreed to marry him.

He gripped his notepad. Erin wasn't his problem. As far as this town was concerned, he had no business getting anywhere near her.

Not only weren't the Lowerys in the same league as the

Marshalls, they'd been virtual outcasts since his father, a former policeman, was arrested and convicted of murder eleven years ago. The fallout had destroyed his relationship with Erin. It had destroyed his father, too.

Although Joseph and his mother had stood by him, very few people shared their belief that Lewis Lowery had been framed. After he died in prison and the years ticked by without new evidence emerging, the chances of clearing his father's name had become negligible.

Erin was another matter. If she'd just become engaged, surely she had confided the happy news to someone. There was no reason to rely on Chet's testimony.

"Is there a friend you might have talked to that day?" he asked.

"My boss, Bea," Erin said. "We were working together at the carnival."

"Do you know her phone number?"

"It's in my organizer."

He retrieved her purse from a chair. "May I?" It might take her a while to get those gloves off.

"Go ahead. It's in the side pocket."

He found the number and dialed her cell phone. While it was ringing, Joseph handed it to Erin.

After a moment, she exchanged pleasantries with her boss. He heard her ask if, before the accident, she'd mentioned her engagement.

"I don't understand," Erin said. "What do you mean you didn't know I was engaged?… Well, to Chet, of course. You received the invitation, didn't you?… What?"

He'd thought she was pale before, but some previously unsuspected color drained from her cheeks. "Oh, my gosh," she said. "Oh, Bea. You won't believe—well, I don't have time to explain. Thank you. Yes. This helps a lot. I'll be in touch." She clicked off.

"Well?" Joseph said.

She swallowed hard. "I didn't promise to marry Chet. I told Bea I was going to turn him down."

Much as he welcomed the news, Joseph had to make sure it was valid. "Could there be a misunderstanding?"

"She talked to me that afternoon, right before I got hit." Erin spoke in a dull, shocked tone. "I said the whole thing with Chet was a mistake. I planned to give him the bad news in person the next day."

Joseph couldn't believe Dever had lied so baldly. "Maybe you accepted him and then had a change of heart."

"I don't see how that could have happened," Erin said. "Chet described how overjoyed I was when I called. He said I could hardly wait to walk down the aisle. I'm not the kind of person who would say that and then change my mind a few hours later."

"When he told you, didn't you wonder why you'd agreed? I mean, you ought to know whether you love him or not." He knew he was being rough on her, but it was nothing compared to the storm that would sweep over Sundown Valley if Erin Marshall left Chet Dever at the altar.

"I believed everything I was told. I couldn't rely on my memory or my feelings." She sounded dazed. "I didn't trust my perceptions."

What a violation! What Dever had done might not be a crime, but it ought to be. "You can't marry him."

Erin dropped her cell phone into her purse. "What a mess! Everyone's going to be so upset. I don't know how I'm going to deal with them."

"The only person you have to deal with is your fake fiancé," he said.

"No." Tears welled in her eyes. "There's my mom. And all those people out there." She started to shake. "I'm sorry. I know I ought to be able to take care of myself, but I can't think straight."

Joseph couldn't help it. He knew he was compromising his

investigation, but he wrapped his arms around Erin and pulled her against him.

She needed him. He'd never believed such a thing could happen, in view of their past and their relative situations in this community. Regardless of whether he crushed his career along with her wedding dress, he refused to let her down.

"Come with me," he said. "I'll help you sort it out."

"You don't have to." She rested her cheek on his chest. "This isn't your problem."

"Tell me how many people you trust right now, besides me."

"My mom," she said.

"Even if she's under Lance's influence?"

"No."

"So there's just me," Joseph pointed out. "That makes it my problem."

Soon enough, she'd have all the support she needed— from lawyers, security guards, accountants, whatever. But for this small, precious space of time, she needed a friend and she'd turned to him. "Let's get the heck out of here."

"Thank you." Erin's eyes looked huge as she peered up at him. "I can't tell you how much this means."

"Cops are the modern equivalent of knights in shining armor, aren't we?" he teased, and reached for the door.

Eerily, the knob turned just before he touched it, and someone in the hall pulled it open.

Chapter Three

Erin stared in dismay at the man standing in the doorway. In his tuxedo, Chet loomed larger than life, his chiseled face set in an unaccustomed scowl.

He was a big man, several inches taller than Joseph although less tightly knit, with anchorman-perfect dark blond hair and an air of authority that swept people before him. Until now, Erin hadn't dreamed of standing up to him—at least, not lately.

Since she'd awakened in the hospital, Chet had taken command of her life the way her father used to do. Bruised and aching, uncertain about what had happened, she'd been grateful for his strength.

She wasn't ready for this confrontation. She hadn't weighed her plans or gathered her courage. On the other hand, that might take days, and she needed to stop this wedding in its tracks.

Behind Chet in the hallway, Tina hovered uncertainly. Whatever she'd told the groom, the news had annoyed him. His guilty conscience had to be pricking, Erin thought with a trace of her old resilience.

"What's going on?" he demanded. "I do not want my bride harassed."

"I don't believe we've been introduced." Joseph thrust out his hand. "I'm Detective Lowery."

Chet ignored his hand. "I know who you are." It was unusually churlish of him, Erin thought.

"Everyone knows who you are." This last came from Tina's brother, Gene. Thin-faced and sharp-featured, he, too, wore a tuxedo, since he was Chet's best man as well as his campaign manager. He and Joseph had disliked each other in high school, she recalled.

Joseph's eyes flicked over Gene with the barest of recognition and returned to Chet. His air of quiet watchfulness impressed Erin. "Miss Marshall is assisting with an investigation."

"Well, Detective, your time is up," Chet said. "We're having a wedding here and I don't recall your being invited."

"If you're looking for trouble, take it elsewhere," Gene added.

Tina's cheeks reddened. "He just wanted to ask a few questions."

"He's exceeding his authority," returned her brother. "And he knows it."

Erin felt the tension in Joseph's body. It was obvious that Chief Norris would hear about his intrusion, given his son's attitude.

If she planned to retake charge of her life, Erin decided, she had better start now. "Joseph was just leaving, Chet, and so am I. I'm sorry but I can't marry you. In fact, under the circumstances, you're the one who should be saying you're sorry."

The groom's reaction was subtle but unmistakable: a tightening around the eyes, a flare of the nostrils. Erin's chest squeezed. Something about him frightened her.

Tina gasped. "Five minutes ago, you were fine. What on earth is going on?"

"Five minutes ago, I was deluded," she said. "Tina, I was going to turn Chet down the day of the accident. He lied to me."

"Tell me what kind of nonsense this man's been spouting." Chet reached for her shoulders, a gesture he frequently used, she realized, when he wanted to assert control.

She stepped away. "He didn't have to tell me anything. I called my boss in Tustin. According to her, I was planning to turn you down before I got hit. I never promised to marry you. You lied to me."

At some level, Chet must have been prepared for her accusation, because he immediately changed tactics. "You've been promising to marry me for the past six weeks. If anyone lied, it was you."

Erin could hardly believe his nerve. "I was flat on my back in the hospital with a head injury! You convinced me we were engaged."

"The hospital released you a month ago. You could have called off the ceremony at any time. No one forced you to do anything, Erin." He spread his hands placatingly. "Look, this is an obvious case of prewedding jitters. We've got a whole ballroom full of guests waiting for us to walk down the aisle. Do you want to humiliate your mother in front of her friends?"

This last statement stopped her. By refusing to move home again after her father's death, she'd already let her mother down once and left her vulnerable to an opportunist like Lance. The last-minute cancellation of her daughter's wedding would embarrass Alice in front of Sundown Valley society. She didn't deserve to be treated that way.

That wasn't a good enough reason for Erin to marry the wrong man, however. And if she hadn't already been convinced there was something amiss, Chet's behavior these past few minutes had made it crystal clear. Instead of showing concern for her happiness, he'd done nothing but try to finesse her.

"When I told you I didn't want to rush things, you described how eagerly I accepted your proposal and how I in-

sisted we get married right away," she said. "You stage-man-
aged the whole thing."

"This is a misunderstanding. This policeman's been playing on your vulnerability. I don't know why he's done it but
I'll find out." Despite Chet's conciliatory tone, his pale blue
eyes had turned to ice. "What I don't understand is how you
think you're going to get away with this."

She couldn't seem to drag her eyes from Chet's. It was like
staring at a cobra. "Joseph?"

"I'm here." His evenness broke the spell.

"You can't stop me."

"The problem is, you're not stable," Chet said in that same
persuasive tone. "We've all tried to smooth things over, but
your behavior this past month hasn't always been rational.
You need someone trustworthy watching over you."

"I'm an adult," she told him. "I can watch over myself."

"Unfortunately, there's a lot more at stake here than a
young woman's whims," he said. "You're half owner of a
major company. If you go off half-cocked, you could not
only endanger your inheritance but threaten the stability of a
large chunk of this town's economy. Maybe it's time someone asked a judge to appoint a trustee until you regain your
mental health."

To have a judge declare her incompetent—what would
that mean? She couldn't be forced into a marriage, but could
they lock her in a psychiatric facility? The prospect terrified
Erin.

She moved closer to Joseph. He was a police officer and
her friend. She just hoped he hadn't changed his mind about
helping her.

His next words were reassuring. "Miss Marshall is under
my protection. If she wishes to leave the premises, that's her
right. You want to talk to a judge? Fine. My mother works for
a lawyer. We'll make sure Erin's properly represented."

"You used to be her boyfriend," Gene put in. "For all we

know, you're playing on her weakness for your own advantage."

"Oh, for heaven's sake!" Tina blurted. "She's not crazy and Joseph isn't here to trick her."

"Stay out of this," her brother warned.

"Why? What's it to you?"

"Let's save the family quarrel for later, okay?" Chet was too intent on his goal to let the conversation get off course. "We've been going together for a long time, Erin. I could tell when I proposed that you intended to accept. I just simplified matters at the hospital because you needed someone to take care of you. What's wrong with that?"

Thank goodness he'd backed away from making threats. At the same time, she marveled at how skillfully he twisted the facts. "I'm sorry if I've disappointed you," Erin said. "But it's useless to argue."

"You're going to run off and leave your mother to handle the fallout?" Chet pressed. "Do you have any idea how upset she's going to be?"

His renewed attempt to corner her annoyed Erin. "I think I know my mother better than you do."

"Is that why you've been asking me to run interference with her this past six months?" It wasn't a question but a challenge. "You don't have the first notion what Alice is going through."

Angered flipped a switch. Andrew Marshall would never have allowed an employee, even a CEO, to address him in this condescending manner. "I've been dealing with my mother since long before you came to work for us." Erin heard her father's commanding inflection in her voice. "I can handle her without your help, thank you."

Chet flinched. It was all the encouragement she needed. "Let's go," she said, and caught Joseph's arm.

She did indeed owe Alice an apology. If that meant she had to endure a tongue-lashing, it couldn't be any worse than facing up to Chet had been.

Adrenaline carried her along the carpeted hallway and outside into the October afternoon and down a walkway toward the guest wing, where her mother had taken a suite for the day. The hacienda-style country club, built sixteen years ago by the Marshall Company, opened onto a landscaped courtyard.

Ordinarily, Erin relished its lush vegetation. Today, she was in no mood to admire the flowers.

Joseph slanted her an admiring grin. "I love the way you pulled rank on him."

"Is that what I did?" She would have found the notion amusing, except that Chet's warning still rang in her ears. *What I don't understand is how you think you're going to get away with this.* What exactly had he meant?

"He jumped as if someone yanked the carpet out from under him," Joseph said. "I think you missed your true vocation. You should have been a drill sergeant."

The darkness inside Erin dissipated. "He scared me. I couldn't have done it without you standing there."

"Don't underestimate yourself." The autumn breeze ruffled his light brown hair, which always seems to stick up no matter how short he trimmed it.

"Do you think he was right?" she asked.

"About what?"

"I *have* been out of the hospital for a month," she said. "No one forced me to do anything. I could have called it off. I don't honestly know why I didn't."

"The Tustin report mentioned amnesia and post-traumatic stress disorder," Joseph said.

"That's what my doctor said," Erin agreed.

"Mind telling me your symptoms?"

"I've had nightmares, and I haven't been able to think straight. Sometimes the people around me seemed like strangers, even my mother. When it came to Chet, I drew a blank, but I figured that was temporary. Why didn't I recognize that I don't love him? It seems so obvious now."

"Trauma victims often feel detached from their emotions," Joseph told her. "Does that fit what you're talking about?"

She nodded. "I didn't really come alive until today. But I'm not sure that's an excuse."

"You've always doubted yourself," Joseph said. "In high school, even when you knew your parents were trying to micromanage your life, you needed reassurance before you would trust your instincts. Between the trauma and your lack of confidence, Chet played you like a violin."

"You think he did it on purpose?" He'd made a convincing case about believing he was following her wishes.

"He's as ruthless as they come," Joseph said. "If you want my opinion, the man's capable of anything. Of course, I'm not the world's biggest fan of politicians."

"He seemed convinced I mistreated him."

"He may really believe it. In his view, anyone who doesn't give him his way is mistreating him."

"That's true!" She'd forgotten what a great sounding board Joseph made. "You have a gift for putting things in perspective."

"And you have a gift for being so sweet-natured, you give the world your heart on a platter," Joseph said. "The problem is, the world's a tough place, Erin."

"I don't want to be tough," she said.

"And I don't want you to be." His voice grew gentle. "But you may have to, for your own protection."

Stumbling on the rough walkway in her satin slippers, she brushed against him. The contact sent sparkles shimmering through across her skin and Erin registered that she'd been right about one thing. She *did* remember how he smelled: like a woodland in a spring rain.

He righted her, but otherwise kept his hands to himself. There were none of the casual caresses that had come so naturally when they were younger.

She knew better than to expect a return to their old closeness. Joseph had done more than enough for her already.

When they reached her mother's suite, Erin saw that the curtains were drawn against the afternoon brightness. Alice had to be feeling ill again, she thought worriedly.

This news was going to be hard to break. Her mom had always been a formidable figure, able to intimidate Erin with a mere lift of the eyebrow. Only since her father's death had it become apparent that beneath the resolute exterior hid an uncertain sense of self.

Even so, Erin figured she was in for a rough time.

At her knock, the door cracked open and Brandy Schorr, her mother's housekeeper, peered out. Despite her smooth bun and trim blouse and skirt, the pouches beneath Brandy's eyes gave her a dissipated air. "Is the ceremony starting, Miss? I'll send her right out."

"No, thank you. I need to talk to my mother," Erin said.

Brandy spotted Joseph. She didn't even try to disguise her antipathy. "What's he doing here?"

"I'm assisting Miss Marshall," he said. "At her request."

The housekeeper chewed her lip before responding. "Mr. Bolding told me your investigation was finished. He said he doesn't want you near Mrs. Bolding."

"He isn't here about her accident. He's with me." Erin pushed the door wider, ignoring Brandy's half-hearted protest. Although she'd found the housekeeper pleasant during the past month, she had no particular ties to the woman, who'd only worked for the Boldings for a few months. Apparently, Lance had driven away the previous one.

"I can't let you…" Brandy let the sentence trail off as Erin quelled her with a glare worthy of Andrew Marshall.

"Mom?" she called into the interior. Despite the brightness of the day, the front room lay in darkness save for one small lamp beside the couch. "I need to talk to you."

"What is it?" The familiar rasp of her mother's voice rang out as Alice materialized from the shadows. "Is something wrong?"

For weeks, Erin had feared her mother was letting herself

go. Today, her upswept strawberry-blond locks emphasized both her patrician features and the sharp protrusion of cheekbones. Her peach-colored dress with its pearl-seeded jacket clung to a figure that was much too thin.

"Mom, I've called off the wedding," Erin blurted.

"What?" Alice, who'd been eyeing Joseph dubiously, turned her full attention on her daughter.

"I can't marry Chet. I don't love him." The words poured out of her. "I never accepted his proposal. He lied to me about that. I trusted him because I couldn't trust myself, if that makes any sense. It's lucky I found out the truth in time."

She braced herself for a needle-sharp rebuke. She knew full well that the cream of Sundown Valley society was gathering and that countless hours of hard work had gone into whipping up the wedding.

"Have you told Chet?" Alice asked.

Erin nodded. "Of course."

"Well." Her attention returned to Joseph. "What is this detective doing here?"

"I had a few questions for your daughter," he said.

"Mom, I'm sorry," Erin rushed on. "I don't think I can face all those people. Is there any way…could someone else…"

Alice sighed. "Lance will tell them. You come home with us, sweetheart, and we'll take care of you."

Erin threw her arms around her mother and started to cry. "Thank you." She should have known her mother would come through when her daughter needed her most.

"We'll work this out." Despite her casual tone, her mother's tight smile seemed pained.

Fearing she might be hurting her, Erin let go. She hadn't realized until she felt the delicate bones how frail Alice had become. Although she was only forty-nine, the events of the last few months had taken their toll.

Lance had done this to her. Erin couldn't let Alice stay there alone with him.

"I'm not going home," she said. "Neither are you."

"Of course I am."

"It isn't safe," she said. "Think about what's happened to both of us. The accidents."

"We've had a run of bad luck but it's over." Alice retreated into haughtiness. "You know your father never approved of running away from problems. What do you think he'd say about all this?"

A noise inside the suite made Erin's heart leap into her throat. Her stepfather thrust his way out of the bedroom, tugging irritably at the bow tie of his tuxedo.

Although for the past few weeks he'd behaved courteously, today his fleshy face wore a peeved expression. "I heard voices. What the hell are you up to now?" he demanded. Erin had never heard anyone speak to her mother that way.

Alice took a shaky breath. "Erin's called off the wedding. She's got that policeman with her."

Lance thrust forward with such fury that Erin retreated onto the doorstep. "I told you to get lost!" he roared at the detective. "You've got no business showing up on my stepdaughter's wedding day."

"It's not my wedding day anymore," she said.

The corner of Joseph's mouth quirked as he joined her on the step. "She requested my assistance with the bridegroom."

"Erin, get in here. If there's a problem with Chet, we'll deal with it," Lance snapped.

"I've already dealt with it," she said. "Mom, come with us."

Her mother uttered a short, mirthless laugh. "I'm fine, believe me."

"Mrs. Bolding, if you need assistance…" Joseph began.

Lance blocked their view of his wife. Arms folded, he glowered. "She doesn't need help from either of you. Erin, you may not like it but I'm Alice's husband now and I'm tired of your attitude. In the future, if you want to talk to her, you can go through the board secretary at the Marshall Company." He slammed the door.

Erin stood there, too shocked to stir. Her stepfather had just banned her from talking to her mother, and Alice hadn't said a word.

Desperately, she turned to Joseph. "She's obviously terrified. Can't you do anything?"

He made a frustrated noise. "Not unless I can demonstrate abuse."

"He almost drowned her!"

"I can't prove that, and believe me, I tried." Joseph steered her away from the building. "Unless he does something overt or she asks for help, our options are limited."

Erin could hardly bear to walk away, knowing that once again she was failing her mother. "She was always so strong until Dad died. I don't know what's happened to her."

"You can't predict how people will react to losing a spouse." They kept to the edges of the country club as they circled toward the parking lot, avoiding the golf center where people might gawk at her bridal gown. "I thought my mother would fall apart when Dad died in prison. Instead, she went back to work as a legal secretary and made a new life for herself."

Suzanne Lowery had been a full-time mom, devoted to her family and always kind to Erin. She'd suffered when her husband's alcoholism ended his police career. She'd supported him through rehab and encouraged him to apply for a job at the Marshall Company, where he'd risen to chief of security.

Then, during Joseph's senior year in high school, his father had been accused—falsely, Erin believed—of robbery and murder. She'd tried to stand by the Lowerys but Joseph had pushed her away. She wished now that she hadn't let him.

"I'm glad she's okay," Erin said. "For my mom, Dad's death was like the bottom dropped out of everything. I guess I should have let her lean on me, but I was selfish. I took a month's leave and went back to work."

"It isn't selfish to grow up," Joseph said. "You couldn't have known what would happen."

Erin wanted to accept his absolution, but she retained a brutish image of Lance storming at her mother. What good was being rich if she couldn't protect the person she loved most?

Joseph had left his aging sedan in a side lot. "I figured my dent magnet would stand out like a sore thumb next to all the Lexuses and Cadillacs in front," he said, unlocking it.

"Is this an undercover car?" Erin moved aside a couple of files and a fast-food bag before shifting into the seat. At least there was plenty of legroom for her full skirt.

"Nope, it's mine. Not much to look at, but it's paid for." After tucking her inside, he closed the door.

In Tustin, Erin had driven a low-priced model bought with her own earnings, but she knew it wasn't the same thing. In the hospital, realizing how much trouble it would be to deal with the car while recuperating, she'd donated it to charity. Once she got permission from the doctor to drive again, she could always buy a new model. Joseph didn't have that option.

Money only made a difference if you let it, she thought. In essential ways, the two of them were equals.

When he settled behind the wheel and stretched his shoulder muscles, the vibrations traveled along the bench-style seat. Erin relaxed. She used to love riding beside him.

"Let's stop by your parents' house," he said. "While they're out, it's a good time for you to pick up a few clothes. Then tell me where to take you."

"I have no idea," she said.

"No hurry. Give it some thought."

She fell silent as they headed between the emerald slopes of the club's golf course. Beyond it, atop a steep rise, stood the grand house where she'd grown up. Her father had built it to command a spectacular view.

She missed it, although she was glad Lance Bolding didn't get to preen himself in the mansion Andrew Marshall had cherished. The house now belonged to Dr. Ray Van Fleet and his socialite wife, Jean, old friends of her parents. They were probably sitting in the ballroom right now, waiting for the wedding to begin.

The wedding. Already, it seemed unreal. Erin had virtually sleepwalked through the past weeks, as if the preparations and the wedding belonged to someone else.

Now she tried to think of a place to go. Although the Marshall Company owned a number of apartments, she didn't like the notion that Chet could get a key to any of them. A hotel room? Employees could be bribed, she thought.

Joseph had asked who might want to kill her. If that was really a possibility, she needed to be careful. Very careful.

She started to tremble. Everyone in Sundown Valley seemed to pose a threat. Except for Joseph, of course.

As for Tustin, she didn't want to be fifty miles away if her mother needed her. Besides, she'd been attacked there.

She tightened her grip on her purse. She wasn't going to get hysterical in front of Joseph. She'd think of somewhere to go.

His next words drove that concern out of her head—and replaced it with a more immediate one.

"Don't get excited," Joseph said, "but I think someone's following us."

Chapter Four

"What?" When Erin twisted in her seat, her face betrayed her alarm. Joseph disliked upsetting her. The words had slipped out before he'd had time to think.

He'd noticed the luxury sedan in his rearview mirror on the way around the lake. It had shot off Golf Club Lane some distance behind them, speeding away from the country club until it caught up and then slowing to trail a dozen car lengths behind.

"Do you recognize it?" he asked. "I thought maybe it was a friend of yours."

Erin shook her head. "I don't think so."

There were too many curves and trees for him to make the plate, and the car was painted a neutral shade. The driver appeared to be alone, although Joseph didn't discount the possibility of someone hunkering down.

He wasn't ready to phone in a report, however. Joseph didn't want to get the department involved in what might be simply a Marshall family dispute.

"It's probably nothing," he said. "Just some golfer going home."

"If you think he's following us, he probably is." Erin's hands clenched.

"I shouldn't have mentioned it."

"Don't treat me like an invalid! Even if I am one, sort of."

"I won't. But it was premature to say anything." Joseph hadn't intended to make his friend any more paranoid than she already was. He felt edgy enough himself after those unpleasant scenes at the country club.

They passed Rainbow Lane, which led to the old fishing area where Joseph and some of his high school buddies used to sneak forbidden beers. But the pier had been declared unsafe years ago, and Joseph had given up drinking after alcoholism cost his father his police career. Joseph didn't intend to run that risk.

When they swung right on Aurora Avenue toward the Marshalls' property, the luxury car continued on along Via Puesta del Sol. "False alarm," Joseph said.

"Good." Erin beamed. He wondered if she had any idea of how appealing she struck him with those lively eyes and a mouth that fit naturally into a curve.

She'd never been vain about her appearance or her social position. Sometimes Joseph used to forget she came from a rich family. It hadn't mattered so much when they were kids, but he'd learned long ago that it mattered to adults.

They passed a cluster of cottages. Farther along the pavement, a Do Not Enter sign marked the point where the road became private.

They curved past a stand of eucalyptus on the sprawling estate. When the Boldings' house emerged into view, Joseph didn't like it any more than he had the first time he saw it six months ago. Maybe less.

He'd arrived the night of Alice's near drowning to see police spotlights playing across the water and red lights blinking atop a welter of emergency vehicles. The structure sat in a hollow, its jutting roof giving it the appearance of a brooding misanthrope with hunched shoulders.

He wondered again how Lance Bolding had persuaded aristocratic Alice Marshall to give up her palace for this low-slung house on the far side of the lake, away from her friends and the country club. Although the wooden structure, painted tan with brown trim, had its own pier on the glittering lake, he found it depressing.

The place hadn't grown on Joseph during his investigation. After reading about Erin's accident, he'd disliked the thought of her staying out here. He found the atmosphere toxic, both literally and figuratively.

He halted on the turnaround. A covered porch the width of the house supported a glider seat and small table. "This place reminds me of a Louisiana plantation gone to seed."

"It is gloomy, isn't it?" Erin made no move to get out. "But the lake's pretty."

"That depends." He decided not to make any further reference to her mother's close call. "You've got a key, I hope?"

"Yes." Erin reached into her purse. Joseph came around to escort her.

As she emerged, sunlight picked out the blue-white clarity of the diamonds in her tiara and choker. "You'd better leave those behind unless they belong to you," he said. "I wouldn't put it past Lance to file a theft report."

"Actually, they were a wedding present from Chet."

"Chet makes that kind of money?" He stopped short of asking how much they'd cost. Maybe they were artificial, but he doubted it.

"We pay our CEO well," Erin told him. "I'll send them back, of course."

When they entered the house, the smell that hit Joseph was a mixture of furniture polish and stale air heavy with moisture from the lake. Drawn curtains plunged the living room into semi-gloom.

At least Alice had brought with her the beautiful antique furnishings from her former home. Chosen with taste, the curving divan and beveled-glass china cabinet retained a lightness that brought to mind happier times. Inside the cabinet, row after row of charming bells—glass and ceramic and metal, lovingly collected over many years—sat silent.

He knew from his investigation that no servants lived on the property, and the only full-time staff was the house-keeper. Even so, Joseph called out "Hello?" a couple of times and listened to his voice echo through the rooms. No one answered.

"Wait while I check it out," he told Erin.

She frowned in confusion. "There's nobody here."

"Humor me." Drawing his gun, he moved quickly from room to room. It wasn't a proper search. He would never go through a house alone if he believed there was someone lying in wait. But it reassured him that they weren't likely to meet any surprises.

"Go ahead," he told Erin on returning to the front room.

"I have to change," she said. "I'll work as fast as I can."

"Need any help?"

"Changing?" She started to smile. "That's quite an offer."

"I didn't mean…" Joseph ducked his head. "I was think-ing your dress must be complicated. But you wouldn't want me fumbling with it. I've got butterfingers." And a tongue tied in knots, he thought in embarrassment.

When she was amused, Erin glowed. It should happen more often, he thought. "You don't have to tell me! Remem-ber that Santa Claus costume? When you first put it on, you had a beard growing out of your ear."

"I did not!"

"Yes, you did. It was cute." Her face tilted toward him. For a moment, she became again a laughing girl of fifteen and he was seventeen, so much in love he couldn't see straight. He had to kiss her.

Joseph stopped. He wasn't a kid, and besides, he'd come here to protect Erin, not indulge himself. "Better hurry. We don't want to be here when your parents get back."

"Oh." With a visible effort, she recovered her poise. "I

won't be long." She whisked away, leaving a floral scent in her wake.

Since he considered himself to be on an investigation despite the chief's orders, Joseph scanned the area. In violent households, one might expect to find a broken lamp or a dent in the wall. He saw none.

Moving to the lake side of the house, he glanced into the sunroom. Through a wall of windows, daylight gleamed across enough wedding presents to stock a department store. Despite the brevity of the engagement, friends had showered the bridal couple with heaps of silver, crystal and china.

After checking through a front window to make sure no cars had pulled in, Joseph paced the living room as the minutes ticked by. Finally Erin rejoined him, toting a suitcase and an overnight bag. She'd swapped the wedding gown and diamonds for a pair of jeans, a pink sweater and a simple pearl necklace.

"I hope I didn't take too long." She glanced past him to the table covered with gifts. "Oh, my! Those all have to be returned. I should write notes to the guests, too."

"Unless you plan to hire a moving van, I suggest you let your mother take care of it," Joseph said. "Besides, no one expects you to write notes in your condition."

"But it's my responsibility."

"Who appointed you the world's only perfect person?" It was a phrase he'd used often when they were teenagers.

"I'm being Little Goody Two Shoes again. You're right. Without your healthy corrupting influence, I slipped right back into the role," she teased.

He didn't bother to ask how a corrupting influence could be healthy. He understood what she meant.

On a message pad, Erin wrote a message to her mother. "Okay, how's this? I'm asking her to return the gifts and give the diamonds to Chet. She can leave them with Betsy—she's the board secretary at the office."

"Sounds good." Joseph was glad she didn't insist on handing them to Chet herself. No matter what the etiquette books said, as far as he was concerned, the less contact between them, the better.

"Well, that's that." Erin signed the note. "Mom can reach me on my cell phone."

"Have you decided where you're going?" Taking the suitcase, Joseph led her onto the porch.

"Not yet." After locking up, she dropped the key through the mail slot. Joseph would have advised her to hold on to it in case of emergency, but she'd beaten him to the punch. "Before I know what I can afford, I need to consult Stanley Rogers at the company. In addition to being the chief financial officer, he manages my trust fund. Until he gets in on Monday, I don't have much money with me."

"Excuse me?" A multimillionaire, and she made it sound as if she were broke!

"I'm not trying to plead poverty. It's kind of complicated." Erin beat him to the car and let herself inside. But once there, she sank back as if she'd expended most of her energy. She must have been operating on adrenaline, Joseph reflected as he stowed her possessions in the trunk.

When he got in, Erin resumed her explanation. "The fund makes a quarterly deposit in my account, and I turn it over to the Friend of a Friend Foundation. That's confidential, by the way."

"You're behind the Friend of a Friend Foundation?" The organization had made a generous grant to the after-school tutoring program founded by his mother and a close friend of hers, a teacher.

"Even Tina doesn't know that."

"Obviously not." Tina volunteered at The Homework Center, and she'd been as mystified as anyone about who was behind the donation.

"I've been living on what I earn at my job," Erin said. "Believe me, that doesn't go far. My bank account in Orange

County has a couple of hundred dollars at most. Of course, there's always my credit card."

"Card, singular?"

"I told you, I've been living on my income," she said. "I'm not sure when the next quarterly payment is due, but maybe I can get an advance."

"You could call this financial guy at home."

"I'm not that desperate," Erin said. "I don't think it's right to force an employee to go into the office on his day off just to suit my convenience."

As he drove, Joseph reflected on the contradictions in her attitude. On the one hand, she saw herself as an owner with an obligation not to abuse her authority. On the other hand, she seemed to doubt her ability even to tap into her resources for a small advance. She owned a half interest in the Marshall Company, for heaven's sake!

Well, these decisions belonged to her, not him. What she needed from her old friend, he mused, was emotional support and physical protection.

He knew he tempted fate by getting involved where no one except Erin wanted him, and he wasn't entirely sure how she felt. Perversely, the prospect of defying the rest of the world appealed to him. If he ever stopped leaping before he looked, life could get awfully boring.

"Well, if you still haven't decided where to stay, I'm taking you to my house," he said.

Erin didn't answer.

"If that's all right," Joseph added.

She gave him one of those sweet, enigmatic expressions that made him want to kiss her and poke her in the ribs at the same time.

"Or I could drop you at the mall," he said with mock solemnity. "Considering that you more or less own it."

"There's a tempting thought. I could pitch a sleeping bag in the food court." She made a face.

"Well?"

"I'd love to go to your place, but I don't want to get you in trouble," Erin said. "You worked hard to get where you are." She might not know the details, but she obviously suspected the hurdles he'd had to leap to get hired on the force, not to mention making detective so quickly. After what had happened to his father, some people had been waiting for him to fail. They still were.

"It's only for the weekend." Joseph negotiated the curving side streets toward Old Lake Highway, the most direct route into town. "It's too isolated for you to stay there next week while I'm at work."

"Where exactly do you live?" she asked.

"In the woods."

"You always said you wanted to be close to nature," Erin recalled. "If I remember right, at one point you talked about becoming a forest ranger."

"I'm too stubborn for that," Joseph said.

"Too stubborn?" After a moment, Erin answered her own question. "You mean, if you left town, everybody would think you were running away."

"Exactly."

"You gave up your dream to prove a point?" she demanded.

"I'm stubborn, but not that stubborn," he said. "I like being a cop."

"You don't have to convince me about being stubborn."

"I thought I was downright accommodating in the old days." After all, he'd poured his earnings from a lawn-mowing job into movie tickets and hamburger dinners, not to mention a couple of tuxedo rentals that nearly broke his personal bank.

"You were, except when we broke up," she reminded him. "I wanted to talk things over. I wanted to give our friendship a chance. You insisted it was hopeless."

"Don't remind me. The past is dead and buried, Erin. If you're going to be staying with me, we have to agree on that." He didn't want things hitting too close to home.

Just being around Erin made Joseph want things he shouldn't. He'd long ago made his peace with the injustices of the past. He didn't need a nest of stinging emotions stirred up again.

"Okay," she said after a long pause. "I agree. Under protest."

"Duly noted."

They fell into silence. During the eight-mile drive into town, the gentle rocking of the car, combined with her exhaustion, put Erin to sleep.

A lock of her shoulder-length brown hair, crinkly where she'd brushed it out of its twist, floated in a draft. Joseph imagined how it would feel against his cheek, as silky as a whisper in the night.

In the old days, he'd have slung his arm across the back of the seat and she'd have scooted close. It was ridiculous how natural it felt to be riding with her again, as if the intervening years had evaporated.

He'd expected to fall in love with someone else by now. When one potential relationship after another failed to develop, he'd attributed it to the rigors of a policeman's schedule and to the difficulty of trusting anyone.

Maybe taking her home with him ran the risk of reigniting an old flame. But under the circumstances, what else could he do?

He returned his attention to his driving. As they made their way through the heart of town, Joseph spotted a luxury sedan like the previous one, again lagging a few car lengths behind them. If it had followed them on the highway, he hadn't noticed.

He made a couple of turns, and the car disappeared. Gone, he hoped. Most likely a different vehicle.

On Little Creek Lane, which wound through a grove close to his cabin, he caught sight of it again. He hadn't imagined it; they were being followed.

Erin's eyes blinked open. "What's wrong?"

"I thought you were asleep."

"I was dozing. I felt the car speeding up."

"We're being tailed again." Before she could sit up, he added, "Stay low." He didn't expect the guy to start shooting, but you never knew.

Erin obeyed. "Can you see who it is?"

"Not yet." Joseph considered his options. The other car hadn't broken any laws, so he could hardly call dispatch. Normally, he'd pull into a public place such as a gas station, but there was only woodland on both sides and the road was too narrow for him to reverse course.

Although he carried a gun, he didn't want to risk a shoot-out in the middle of nowhere. While he hated to lead whoever was tailing them to his house, his property would offer cover and a chance for Erin to escape inside.

The funny thing was, the vehicle seemed familiar. Not just because he'd seen it earlier today, either. That particular make, that beige paint—well, they were common enough. The only thing he could say for sure was that the figure behind the wheel didn't appear as large as Chet.

Maybe it was another resident. Although the houses were set far apart, including vacation cabins that frequently lay empty, it was possible the guy lived nearby. Maybe that was where Joseph had seen the car before.

They passed one driveway, then another. The vehicle didn't turn. Finally, the only one left was Joseph's.

"Looks like we've got a visitor."

"Can't you call someone?" Erin kept low, as he'd instructed. "Cops can call 911, can't they?"

"Sure. Or I could use my radio. But I've been out conducting an investigation against the chief's orders, and I've got a feeling whoever's behind us wants to talk about it," Joseph said. "I'm not real eager to bring in the rest of the department unless things get sticky."

"Okay," Erin said. "I didn't mean to cause trouble for you."

"If there's any trouble, I caused it for myself."

He hoped his decision not to call for help wasn't putting her in unnecessary danger. For himself, Joseph never worried. Except for the pain it would cause his mother, he didn't fear death nearly as much as disgrace or false imprisonment, the fate his father had endured.

His driveway wound uphill through dense woods. Normally, Joseph enjoyed the sense of leaving civilization behind. In all but the worst weather, he rolled down the windows to enjoy the twitter of birds and the scent of pines. Not today.

With Erin at risk, he had to assume that whoever was tailing them might turn nasty. He made some quick calculations.

"You may have to duck inside," he said. "There's a spare gun in the bedroom, in the nightstand."

"I don't like guns," Erin said.

"Ever fired one?"

She nodded. "My dad took me to a shooting range a couple of times. He said I needed to know how to protect myself."

"Watch out for the recoil," he told her. "It's a .38. That's powerful but we don't know if this guy's on drugs, so if you have to shoot him, fire at least two or three rounds. One bullet might not stop him."

"You're scaring me."

"Don't get scared. Get mad." He'd adopted that slogan as a teenager, and it had served him well. "Okay, enough of the pep talk. When I turn off the motor, I'll hand you the keys. There are two, one for the car, one for the door. Stay out of sight until I give the word, then bolt for the house. He may not know you're here, so you've got surprise on your side. The bedroom's the first door to the right."

"Thanks," Erin said. "I'll be okay as long as I know the plan." She sounded steady and determined. Joseph respected people who kept their heads in an emergency.

Cresting the hill, they came within sight of the cabin. A gravel clearing fronted the wood-and-stone building, which had a carport situated on the far side.

"I'm going to stop in front of the porch," Joseph said. "If you have to duck out the door, you'll be right there." Pulling into the carport would have given him more cover but would slash Erin's chances of making it inside. "Don't go until I tell you to."

"I won't."

So far, there'd been nothing threatening about their pursuer other than the fact that he was following them. Unexpectedly, the other car jolted forward, almost hitting Joseph's bumper. It felt like a threat.

In the rearview mirror, the driver's eyes met Joseph's. Cold fury radiated at him.

At least he understood why he'd recognized the car. The man behind the wheel was Edgar Norris.

Judging by the chief's taut jaw and the angry gesture with his car, he was royally ticked about having his orders disobeyed. That didn't explain why he'd left the wedding and lit out after them. Or why he emerged from the car with one hand hovering near his gun.

Eleven years ago, as detective lieutenant, Norris had headed the investigation into the robbery-murder of jewelry store owner Binh Nguyen. It was Norris who'd evaluated the evidence against Lewis Lowery, recommended that he be charged and sat at the prosecutor's side during much of the trial.

He'd never liked Joseph, but he'd always treated him fairly. In return, Joseph had given the chief the benefit of the doubt. Although he was certain his father had been framed, he'd assumed Norris simply failed to recognize that.

Now he wondered if he'd been wrong. And whether his shortsightedness was going to get him and Erin killed.

Chapter Five

Joseph stopped in front of the porch. "Remember the plan," he told Erin in a low voice.

"You bet." She didn't chatter or seek reassurance. Not that he would mind comforting her, but not under the circumstances. "Can you tell who it is?"

"It's the chief."

"Why would he follow us?"

He kept his face averted as Norris approached, so he couldn't be seen conversing. He hoped the chief believed that he'd left Erin at her mother's house, and he intended to keep it that way. "I don't know. He looks mad."

"He wouldn't shoot us, would he?"

"Let's hope not."

After slipping the keys to Erin, Joseph opened his door and eased out to face his boss. He had a good three inches on the chief, but you didn't judge a man like Edgar Norris by his size. Or by the spare tire around his waist or the fact that he dyed what was left of his hair. He had kick-butt body language and the grit to back it up.

Norris's fist pounded Joseph's trunk, making the car creak on its aging springs. "What the hell did you think you were doing when you barged into Erin Marshall's dressing room?"

"I wanted to wish an old friend well," he replied evenly.

"Don't lie to me," the man growled. "I told you to leave

Alice's case alone. You're harassing one of this town's leading families, and now you've managed to screw up the wedding of the year."

"I needed to clarify some points to wrap up my report," he said. "I didn't expect to discover that her fiancé had pulled a con job on her."

"Nobody forced that woman into a bridal gown."

"There's more than one kind of force," he said.

"You don't know understand the kind of fallout there's going to be," the chief snapped. "Do you have any idea how a public humiliation like this is going to hurt Chet Dever's campaign?"

"What does Chet Dever's campaign have to do with the Sundown Valley Police Department, other than the fact that your son is managing it?" Joseph shot back. It wasn't the smartest remark to make under the circumstances. Sometimes retorts flew out of his mouth before he could stop them.

Although the chief's face darkened, he kept himself under control. "You're injecting your personal feelings into police business. When it comes to the powerful people in this town, there's a chip on your shoulder and everyone knows it."

"Everyone being Gene?" He'd gone too far, Joseph thought. "I take that back."

"You're going to wish you could take a lot of things back," Norris said. "You've made enemies all over town, embarrassed this force and contradicted my direct order. As of right now, I'm busting you back to patrol."

"Wait a minute!" A demotion made it unlikely Joseph would ever advance in this department or, possibly, any other. Thank goodness the police union had established protections for its member. "I have the right to appeal."

"I'll throw in a few more charges to make it look good." Satisfaction was written all over the chief's face. "Like the fact that you drew a gun on me."

"I haven't touched my weapon!"

"It's my word against yours. Who do you think people will believe?"

Joseph's passenger door swung open. Before he could call out that the situation might still be dangerous, Erin's resolute face appeared above the car. "I think they might believe me," she said. "I heard the whole thing."

The chief's Adam's apple performed a couple of rapid bobs. "Miss Marshall. I didn't see you."

"So I gathered." She studied him levelly.

"This officer violated a direct order." Norris recovered a trace of his bluster. "I have an obligation to discipline him."

"What I don't understand," Erin said, "is why you accused him of drawing his gun when I can see that it's still in its holster."

She probably couldn't see that, since Joseph's holster was beneath his jacket. It didn't matter. She'd made her point.

The chief gritted his teeth. He wasn't accustomed to backing down and Joseph knew he'd take his pound of flesh one way or another. Finally, he said, "You're on administrative leave for a month, Lowery. Paid leave," he said in Erin's direction.

"You need to rethink your priorities," he continued, turning toward Joseph, "and decide whether you're ready to follow the chain of command or whether you'd rather work somewhere else."

"And when I come back?"

"There'll be no action taken unless you do something else to deserve it." Shutting off further discussion, Norris returned to his car. He gunned the motor, shot backward and spun away. Gravel spattered off Joseph's car.

The chief's order took a minute to sink in. Joseph was on leave. His pressing cases would be reassigned and disposed of. Especially the Alice Bolding case. But at least he wasn't busted back to patrol.

"Did I do more harm than good?" Erin asked.

"No way. You got me a month's paid vacation." He summoned a grin for her benefit. "What's to complain about?"

Joseph retrieved her suitcase and overnight bag. If the chief's gravel shower had left a few new dents in the car, it was impossible to tell, he reflected as he slammed the trunk.

But he hadn't told the whole truth. Chet Dever wasn't the only guy around here who'd been humiliated today. By Monday, every cop in Sundown Valley was going to know that the son of the town's most infamous ex-officer had screwed up.

ERIN FOUND the inside of the house brighter and warmer than she'd expected. From the rough-hewn front, she'd formed a mental image of small, undistinguished rooms, but Joseph opened the door into a large chamber that stretched the depth of the house to a rear wall composed mostly of glass.

The huge window showed a grassy rear yard dappled with wildflowers. Beyond it lay a vista of raw, plunging canyon depths in one direction and, in the other, a gentler, wooded slope. Even with twilight closing in, the scene took her breath away.

Inside, soft colors rippled through the room as if a sunset had floated there. From the modern furnishings to a block-glass bookcase that partially divided the room, nothing hindered the flow of light.

"This is gorgeous." Erin touched the velvety texture of the couch, which faced an entertainment center. "Don't tell me you designed this yourself."

"Not all of it. I had a female consultant." Before she could draw any inference, Joseph added, "My mom."

"How is she?" Erin asked.

"Incredibly busy," he said. "Happy, too, I think."

He hefted her luggage through a doorway to the right. That, Erin remembered from his earlier instructions, led to the bedroom.

As soon she was alone, scenes from the past few hours

sprang vividly into her mind. Chet, all wounded pride and self-importance. Lance storming past her mother. The chief threatening Joseph. Which of them were her enemies? Did one of them want to kill her?

You're getting paranoid again. Put a lid on it.

Squaring her shoulders, she followed in Joseph's wake. As soon as she crossed the threshold, she registered that this was unmistakably his room. She knew it not only from the masculine furniture and high school wrestling trophies, but from the heady male scent in the air.

He'd set her stuff on the bed's bright comforter and turned away to clear space in the bureau. Where he'd removed his jacket, she noticed his tailored white shirt clinging to a muscular back and broad shoulders.

Awareness sizzled through her body. Softly swollen breasts and a speeding pulse tempted her in ways she hadn't been in years. This was dangerous, alluring, crazy.

The temptation to curve herself against Joseph nearly overpowered Erin. She fought it and won, because she had to.

"I can stay in the other bedroom," she said.

"There is no other bedroom." Joseph removed linens from a drawer and set them on the queen-size bed. "The previous owner turned the back bedroom into part of the living room. Not very practical but I like the expansiveness."

"I'll sleep out there," Erin said.

"No." His tone brooked no argument. "It's easier for me to protect you if I'm out there. By the way, don't open the door to anyone or answer my house phone. I'd rather as few people as possible know where you are."

"I can't imagine anyone harming me here."

"There's always a risk." Joseph shoved his clothes to one side of the closet. "I want to keep the blinds closed throughout the house so no one can get a fix on you."

"A fix? As in a rifle sight?"

"Forget I mentioned it."

As if that were possible! Erin dropped onto the edge of the bed.

This morning, she'd awakened with her head full of wedding plans, the whole day and possibly her life laid out before her like a garden path. She'd been sleepwalking, of course, but there'd been comfort in that. "I wish I were numb again," she blurted.

After pushing the suitcase aside, Joseph sat beside her. His hands chafed her smaller ones, making her realize how cold she was.

"Scared?" he asked.

"Petrified. That remark about someone getting a fix on me wasn't exactly comforting."

"I'm not here to comfort you. I'm here to keep you alive." His breath whispered across her cheek.

"I didn't realize you'd volunteered to be my bodyguard." She fought the impulse to turn and touch her lips to his.

"I guess I have, by default." He shifted away. Perhaps he was battling the same urge, she thought "There's a positive side to my being on leave. Since I won't have to work, there's no danger of leaving you here alone."

"Does that mean I can stay?" Erin asked, elated. Then, guiltily, she added, "But I'm putting you out of your bed. Once I meet with Stanley, I should be able to move somewhere else."

"If you like, I can put you in touch with a top-level security service." He fingered a loose strand of her hair. "Or you can stay, if you prefer."

She did prefer. Very much. "Yes. I'd rather be with you."

"We can handle this investigation together. After that stunt Chet pulled with the hurry-up wedding, I have to believe something's seriously amiss. Whatever it is, we need to find out."

She remembered the chief's threat. "That might get you fired. I'll hire a private detective."

"Like hell you will!" Fervor lifted Joseph to his feet. She

missed his warmth. "It'll take him days or weeks to get up to speed. Besides, this is my case. With or without you, I'm using this time to find out what's going on. The more the chief orders me to back off, the more I want to find out what he's hiding."

"This is my battle," she insisted. "And he might not be hiding anything. He's always tried to stay on my family's good side."

Grabbing a cane-bottom chair, Joseph swung it backward and sat facing her with his arms folded on the chair rail. "Out there, I saw something in the chief's face that stopped me. Rage. The worst kind of rage, the kind that stems from fear. I want to know why."

"What could the chief have to fear?" Tina's father had always moved with a swaggering confidence a bit like his son's. To Erin, he seemed unshakable.

"He headed the investigation that sent my father to prison," Joseph said. "What if he wasn't just doing his job? What if he did something back then that he's ashamed of and I'm the one person who can bring it to light?"

"You think he railroaded your dad?" Although she'd never entirely liked the man, she'd never doubted his integrity "And that this is somehow connected to his not wanting you to investigate whether somebody tried to kill my mother and me?" She braced her hands against the bed as if afraid she might lose her balance. The implications were bizarre. And terrifying.

"I guess it does sound far-fetched," Joseph said.

"I hope so." She blinked, and discovered that her eyelids were heavy. Apparently, the nap in the car hadn't taken the edge off her weariness after all. "Just because the guy's short-tempered doesn't make him a criminal."

Joseph shrugged. "I'll admit, the chief doesn't need an excuse to dislike me. It's no secret that he didn't want me on the force. Like father, like son, he figured. Your dad felt the same way."

"Whoa!" His words stopped Erin cold. "Are you saying he objected to the police department hiring you? I can't believe that. I mean, that was, what, six years after your father's trial? And my dad never blamed you."

"He must have found it painful even to hear my name. Don't forget, my father was his employee. It was like a betrayal," Joseph said.

"What makes you think he had anything against you personally?" Erin asked.

"Rick overheard a conversation between the old chief and Norris about my application. That's back when Norris was still a captain."

Chief Manuel Lima had retired three years ago, Erin remembered. "They discussed whether to hire you, right out in the open?"

"Rick was in an alcove in the break room, getting coffee," Joseph said. "You can't see somebody in there. Can I tell the story or are you going to keep interrupting?"

"Sorry."

"According to Norris, they'd discussed my application on the golf course and your father opposed it. So he passed the word along to Chief Lima."

"Dad always liked you," she said. "And men don't usually like the boys who date their daughters, do they? Besides, you did get hired. That ought to prove something."

"It proves Chief Lima wasn't in thrall to the town's VIPs the way Norris is," Joseph said. "I had the highest score on their aptitude test, and he gave me a chance. Look, I don't know why your father felt that way. Maybe he thought I'd be better off working in another town. He might have figured he was doing me a favor."

Erin rubbed her temples. "I'm sorry. I think I'm on overload. I just hate to believe Dad would say something like that."

Joseph rocked forward in his chair and for a moment she

thought he was going to reach out. She wanted him to touch her. She wanted him to make the pain go away.

Instead, he said, "You're right. I'm asking too much of you. You need to sleep." When she opened her mouth to protest, he said, "Don't argue. By the way, when's the last time you ate?"

Erin tried to think. "Lunch, I guess. I had some soup at home. I ought to be starved."

"You may not know this, but I'm a gifted gourmet cook," he said.

She spotted a playful quirk around the edges of Joseph's mouth. "Are we talking Fiddle Faddle with chocolate milk?"

He clapped a hand to his heart. "Your skepticism wounds me."

"Frozen lasagna?"

"Ye shall be surprised." He moved her suitcase to the floor. "I'll have dinner ready when you wake up."

"As long as the food doesn't bite me back, I'll be happy."

Joseph left without any further fuss. Yet she felt more cared for than if he'd hovered over her.

Slipping off her shoes, Erin crawled gratefully under the covers. As her body relaxed against the sheets, she wished she could remember what had happened the day of her accident. If only she could describe the driver, it might help them solve this puzzle.

When she was eleven, she'd had a tonsillectomy. She remembered lying in the operating room before the surgery. One minute the anesthesiologist had been murmuring words of comfort and the next minute she'd awakened in the recovery room. She could have sworn she'd simply closed her eyes and then opened them again.

The Saturday six weeks ago was like that. She had to have awakened in the morning, dressed and gone to the carnival. She'd obviously talked to Bea at one point. No one had given her anesthesia, yet it was all a big blank. Vanished without a trace.

Why didn't she remember setting the cash box on the pavement? Why couldn't she recall a darn thing?

Chocolate. And nuts. A big, thick bar.

Erin almost tasted it. She doubted it had anything to do with that day, however, because she'd sworn off unhealthy treats long ago. It had to be her hunger pangs talking.

Focusing on the promise of a meal to come, she drifted off.

OKAY, SO HE'D exaggerated his culinary skills, but they weren't bad if you considered the circumstances. When Joseph was younger, his mother had done all the cooking, and during college he'd been too busy working and studying to do more than grab a burger now and then.

During the past few years, as he entered his late twenties and began hearing the unwelcome news that youth didn't last forever, he'd decided he needed to eat right. So he'd done what any red-blooded American male would do: He'd asked his mom for cooking lessons.

She'd declined.

What a shock, Joseph reflected as he took out a package of frozen burritos. From the cabinet, he retrieved a can of low-fat refried beans and a box of Mexican rice. With fat-free sour cream, grated cheese and a salad, they'd have a passable meal.

He'd figured out by himself how to throw a meal together. It was definitely the hard way to learn to cook. He'd eaten more burned, bland and just plain lousy food than he cared to admit. On a policeman's salary, he couldn't afford to throw anything away unless it verged on medically hazardous.

Suzanne Lowery hadn't been trying to give her son a hard time when she turned him down. She was too busy, she'd explained apologetically. Between working as secretary at a law office and heading up her homework organization, she rarely cooked even for herself.

Even so, she was a great mom. Without her, Joseph couldn't imagine how he'd have kept his balance through the shock of what had happened to his father.

She'd never grown bitter, despite the devastating loss of her husband, who'd been killed in prison when he tried to break up a fight. She'd moved on, because there was no point in doing anything else. And, perhaps, to set a good example for her son.

She'd succeeded, Joseph mused while waiting for the water to boil for the rice. He'd put the past behind him, too. Well, except for a bit of digging through news articles from the time, since he didn't dare request a copy of the old police reports.

He'd found precious little.

The known facts weren't complicated. One night when Joseph was seventeen, a merchant named Binh Nguyen, who designed and sold jewelry at the Mercantile Building—one of the Marshalls' properties—had received a shipment of gems valued at $2.5 million. He'd put a deposit on them, expecting to pay off the balance with profits from custom jewelry orders.

Aside from the Nguyen family, only the police department and Marshall Security had been notified of the shipment. In case their watchfulness wasn't enough, Binh Nguyen had made a last-minute decision to sleep over at his shop that night.

It had proved to be a fatal mistake.

That night, someone had disabled the alarm and sneaked into the building. Confronted by a baseball-bat-wielding Nguyen, the robber or robbers had grabbed the weapon, beaten him savagely and escaped with the jewels.

In the morning, police had found him dead. In a nearby alley, they'd located Lewis Lowery, with alcohol in his system and a head injury he apparently suffered when he'd tripped and fallen.

Lewis claimed he'd gone to the building to make sure everything was all right and that someone had attacked him. He'd attributed the trace of alcohol in his blood to someone pouring it down his throat, but the prosecutor had persuaded the jury he'd been roaring drunk the night before.

The night watchman assigned to the Mercantile Building, one Alfonso Lorenz, testified that Lewis had ordered him to stay away that night. He'd presented a convincing, cohesive story and never strayed from it.

When police found Joseph's father in the alley, he was carrying a photocopy of security plans for the building that included the alarm code. The murder weapon, left at the scene, bore his fingerprints.

The prosecutor had argued that after an unexpected confrontation, Lewis had killed Nguyen and then been so overwhelmed with guilt that he'd drunk himself into a stupor. His motive for the robbery—this had bothered Joseph more than anything—had supposedly been the desire to fund his son's college education.

The jewels had vanished. Only a few had ever been identified, years later, and they'd been sold overseas.

The evidence and testimony had been strong enough to convince the jury. Later, Lorenz had departed for a Caribbean island that lacked an extradition treaty with the U.S. Although he was certain the man had been involved, Joseph didn't believe Lorenz was smart enough to have pulled off the job alone.

The only other suspect had been a small-time crook named Todd Wilde who, a few days before the crime, was released from the county jail after serving a sentence for theft. Detectives had questioned him routinely but found no link to the murder of Binh Nguyen.

On the Internet, Joseph had learned that, six years ago, Wilde had been convicted in Los Angeles for a string of burglaries. He'd gone to prison for a long stretch.

It all brought matters back to square one. Joseph's vague suspicions about the chief didn't amount to a hill of beans. Or a can of refried beans, for that matter.

On the stove, the water boiled furiously. He'd better pay more attention to his cooking.

After stirring in the rice, Joseph went to check on Erin. She slept with the covers pulled up to her chin, her chestnut hair spread across the pillow. This was supposed to be her wedding night, he remembered. If not for his interference, she'd be Chet Dever's wife now.

A wife taken by fraud and deceit. Joseph would never regret what he'd done, even if it harmed his career. Erin belonged here until they cleared up this mess.

He refused to torture himself with delusions about them having a future together. That diamond choker and tiara had said it all. He didn't belong in a high-stakes world like that, and he didn't want to.

He cared passionately about his work: the abused wife he'd convinced to take her children and flee to safety. The heart attack victim he'd kept alive with CPR until the paramedics arrived. The little girl he'd found, lost and frightened in the woods, because he'd called softly while earlier searchers had terrified her by making a racket.

He'd made a life for himself. But there was something missing.

Gazing at Erin, Joseph wished they were just two people whose bodies got excited every time they brushed each other. Just two people who, as teenagers, had been willing to take it slow because they had all the time in the world. Just two people who might be falling in love again.

Refusing to dwell on what might have been, he decided to check on the rice. He'd just stepped into the kitchen when he heard the rumble of a car. Because of the way sounds echoed in the canyons, it was impossible to tell whether it was moving toward the house, down the street or on another road entirely.

After switching off the burner, Joseph went to peer out the front. Below and to the left, at the nearest house, he glimpsed a midsize sedan, possibly green, moving through the dusk. The house, a rental, had been vacant for weeks. Perhaps the owner had found a new tenant.

In the kitchen, the phone rang. As he hurried to grab it, he reflected in annoyance that he should have turned off the ringer on the bedroom extension. Worst-case scenario: Erin would awaken sleep-dazed, forget where she was and answer.

Sure enough, he heard her voice a split second before he, too, said, "Hello?" into the mouthpiece.

On the other end, the caller hesitated. Someone was there. He could hear breathing.

The line cut off.

Joseph hung up and counted to ten. If it was his mother or a friend confused by hearing a woman's voice, the phone would ring again.

It stayed silent.

He dialed Star-69 to return the call. It didn't go through. The caller must have turned off his cell phone.

It could be anybody. There might be no correlation between the car next door and the phone call. Or maybe there was.

Joseph checked a slip of paper on the refrigerator and dialed the rental owner in Santa Barbara. The man, pleased to have a policeman next door, had given it to him in case a tenant created a disturbance.

When the owner answered, he said he hadn't rented the place nor had he authorized anyone to use the cabin. Of course, the car might belong to someone who'd noticed the For Rent sign and decided to inspect the premises.

Joseph promised to keep an eye on things and rang off. Uneasily, he headed for the bedroom.

Whoever had phoned knew Erin was there. If this meant trouble, he intended to be ready for it.

Chapter Six

When the dial tone sounded in her ear, it occurred to Erin that she wasn't supposed to answer the phone. She hoped it had simply been one of those careless callers who didn't have the decency to apologize for a wrong number.

Her mind still sleep-fogged, she rose, smoothed out her clothes and dug the brush from her purse. Inside the bag, something slid over her hand. A gold chain. She'd brought the jagged-heart pendant from her mother's house.

She wondered what Joseph would think if he saw it. Perhaps he'd forgotten about it entirely. He'd obviously moved way past their high school days.

She tucked the pendant into a drawer and pulled the brush through her tousled hair. After restoring a semblance of order, she freshened her powder and lipstick.

Even in adversity, Erin took pains with her appearance. Alice had forbidden her to run outside barefoot as a child or, as a teenager, to leave the house without inspection, saying Marshalls had to maintain their dignity. It was a good thing she hadn't seen Erin posing as Mrs. Santa Claus or fraudulently decked out as a Girl Scout during another escapade.

A tap at the door heralded Joseph's entrance. "What's so funny?" His eyebrows puckered in the middle, making him appear half-amused and half-dubious. The indentation begged to be explored by Erin's finger—and her lips.

"I was remembering stuff," she said. "Like when Letty Brownling arrived for a Friends of the Library speech and was too publicity shy to meet with reporters."

The two of them had decided to score a coup for the school newspaper by interviewing Letty, one of their favorite young-adult authors. Since she'd written about her love for Girl Scout cookies, Erin had borrowed Tina's uniform and she and Joseph had ferreted out the number of Ms. Brownling's hotel room.

They'd sold four boxes of cookies and landed the interview. Letty had also given them an autographed copy of her latest book, which Erin, pricked by her conscience, had donated to the school library.

"That was fun," Joseph said. "Sorry to bring this up, but about that phone call…"

"I made a mistake." She returned the makeup to her purse. "I forgot I shouldn't answer."

"I know. It's not your fault, but there may be a problem." He glanced out her window through the blinds. "A car just pulled up to the neighbor's house, which is supposedly empty."

Erin went cold inside. "What should we do?"

"It may be a potential renter, but I'm going to take my binocs outside for a closer look. Lock yourself in the bathroom until I get back."

Erin refused to crouch in the bathroom like a hunted animal. She'd already wasted a month blaming herself for her vague suspicions when they apparently had a basis in fact. Instead of terrifying her, the situation made her angry.

"I'll stay inside if you like, but I'm tired of playing the victim," she said. "If someone breaks in, I'll go for the gun."

Joseph's mouth twisted. "You're getting feisty."

"You've inspired me."

"Far be it from me to try to keep you down." He dimmed the lights and peered out again. "I don't see movement. If anything happens, dial 911 before you start playing Rambo."

"Got it."

"Stay clear of the window, too. Stray bullets can kill." About to leave, he glanced out again. "Oh, hell."

"What?" Her heart gave a painful skip.

"Someone's coming up the hill on foot from the next house."

Erin came and looked out. Trees striped the slope, black against gray in the near darkness. After a moment, she detected a figure slipping furtively up the uneven ground, accompanied by a moving pinpoint of light. It stumbled, and she heard a man curse loudly.

"I think we can rule out a professional assassin," Joseph murmured.

A chill ran along Erin's spine. "Was that what you expected?"

"Where there's big money, it's possible." He glanced out again. "Weird guy. He reached the driveway and he's continuing right out in the open. I'd better give him a welcome. Maybe he's just lost."

In the living room, she inhaled the scent of Mexican food and discovered she was hungry. Having to delay dinner made her even crankier at their uninvited guest.

Joseph snagged his holster from an end table and strapped it on. By the door, he flicked a switch and lit up porch.

He fitted his eye to the peephole. "Here he comes."

"Who is it?"

"I can't tell," Joseph said. "Please look out the back. Either this guy isn't up to anything or it's a trick, in which case he may have help."

Erin hurried to obey. Her gaze swept over the redwood deck and yard, which were also illuminated. "Nothing that I can see."

The doorbell rang. She twitched instinctively.

Joseph pointed to a high-backed swivel chair near Erin. If she sat facing away from him, she realized, she'd be hidden from view.

As soon as she complied, Joseph snicked open the bolt. "Have trouble finding my driveway?" he asked someone.

Erin waited to hear who would answer.

"I didn't want anyone to see my car parked in front of your house," the reply came in a familiar, slightly nasal voice.

Gene Norris. His father must have told him she was here, but what on earth did he want? It certainly wasn't a social call. Although she'd known him for years, Erin didn't think the two of them had ever conducted a one-on-one conversation in their lives.

"By anyone, you mean all those thousands of people who drive by?" Joseph asked. "Or maybe the gossipy pigeons in the trees?"

"You never know who'll drop by," Gene said stiffly. "I have sensitive business to discuss. Where's Erin?"

"Why?"

"What do you mean, why? Is there some reason I can't talk to her?" He ought to lose the whiny tone, she thought. Heaven help him if he had to make a speech on Chet's behalf.

"That depends," Joseph said.

"On what?"

"First of all, did you call here and hang up?"

She found herself hoping he'd say yes. At least that would resolve one nagging worry.

"I didn't hang up," Gene said. "I got cut off. The service is crummy in these canyons. I just wanted to make sure you were home."

"So you could park at my neighbor's house and sneak up." Joseph wasn't cutting the guy any slack. Nor should he.

"I need to talk to her about Chet." Gene had apparently decided on the direct approach.

"He's using his campaign manager as a go-between?"

"I'm also the best man," Gene reminded him. "Don't worry, I'm not going to try to persuade her to take him back. That's his job."

Erin decided that, with Joseph standing by, he posed no immediate danger. She swung the chair around. "I'm right here."

Across the large room, Gene, still in his tuxedo, made an odd picture beside Joseph's taller, more powerful form. Despite the dirt on one knee and a leaf clinging to his dark blond hair, there was nothing laughable about Tina's brother.

His thin face and wiry form burned with the same nervous energy that, in high school, he'd applied to trying to make other kids feel inferior. Since he was whip-smart, that hadn't been difficult. She'd been glad when he left to attend UC Santa Barbara, after which he'd worked as a stockbroker for a while alongside Chet.

Gene had found his calling when he volunteered in the re-election campaign of a local assemblyman and did so well he was offered a job. After a stint in Sacramento, he'd returned to link up with his former co-worker.

Erin wondered how far he would go to protect his candidate. It hadn't even occurred to her until Chief Norris mentioned it that her actions might have harmed Chet politically.

Gene scowled on seeing her but quickly rearranged his features into an approximation of civility. "I have a request."

"From you or from Chet?"

"Both."

Joseph assumed a watchful stance. His caution reminded Erin not to let down her guard.

"I'm listening." She kept her distance. The acoustics were fine from across the room.

"Chet wants your family to issue a press release to the effect that you suffered a relapse and the wedding has been postponed."

"Postponed?" Joseph said.

"Indefinitely."

"And you expect the press to accept that and go away quietly?" Erin didn't try to hide her skepticism. "They're not gullible."

Gene had a ready answer. "The release will explain that you'd deliberately planned the ceremony to take place before the campaign got into full swing. In view of your condition, he doesn't want to expose you to the stress of an election, so it won't be rescheduled until after March. By then, the whole business will be old history and you can quietly call off the engagement."

Joseph's eyebrows did their bunching thing. He wasn't convinced of the necessity of this ruse, she gathered, and neither was she. If Chet had come up with this scheme in order to keep her dangling, she wanted no part of it. "I need a reassurance that he'll leave me strictly alone. I am *not* going to marry him."

"Don't you get it? This isn't about marching you down the aisle; it's about protecting my candidate from embarrassment." Gene paced back and forth, gesturing choppily for emphasis. "All it takes is one comedian making *Runaway Bride* jokes, and he gets laughed out of the running."

He had a point. Erin wanted out of the relationship and she resented Chet's manipulations, but she wasn't vindictive. "All right."

Gene hesitated. "You're agreeing? Just like that?"

"That's what 'all right' usually means," she said.

Joseph gave his head a small, almost involuntary shake. "Erin, are you sure about this?"

"Stay out of it!" Gene's hands balled into fists. A second look at Joseph made him drop the pugnacious posture, but it didn't stop him from glaring.

Ignoring him, Joseph addressed Erin. "I understand your not wanting to embarrass Chet, but this means you'd still be engaged to the man. As your fiancé, he could find ways to pressure you. No matter what Gene says, Chet hasn't given up on marrying you."

Erin expected an outburst from their visitor. Instead, he

said reluctantly, "I suppose you've got a point. Frankly, it's an area where I disagree with the candidate."

"I'm glad to hear that. I think," she said.

Gene picked a leaf off his trousers. "If you don't want to marry him, he should move on. The man thinks he's in love but if it isn't a two-way street, he's wasting his efforts. He doesn't need your money, if that's what you're thinking."

"Politicians always need money," Joseph said.

"Chet Dever isn't a politician, he's a statesman." The words might be more suitable for a stump speech than for a discussion, but Gene imbued them with earnestness. "People recognize that he's going places. He's got supporters around town, including the Boldings. And he's well fixed in his own right. He's loaned his campaign a bundle."

"He wasn't born wealthy. According to the newspapers, his father owns a bookstore in Los Angeles," Joseph countered.

"Three bookstores," Erin said. Chet had taken her to dinner with his parents once and she'd heard all about their vast selection of science fiction and mystery novels. They'd spent the rest of the meal bragging about their son.

"As for where he got the money, he's a financial wizard." Gene certainly didn't blush at hyperbole, Erin noted. "He graduated from UCLA at twenty and earned an MBA by the age of twenty-two. When I met him, he was the most outstanding broker in the history of H&B Financial. Frankly, I thought he was taking a step down when he went to work for Andrew Marshall, but the man recognized his gifts and was smart enough to promote him to CEO."

"I'll accept that he's well off, but don't political campaigns cost millions?" Joseph pressed.

"They can," Gene agreed. "Even a small congressional race like this one isn't cheap. But he's made some incredible investments over the years."

"Do you know that for a fact or are you taking his word?" Joseph asked.

"What do you think he did, rob a bank?" came the retort. "Of course I take his word."

Erin's head started hurting again. She was tired of talking about money and Chet and weddings and elections. The fact that she'd hardly eaten all day wasn't helping, either. "Fine. He can raise his funds any way he wants to, as long as I'm out of the picture."

"More or less out," Gene noted. "You might need to repeat the story about the postponement if any reporters show up. But hopefully they won't bother you."

"Excuse me for mentioning this." Joseph's apology was clearly aimed at Erin, not their visitor. "However, since Miss Marshall is being so cooperative, I think she might have a few requests of her own."

"I figured you'd want to bargain." Gene folded his arms. "Go ahead."

What should she ask for, other than to be left alone? Erin wondered. Then it hit her. "My mom! Chet can arrange for me to see her when Lance isn't around."

"I'm sure he'll do his best," Gene said. "In fact, he figured you'd be concerned about Mrs. Bolding. He told me he's run interference since her accident, and he'll keep doing it if you want. Whether or not you agree to his request."

Erin was relieved "Please thank him for me."

"Will do."

"I'll be in touch with him later." She couldn't handle any further negotiations with her head aching.

"I have another request," Joseph said.

Gene eyed him dubiously. "Yes?"

"Don't worry. All I want is your opinion."

"I've got plenty of those."

"Regardless of what your father thinks, I believe Erin and her mother are in danger," he said. "Do you know anyone who might want to harm them?"

"No. If I did, I'd say so," Gene answered promptly. "I can

assure you, if you have any suspicions about Chet, forget them. He would never hurt Erin. Even if he fudged about the engagement, his heart's in the right place."

Joseph didn't look entirely satisfied, but he nodded.

"I think we've got a deal," Erin said.

"I want you to understand something," Gene added. "I'm glad this is a win-win situation. But if push came to shove, I'd do anything for Chet. His career is my career now. Being part of his team is the best thing that ever happened to me, and I plan to ride it all the way to Washington. Maybe even to the White House."

"At least you don't think small," Joseph said.

"That's right." Tina's brother rubbed his chin reflexively. "I may not be a popular guy like you, a man's man like my father wished." He didn't seem to notice Joseph's mystified expression. "I like wheeling and dealing, and that makes me good at politics. I'm riding the big one and I'm not getting off."

"Good luck," Erin said.

Gene tilted his head in acknowledgment. "It goes without saying that this conversation will remain confidential."

"Agreed," Joseph said. "By the way, if you need to drop by again, come up the driveway. Sneaking around is likely to get you shot."

Their visitor shrugged. "Yeah, I went a little overboard there. But it pays to be careful."

"Can you reach your car okay? It's full dark."

"I've got a flashlight." Gene was too proud to ask for a lift, Erin thought, and Joseph made no further move to volunteer. "I'll be in touch." He shook hands with them both.

After he left, Joseph said, "I hate to think what that tuxedo is going to look like when he's done sliding down the hill. I hope the rental shop won't have a fit."

"I'm sure he owns it," Erin said. "Probably several."

They went into the kitchen, where Joseph finished cook

ing dinner and baked cookies from refrigerated dough. The odors percolated through Erin's system, wiping away all thought of anything but food.

They ate at the round table in the main room, with boldly colored dinnerware and cloth napkins. The food tasted fantastic, and Erin's headache lifted. She felt comfortable here in Joseph's beautiful house.

Everything from the furnishings to the festive plates indicated he'd nested. If so, it surprised her that he'd chosen a place with a single bedroom.

Didn't he plan to marry and have kids? He had to be twenty-eight by now. She wondered why he'd never met the right woman. And refused to allow herself to accept the answer that tantalized her.

Joseph Lowery hadn't been carrying the torch for Erin all these years. He'd never even tried to visit until police business required it. The gulf that had opened between them eleven years ago had only widened over the years.

Being thrown together like this was proving an unexpected joy, but she knew better than to read anything into his protectiveness. That was just the way he was—a man's man, as Gene had put it. But he wasn't her man. Not anymore.

"I can understand why you're so popular," she said aloud. "I'm glad Gene recognizes it."

Joseph set down a cookie he'd picked up. "He's dreaming."

"People always liked you."

"Not always."

"The kids at school were uncomfortable. They didn't know what to say to you," she told him. "And you walked around mad at the world. But you aren't an outsider anymore. People admire your mother and I'm sure they respect you."

He picked up the cookie again. "I've learned not to rely on other people's good opinions. Too many folks sway with whatever breeze comes along. I suppose I should be grateful

I'm cured of that." He finished the cookie and changed the subject. "Did you know Chet had that much money?"

"No," she admitted. "We never discussed finances."

"You didn't have a prenuptial agreement?"

"They're fine for older people or for couples who believe in divorce, but when I get married, I plan to stay married," she said. "I don't want to hold anything back."

"Let's just hope you don't get taken advantage of." Joseph rose to clear the dishes. When Erin tried to help, he waved her away. "You're supposed to take it easy."

Despite the long day, a nap and the meal had revived her. "I feel kind of restless. Cooped up, I guess." The drawn curtains weighed on her spirits. They reminded her too much of her mother's place.

"I've got an idea. Hold on." After stacking the dishes in the sink, Joseph retrieved two comforters from the linen closet. "Stay there."

He extinguished the interior and exterior lights and disappeared out the back door. The scrape of furniture and the flapping of cloth hinted at his activities.

He peered inside. "You can come out now."

"Is this some kind of magic ritual?"

"It's called making the world disappear. And making us disappear with it."

On the rear deck, Erin found that he'd pushed aside the patio furniture and spread a comforter on the boards. He sat down and gathered the second one around him. "Scoot under here."

She joined him, delighted. Leaning against the house, the two of them made a tent with the covers, leaving only their faces exposed. The bite of October chill against Erin's cheeks intensified her sense of coziness.

From this point, only the deck railing and the tops of pine trees broke the expanse of star-flung sky. "This is great," she said. "And private."

"Remember the night we built a campfire and sat around it telling ghost stories?"

"You made me jump."

"Which story was that?"

"Something about long thin fingers and thick rubbery lips. Don't tell it again!"

He laughed. "I won't. I promise."

When Erin admitted they'd spent the evening alone in the woods, her mother had refused to believe all they'd done was tell stories and had grounded her for a week. After that, she'd reluctantly learned to fib to her mother. It was one of the few things she regretted about that period of her life.

"Remember the time…" Joseph started, but didn't finish.

"Which time?" she asked.

"All of them."

"Yes." They'd had dozens of adventures, enjoying the simplest pleasures as long as they were together.

They'd met when she was a freshman at Sundown Valley High and he a junior. They'd spotted each other early in the year and kept stealing glimpses at lunch and after school, but both had been too shy to walk up and introduce themselves.

To her, Joseph had been the handsome captain of the wrestling team, out of reach for someone as inexperienced with guys as she was. Of course, she knew his father worked for hers, but in the self-contained universe of high school, their relative statuses had been reversed.

They'd met for real one day when she forgot her umbrella. After school, Joseph spotted her dashing into the rain, caught up and walked her to the bus.

They'd ridden home side by side on a damp seat. At first, they'd only discussed their classes, but in the days that followed, they'd talked so intently that once Joseph—who descended sooner—missed his stop and had to hike back. He hadn't seemed to mind.

Many other guys of sixteen had their own cars. She'd been

deeply grateful that Joseph didn't, because it gave them a chance to get to know each other on the bus.

Soon they were hanging out at lunch, too. By spring, the wrestling season ended and he had weekends free to take her to the movies and the occasional dinner. He'd been playful, tender and so gorgeous that she couldn't believe he didn't pressure her for sex.

There'd been one night during her sophomore year, making out in the back seat of his parents' car, when she didn't think she could stop herself. She hadn't had to. Joseph had reined himself in and driven her home.

"You might want this now but you're not ready," he'd said. "We've got plenty of time."

They hadn't, though. Halfway through his senior year, his father was arrested. Other kids, uneasy with the situation, veered away from him. It hadn't helped that everyone knew Lewis Lowery worked for Andrew Marshall.

Joseph had said he didn't want to come to Erin's house anymore to pick her up. He'd become hypersensitive to slights, even unintentional ones. After a fistfight, he'd been suspended from the wrestling team, along with his opponent. Brooding and angry at the world, Joseph had become irritable and distant, even with her.

"That is not a happy, starry-night expression." His voice broke into her reverie. "I think you're remembering too much."

"Way too much," she agreed. "It's funny, considering that I've forgotten the one day I desperately want to evoke."

"It might come back," he said.

"At least I haven't forgotten the happy times."

The breeze picked up and he drew the comforter tighter around them. Erin moved closer. She loved the ragged sound of Joseph's breathing and the springiness of his hair when she touched it.

He must have felt the same way, because his face glowed

toward hers and his arm came around her. After a moment of hesitation, their mouths met for a long, sweet kiss.

Erin's head began spinning again, but this time she didn't mind at all.

Chapter Seven

Longing stirred inside Joseph, mingling with tenderness. The joyous way Erin's lips met his revealed her own excitement.

Beneath the blanket, they touched each other lightly and swiftly, as if in a few minutes they could banish years of separation. The comforter bunched around them, admitting exhilarating blasts of cold air against his heated skin.

Erin's fingers unworked the buttons on Joseph's shirt as he slid up her sweater and bra. When he bent and licked each pearly tip, she gave a cry of delight.

Joseph ached to mold her to him and remove the last barrier between them. He knew exactly what came next; he hadn't spent the past ten years in a monastery. But he couldn't and wouldn't hurry this. Erin deserved better.

Yet she urged him, trailing kisses down his throat. When he shifted position, she stretched alongside him and played her breasts against his bare chest. The intimacy threatened to shred his self-control.

She wanted him to take her. He knew it just as he'd known it in high school. This time, he didn't want to restrain himself. They weren't kids anymore. They both knew what they were doing.

Disregarding caution, he unsnapped Erin's jeans and lowered them along her hips. When she wiggled, he gripped her derriere and felt it tighten as her hot core brushed his.

The comforter slipped, admitting a chill that slapped him like a warning. "You're on the Pill, right?" Joseph murmured.

"What?"

"The Pill," he repeated hoarsely.

The reluctant answer whispered out of her. "No."

"Don't you have some other kind of protection?" It had been a while since he'd needed any, but surely she'd tucked something into her purse.

"I didn't think about it."

Joseph stopped moving as he tried to grasp the situation. "It's supposed to be your wedding night. Surely you planned ahead. I mean, you and Chet…" He didn't finish the sentence because he didn't like to think about the two of them together.

"We didn't," Erin whispered.

"Didn't what?"

"I never…" Her eyes shone large in the moonlight. "I never slept with him."

That was a relief. And a bolt from the blue. "Are you saying you're a virgin?"

"Well, yes." After a pause, Erin added, "Worse than that, I'm a virgin with no birth control. You don't happen to have any, do you?"

"Sorry, no." Joseph sat up and began buttoning his shirt with stiff fingers. He was grateful for the blanket shielding his midsection. "This is great. Just great."

Erin yanked her jeans into place. "Well, it *was* great until you got all practical on me."

As his ardor cooled, his better judgment reasserted itself. "It's for the best. I've got no business deflowering a virgin, especially under the circumstances. What's more, you're in no state to take such a big step."

"I may not be thinking clearly," she retorted, "but on this particular occasion, I might have preferred it if you weren't thinking clearly, either."

"This has a familiar ring," he said. "I was right to wait when we were kids. Wasn't I?"

"I suppose." She didn't sound convinced.

"I would never have risked getting you into trouble."

"You got me in plenty of trouble!"

"Like when?

"How about the time we deliberately missed the bus so we could hang out at the mall?" They'd walked the few blocks from the high school. "I don't know why it didn't occur to me that Mom would call out the Marines when I didn't show up."

They'd been battling bad guys at the arcade when the mall security guards, every one of whom probably had an image of Andrew Marshall's daughter imprinted on his inner eyelids, rushed up and grabbed Joseph. They'd nearly hauled him off until Erin convinced them he hadn't kidnapped her.

It had been doubly embarrassing that the guards reportedly directly to Joseph's father. Lewis Lowery hadn't had to say a word that night. His father's look of disappointment had cut deeper than any scolding.

They were lucky they hadn't been forbidden to see each other again. According to Erin, her father had stood up to her mother, pointing out that they were merely having some innocent fun. Perhaps he'd held Joseph's misbehavior against him in later years, though.

Erin fumbled with her sweater. "Could you help me with this?"

Joseph felt an urge to acquiesce, to touch the tempting swell of her breasts. They could start over with slow kisses and the gratifying experience of undressing each other, then enjoy each other in ways that didn't require birth control.

Was he out of his mind? They weren't kids to indulge in heavy petting. Besides, sex between them could never be taken lightly, even if it weren't technically consummated.

"You're kidding, right?" He tried to keep his tone light.

"Just making sure you really meant it." She fixed her garment unaided.

"You're a temptress!"

"Actually, I'm feeling kind of giddy." Erin peeked up at him in a manner part seductress and part waif. "But I'll admit, it's getting cold out here."

Although southern California autumn days might be warm, the nighttime temperatures dipped into the fifties. "Come inside and I'll make hot chocolate."

She pretended to weigh his offer. "With marshmallows?"

He didn't have any. "How about chocolate sprinkles?"

"Done!"

They trailed inside where, without a word, they each gripped the ends of a comforter and folded it together, then fixed the other one. They'd honed their skills years ago during picnics at the park and summer trips to the beach fifteen miles from Sundown Valley.

They settled at the small kitchen table. As they sipped the hot liquid, Joseph broached a subject that bothered him. "I'm wondering where Chet really got his money."

"Investments, according to Gene."

"Maybe in the long run, but it takes money to make money," Joseph pointed out. "His family isn't wealthy, so where'd he get his investment capital?"

"He earns a six-figure salary at the Marshall Company."

He shook his head. "He didn't get rich that quickly. He'd have needed to be investing money over a period of years."

She savored a spoonful of sprinkles. "What are you getting at?"

Joseph wasn't sure he wanted to voice the idea that occurred to him. It was, he had to admit, implausible, maybe even twisted. But today he'd started thinking about his father's case and it refused to leave him alone.

He could tell Erin wasn't going to let him put her off, so

he might as well pursue it. "When did Chet arrive in Sundown Valley?"

"Ten years ago, I think." Her forehead creased. "He spent five years as a stockbroker at H&B Financial and five years working for us."

"And before that?"

"He earned his master's from UCLA."

"What year?"

She gazed into the distance. "I'm trying to picture his résumé. I got it!" **She** named the date. It was eleven years earlier.

"Is that right?" Joseph said. "Is there really a year's gap or did we miss something?"

"He took a year off to travel around Europe," Erin told him. "He wanted to experience a little freedom before his career got under way. He said he financed it with money he'd saved from summer jobs and a teaching fellowship."

"Did he ever show you any pictures? You know, him standing in front of the Eiffel Tower, that kind of thing?"

"No, but I didn't ask." She licked a chocolate sprinkle from the corner of her mouth. "Wait. He did play me some CDs he bought over there."

"Maybe he went to Europe for a few months," Joseph speculated. "That would still leave some time unaccounted for."

"During which you suspect he did what?"

"It's a long shot. Probably crazy." He might as well go all the way with it "Eleven years ago, whoever framed my dad made off with $2.5 million in jewels. That's a lot of money, even allowing for the fact that they couldn't be fenced for full value."

"Oh, come on!" Erin smacked the table. "You believe a guy with an MBA is going to risk his entire future by hooking up with some petty criminals to pull a robbery?"

"People have done stupider things."

"Chet isn't a criminal and besides, how would he have known what target to hit? He had no connections here," Erin said. "Come on, Joseph, I'd love to see your dad's name cleared, but this is preposterous."

He couldn't let it go that easily. "Chet must have known someone in town. Otherwise, how'd he get the job?"

"How does anybody get a job?" she countered. "Besides, Gene's a campaign manager. I'm sure he exaggerated how much Chet has."

"All right." Joseph had to admit he'd pushed the theory as far as it would go. "Let's look at this another way. Chet lied and tricked you. People don't usually manipulate and lie in only one area, so even if he didn't steal his money, he may be up to something else as well."

"Such as?"

He gave his imagination free rein. "Gene said your mother and stepfather are contributing to Chet's campaign. What if Chet and Lance are in league somehow? They're both from L.A. so they might know each other."

"Lance is a lot older," she pointed out sleepily.

Joseph couldn't resist following the idea to see where it might lead. "Lance was in business—" he'd owned an industrial video company that had folded shortly before he met Alice "—so let's suppose their paths crossed at a UCLA seminar and they kept in touch. Chet had to have known your mother was going on that cruise, and he could have told Lance. Marriage to a rich widow who was also Chet's boss could benefit them both."

"You sound like one of those conspiracy theorists," Erin said. "Besides, it doesn't make sense. I mean, if there's some huge plot, then the attack on me has to be part of it, right? Six weeks ago, Chet had no reason to want to kill me. I hadn't said no to him yet, remember?"

Joseph tried to find grounds to argue. He failed. "You're right. It doesn't work."

She stifled a yawn. "You're too hard on Chet. According to you, he plotted with Lance *and* he framed your father. Maybe he was behind the Kennedy assassination, too."

"Okay, okay!" He raised his hands. "I concede defeat."

Erin didn't gloat. "We got sidetracked from the issue of who framed your dad."

"Did we?" He couldn't remember where this conversation had started.

"I'm curious," she said. "Over the years, you must have looked into it. Did you come up with any suspects?"

"A couple, but nothing of substance." Joseph told her about Alfonso Lorenz, the guard who'd testified and then left the country, and Todd Wilde, the robber who'd later gone to prison. "It's possible they cooked up the scheme between them. Lorenz would have known about the jewel shipment. Still, I've always believed they must have had help from somebody smarter than they were."

"Why?"

"They got away with pinning a murder rap on a former police officer. It's hard to imagine they had that much dumb luck," he said.

Erin's hand barely made it to her mouth in time to cover another yawn. "I'm sorry. It's not lack of interest, believe me."

"You've had a stressful day," he said. "Let's get you to bed."

"I'll get myself to bed."

That, he mused, was a good idea. "Sleep well, then."

"You, too." She set her mug in the sink and half stumbled away. Joseph considered going to her aid but decided that getting anywhere near Erin and a bed, even in her exhausted state, wasn't a good idea.

A few minutes later, he sat listening to the sound of water running in the bathroom. That morning, he'd armored himself against the knowledge that she was soon to be another man's wife and here she was, ensconced in his bathroom. Who could have predicted it?

Joseph had dropped by the country club when it occurred to him that this might be his only chance to question her without interference. He'd also wanted to see her for one last time while she was still Erin Marshall and not Erin Dever.

He hadn't expected to achieve anything. Or to wreck anything. Certainly not to find himself nearly making love to her tonight.

Her light scent lingered in Joseph's nostrils. He could feel the smoothness of her skin and the silken flow of her hair against his cheek.

From the next room came the murmur of fabric. She had to be stepping out of those jeans in the bathroom. Lifting her sweater, unsnapping her bra…

His groin tightened. He wanted to wipe away any effect Chet might have had on her, even the impression of his mouth on hers. He wanted to replace it with an experience so intense it blotted out anything that came before.

That's just what she needs. A hot and heavy relationship that's going nowhere.

When he was younger, he'd believed himself to be the right man for Erin. In some ways, he still believed it. But even if his family's reversal hadn't give him a jolt of reality, sooner or later he'd have learned better.

To make a marriage work, two people had to share their lives and their goals. Neither he nor Erin fit into the other's future.

Police officers had a hard time maintaining relationships, considering their long hours and the stress of dealing with danger, hostility and tragedy. Home had to be a sanctuary. Their work might not be the sole focus of the family's life, but it had to take a high priority.

Erin faced the responsibilities that came with her immense fortune. The battle she was fighting now, which he suspected had to do with control of the Marshall Company, might be only the first of many power struggles. She needed a husband who moved easily in society, who commanded the respect of her peers and whose main focus corresponded to hers.

Marriage would pull them apart and leave them both feeling like failures. The fact that the community already mistrusted Joseph wouldn't help, either.

To redirect his thoughts, he fetched a pen and notebook and took them into the living room. Working was the best way to keep his mind off Erin.

He wrote down everything they'd discussed that evening, looking for patterns. Despite plenty of tantalizing hints, nothing conclusively linked the jewelry store robbery-murder with recent events. As for the incidents involving Erin and her mother, he'd uncovered no convincing evidence that they'd been anything but unrelated mishaps.

Putting away the notebook, Joseph turned on the local news at low volume. He watched the end of a car chase and a report on a missing child found safe at a neighbor's house. It was ordinary police business. His business, in a sense. No, not his business, not for the next month.

On Monday morning, he wouldn't wake up and head for work. He wasn't going to start his shift by grabbing a cup of coffee before briefing. The guys and women in blue would be attending to their duties without him.

For five years, he'd been a cop. As long as he could remember, even during high school, he'd worked at one job or another. It went against Joseph's nature to sit idly by.

But then, he didn't intend to. Tomorrow, with Erin's help, he'd figure out whom to talk to and how best to approach them.

The chief had given him a month's leave on full salary. He planned to earn every penny of it.

ERIN AWAKENED to a ringing on the nightstand. Barely in time, she remembered she wasn't supposed to answer.

The electronic chime came again, insistently. It was her cell phone, not the house line, she realized foggily. After some groping around, she found the device and pressed the right button.

"Hello?" The word came out raspy.

"Erin?" The crisp female voice didn't immediately ring a bell.

"Yes?"

"This is Jean Van Fleet. I regret calling on a Sunday morning, but I must speak with you immediately."

It was her mother's best friend. Oddly, there'd been no sign of her this past month, but she had been on the wedding's guest list. "It's good to hear from you. I'm sorry about the inconvenience yesterday. I mean, at the wedding."

"Courtesy to your guests doesn't require you to marry the wrong man," Jean said. "I see in the paper that your family claims you had a relapse. It's a good story, but I'm not that gullible. Are you staying at your mother's house?"

"No." Erin decided not to volunteer more information until she learned the reason for this call. She'd given Jean her cell phone number after her father's death in case she had any concerns about Alice. This was the first time Jean had used it.

"Good," her caller said. "I don't want Alice to know about this discussion. And it has to be in person. I have several things to say, and they're not the sort of thing I care to communicate over the phone."

"I'm not sure when—"

"My husband's at a medical convention and I'm not going to church this morning, so you can come over as soon as you're dressed." It was a command, not a request. Jean and Alice had a lot in common.

"I haven't eaten." It was the first thing that popped into Erin's mind.

"We have pastries and coffee. My daughter barely touched them. She's always on a diet." The Van Fleets had a son in college and a daughter, Beverly, in high school.

Erin wanted to hear what her mother's friend had to say. "I'll get there as soon as I can. Say an hour. I'll be bringing someone with me."

"Who?"

"Joseph Lowery." There was no need to explain. Jean couldn't have forgotten Erin's high school romance or the town's major scandal.

"These are private matters," Jean said.

"I can't drive until my doctor certifies I've recovered from my head injury." Realizing that didn't preclude her calling a cab, she added, "Also, it's possible that what happened to me wasn't accidental."

"You mean someone ran you down deliberately?"

"We're not sure," Erin said. "In any case, I feel safer with Joseph around."

"I suppose it can't hurt to bring a bodyguard," Jean conceded. "Very well. I'll see you in an hour."

They said goodbye and clicked off.

Erin supposed she should have consulted Joseph before making plans. But whatever Jean Van Fleet had to say, she suspected it was important.

DRIVING UP THE HILL to the Van Fleets' home, which had formerly belonged to the Marshalls, brought back the turbulent but happy years of growing up. Erin half expected her father, who'd had the house built to his specifications, to be waiting for her at the door.

They cruised by the rose garden whose planting Andrew had supervised. Set into the emerald lawn, the bushes rioted with blooms. She recognized the pale blush of Pristine and the proud, white Honor blooms, as well as dark-red Mr. Lincoln flowers so rich Erin could almost smell them.

At the top, the mansion gleamed like a pearl in the morning sun. The smooth columns of the portico added a touch of Greek elegance to the clean architecture.

"I hope we'll sit outside," Erin said. "It's such a pretty day."

"If we do, I might be tempted to dive in with my clothes on." Although rarely comfortable under her mother's watchful eye, Joseph had enjoyed the pool parties Erin used to host. "Too bad she didn't invite us to bring our swimsuits."

"Really," she said in pretended agreement. They both grinned.

Joseph presented a cool, self-possessed appearance today in a jacket, slacks and polo shirt, she thought. Her father would have welcomed him.

Jean Van Fleet was another story. When she met them at the door with her silver hair sprayed into place and her still-slim figure graceful in a skirt and silk blouse, she barely acknowledged him.

"It's such a lovely day, I thought we'd be more comfortable on the terrace," she told Erin after they exchanged greetings.

She was getting her wish to sit outside. "I'd like that."

"We haven't made many alterations, you'll notice." Their footsteps slapped across the marble-floored entryway, past a sunken pool and classic fountain. "This was always a showplace."

"It couldn't be in better hands." Erin's compliment drew a pleased smile.

To the left of the entrance stretched what Alice used to refer to as the public rooms, a series of living and lounge spaces that led to a catering kitchen. To the right, away from view, lay the family quarters plus guest chambers, a smaller kitchen and a housekeeper's suite.

They emerged onto a curving terrace set with white wrought-iron tables and chairs. Below, ferns edged the meandering pool, which disappeared into a hidden bower where Erin had once kissed Joseph. To one side stood the pool house, which contained a large entertainment room, a kitchenette and dressing rooms. Beyond the pool stretched a spectacular vista of the country club and golf course, all the way to the distant blue serenity of Sundown Lake.

At least, it appeared serene at the moment.

Jean poured coffee and offered them an array of Danishes. When they'd been served, she proceeded directly to the reason for her call

"I was shocked yesterday by the change in your mother," she said. "Erin, she must be ill."

"She has lost weight." Erin set down her cup. "She's been fighting off bouts of bronchitis since she fell in the lake."

"I hope that's all it is," the woman said. "She seemed—well, I can't put my finger on it. I'm seriously distressed."

"How long had it been since you'd seen her?" Joseph took out his notebook.

"Five or six months," said their hostess. "Since her accident."

"You're kidding!" Erin hadn't realized her mother had withdrawn from Jean as well. "I thought I was the only one she cut off."

"We've talked on the phone a few times, but that awful man—" she obviously meant Lance "—doesn't like me hanging around."

"Did he order you to stay away?" Joseph asked.

"Not in so many words. How did he put it? The last time I dropped by, he blocked the doorway and announced that Alice's old friends tired her." Jean sniffed. "She was sitting right there in the living room. I could hear her coughing. Erin, I wanted to say, I've wondered if he's drugging her."

The suggestion hit Erin hard. Her mind searched for anything she'd noticed that might substantiate Jean's suspicion. Could her mother have been drugged right under her nose? It would certainly account for her unpredictable moods.

Joseph wrote something down. "Did you notify the police?"

"Certainly not!" Jean glared as if he'd suggested she burn down the house. "One doesn't do that sort of thing."

"She mentioned she was taking something for anxiety," Erin said.

"It would explain how he's controlling her," Jean said. "Joseph, I suppose it's a good thing you're here after all. You should look into this. Discreetly, of course."

He made another note on his pad. "I have no authority. Chief Norris put me on leave, and I doubt he'd let anyone else investigate. He's very protective of his social circle."

"Chief Norris needs to keep in mind that he's a policeman first and a member of the country club second," Jean snapped. "As her closest relative, Erin, it's up to you to protect your mother."

"Lance won't let me get near Mom, either." She searched for possibilities. "Maybe Chet can help us. He said he would, but I don't want to call on him unless I have to."

"Who else could intervene?" Joseph asked. "Mrs. Van Fleet, I should imagine you know her friends as well as anyone."

"Indeed I do. We grew up together, you know," their hostess said.

Erin remembered pictures from her mother's 1970s-era yearbook at Sundown Valley High. Alice Flanders and Jean Russell, both from prominent families, had been active in numerous clubs.

"Can you give us any names?" Joseph tapped his pen on the table.

"As you know, the obvious person should be your Aunt Marie." Jean addressed Erin instead of him. "But they never got along. She didn't even attend your father's funeral."

"I know." Erin hadn't considered contacting her aunt, who was two years Alice's junior, because of their prickly relationship. "I asked Mom if she'd been invited and she said Dad wouldn't have wanted her there."

"Why not?" Joseph asked.

"Dad never liked her, although he used to tolerate her for

Mom's sake, " Erin said. "After I went away to college, they had some kind of fight. I never knew the details."

She'd figured it was the culmination of a long-standing antipathy. Marie Flanders was a free-spending, flashy dresser who'd landed a series of small roles on TV. It wasn't her career or her grooming that had irked Erin's father, however, as much as her attitude of entitlement.

She'd resented her sister's comfortable life and demanded to borrow money, which she'd never repaid. Andrew, who believed in working hard and in being grateful for whatever good fortune came one's way, hadn't been shy about criticizing his sister-in-law.

Nevertheless, Erin had always had a fondness for her aunt. When she was younger, Marie had sometimes taken her out to a movie or an ice cream parlor.

Jean clinked her coffee cup onto its saucer. "I'm glad I thought of her. Frankly, that's another worry."

"Yes?" Joseph encouraged.

"If someone deliberately hit Erin and if Alice's boating mishap wasn't an accident—well, if someone's targeting both of them, Marie might be in danger, too."

That possibility hadn't occurred to Erin. "Why? I doubt she has much money and we haven't been in touch for years."

"There's always the possibility that someone bears a grudge against the family," Jean pointed out. "Also, your grandparents left both girls a small trust fund. It might be enough to tempt someone in the crowd she runs with."

"What crowd would that be?" Joseph asked.

"I haven't been in touch with her recently," Jean said. "But I do recall one fellow she dated off and on since high school who was always in trouble. About eight years ago, she brought him on a visit and he acted so obnoxious, he and Andrew nearly came to blows. Erin, he and your aunt left in a huff."

That must have caused the rift, Erin thought. She wondered

how the man had managed to antagonize her father, who'd usually been slow to anger.

"Can you give me his name?" Joseph glanced up from his note taking.

Jean reflected. "Todd," she said at last. "Todd Wilde. The Wilde part certainly suited him."

Erin recognized the name of Joseph's suspect from the jewelry store slaying. If he'd beaten a shopkeeper to death, he could certainly pose a threat to Marie. And perhaps to the rest of the family.

"I doubt we have to worry about him," Joseph said.

Jean frowned. "Why not?"

"He was sent to prison about six years ago."

Her eyebrows rose. "Well, he's out."

Joseph leaned forward, his notebook forgotten. "How do you know that?"

"I saw him a few weeks ago," she said. "Right here in Sundown Valley."

Chapter Eight

On the drive back to his house, Joseph kept turning over Jean's revelation in his mind. The Van Fleets had been boating with friends when they'd spotted Todd walking along the shore not far from the Boldings' house, carrying binoculars.

So Todd was out of prison. Why would he be spying on the Boldings? Did he have anything to do with the attacks on Erin and her mother?

The part that both disturbed and excited him was that there really might be a link between recent events and the robbery-murder eleven years ago. Still, he didn't want to make assumptions.

In the passenger seat, Erin sat hugging the high school yearbook she'd borrowed from Jean. A thirty-year-old photo of Todd might not be much help, but it was better than nothing.

"I have to find out when he was released," he said aloud. "These events began five and a half months ago."

"It can't be him who attacked my mom," Erin answered. "She claimed she was alone in the boat. Why would she lie to protect someone she disliked?"

"He might be blackmailing her," Joseph pointed out.

"With what?"

He tried the first surmise that came to him. "He could be holding Marie hostage."

"You think so?"

"It's just a wild guess," Joseph said. "Are there any skeletons in her closet, any deep dark secrets Marie could have confided in him?"

She shook her head. "That's the thing about coming from a prominent family. You can't get away with secret babies or lovers or any of that stuff."

"Don't be too sure." Still, during her interview with Joseph, Alice had maintained a composure incompatible with her having been threatened and attacked. "Let's hope Wilde is violating parole by hanging around here. At least we could get him back into custody."

"I'd like that," Erin said. "He sounds creepy."

Of course, Joseph thought, he'd have to find a way to report the man without revealing that he was continuing to investigate. He had to walk a tightrope or risk harsh consequences. Not as harsh as Erin or Alice faced, however.

He scanned the woods on either side as they approached his house. Now that they knew Todd Wilde was on the loose, it paid to be even more cautious. Although nothing appeared out of place, he checked inside the house too before giving the all clear.

"You should install an alarm system," Erin suggested as they went in.

"Maybe so." He hadn't considered it necessary in such a safe community. With a woman living here, it might be a good idea.

She wasn't going to stay, he reminded himself. The Marshalls' former pool house dwarfed this entire home. The idea of Erin Marshall residing in such a tiny house on anything but an emergency basis was preposterous.

"I'll see if I can track down my aunt." She took out her cell phone.

"Good idea. I'm going to find out more about Todd Wilde."

He sat at his desk on one side of the main room, switched

on his computer and accessed a police database. Fortunately, it still accepted his security code. Wilde, he learned, had been released on parole two months earlier. He was assigned to a parole officer in the Sundown Valley area, so he hadn't left his jurisdiction.

The dates indicated Wilde had been freed before Erin's accident but after Alice's. That seemed to weigh on the side of innocence; if he held a grudge against anyone, it was more likely to be the mother than the daughter. Yet it struck Joseph as an odd coincidence that he'd been walking near the Boldings' house with binoculars. In his experience, violent ex-cons didn't usually take up pacific activities like birdwatching.

It was time to play the what-if game. What if somehow both Chet and Todd had been involved in the jewelry store case? What if, after his parole, Todd had returned to shake down Chet, Chet refused to pay and Wilde attacked Erin as a warning to her fiancé?

Joseph added the idea to his notebook. The theory gave Todd a motive for spying on the Bolding house, since Erin had been recuperating there when Jean saw him. That didn't make it the truth, but it was pretty darn plausible.

Besides, there was nothing to pin on Chet except some doubts about how he got so rich. Joseph had committed the mistake of getting too attached to one theory because it suited him emotionally. Bad idea.

He glanced across the room, past the glass divider to where Erin curled in a swivel chair with the yearbook in her lap. Hair clipped back neatly with a barrette, she sat talking on her phone while doodling on a scratch pad. He wondered whom she was talking to.

A loose strand of hair tickled her nose. She swatted and dislodged it, but a moment later it settled back into place. Although her nose crinkled, she was too absorbed in her con-

She clicked off and noticed him watching her. "What did you find?"

"Todd's been out of prison for two months," Joseph said. "He's not violating parole by hanging around here."

"Two? Well, that's good. Kind of."

"Who was on the phone??"

"Aunt Marie's roommate. I found her number in the L.A. directory," she told him. "Crystal says she left about five months ago to go on a trip with a friend for a few weeks."

"And?"

"She never came back."

"Did this roommate file a missing person report?" Joseph asked.

"I don't think so." Erin tucked the errant strand behind one ear. "She mostly seemed annoyed that Marie had stopped paying rent. Eventually she found a new roommate, but she was out quite a bit. I left her my phone number in case she thinks of anything else."

"Did your aunt mention where she was going or with whom?"

"Neither."

Although troubling, the woman's disappearance didn't necessarily indicate foul play. "Judging by Mrs. Van Fleet's comments, your aunt might be the type to just take off." Most people reported missing turned up on their own sooner or later. "In any case, the friend she left with couldn't have been Todd. He was still behind bars."

"Speaking of him, I updated his picture as best I could." Erin brought over the pad. She'd made a creditable sketch from his high school photo, which she'd altered by shortening the 1970s long hairstyle, adding creases around the eyes and receding his hair at the temples to allow for his age.

The face that stared out resembled a sneering man more than a cocky boy. "Good job. At least now we've got some idea who we're searching for."

"Are we searching for him?" Erin asked. "I mean, we have to keep this low-key."

"There's no law against going for a boat ride." Another idea occurred to Joseph. "Suppose he wasn't spying on your folks. Suppose he was looking for something."

"Like what?"

"Buried jewels? Who knows." Joseph logged off the computer. "I want to check out the area where Mrs. Van Fleet saw him and the section where your mom's accident occurred."

"Didn't you already go there?"

"Yes, and after all these months I know I'm not likely to find anything new." He'd explored that area of the lake both by boat and on foot without finding any evidence. The whole time, however, he'd been haunted by the sense that he was missing a vital clue. "Still, we might come across someone who's seen this guy. If he's staying in the area, I'd better talk to him."

"We just won't mention that you're off the case," Erin said.

"Exactly. Hang on while I arrange a boat rental. You can poke around on the Internet while I'm gone. Your aunt's an actress, after all. There might be some mention of her."

Erin folded her arms. "I'm coming with you."

"I don't want you along if I run into Wilde."

"You said it was too dangerous to leave me here by myself," she reminded him. "Too isolated."

He debated. Since the perils appeared to balance each other out, he decided to give in. "Okay. I can always use another pair of eyes."

"Your eagerness is overwhelming."

"I should have said, another pair of sharp eyes."

"That's better—I guess."

At the noise of a car rumbling up the driveway, he sprang to his feet. Gesturing to Erin to stay back, Joseph parted the front blinds and peered through.

Up the gravel driveway jounced a compact convertible with a long-haired blonde at the wheel. Half the police force would have been tempted to make wolf whistles—until, of course, they recognized the chief's daughter.

"It's Tina," he said.

"Alone?"

"Unless somebody's accordion-pleated himself on the floor, yes," Joseph said.

"It is kind of an impractical car, isn't it?" Erin said.

"My mother said she'd drive a car like that if she looked like Tina."

"Your mom knows her? Oh, right. I forgot they volunteer together." Erin glanced at the yearbook and the sketch of Todd, testimony to their forbidden snooping. "I'd better keep her outside."

"Good idea."

While she scooted out, Joseph flipped through the Yellow Pages to the Sundown Boating and Fishing Center. It was a pretty day to go sailing, if nothing else.

"I WANTED TO MAKE SURE you're all right." Filtered sunlight played across Tina's fair skin. "Gene told me what a good sport you were yesterday about the press release. I heard they issued it last night."

"That was quick!"

"Considering the story made today's front page, they were wise not to wait," Tina said. "Gene liked the way it came out."

"Your brother's put his heart into Chet's campaign. I hope it works out for him." Erin wondered how much else she should say, about anything.

She disliked keeping Tina in the dark, but her old friend still lived at home with her father. Staying there enabled her to save money for a down payment on her own home someday, she'd explained. Since Gene didn't plan to settle in town, he'd been in residence there also since his return from Sacramento. That was all very sensible, but it meant that anything Tina let slip was likely to reach unfriendly ears.

Her friend chattered on. "The guests were really understanding yesterday. I think they all sympathize with you."

"Did they eat dinner?" No matter how much money Erin's family had, she didn't like to see food wasted.

"Most of them did," Tina assured her.

Erin felt awkward standing in front of the house. "I'd invite you in for coffee but we're on our way out."

"What's up?" Tina asked.

Oops. She shouldn't have said even that much. "Joseph and I decided to go out on the lake for a little R&R."

"Rick's got a motorboat. I'm sure he'd lend it to you," Tina said. "I'll give him a call." She reached into her purse.

Erin waved away the offer with pretended nonchalance. "I think Joseph's already made arrangements."

"Are you guys back together?" her friend asked. "I mean, you hadn't seen each other in years and suddenly you're living with him."

"We're just pals." Didn't all the movie stars say that right before they announced their engagements? Erin wondered uncomfortably. "I'm only staying here for a few days while I sort things out."

"Nothing against Joseph, but this is happening kind of fast." A ray of sunlight picked out the freckles on Tina's nose.

"I feel more like myself here," Erin admitted. "Mom's house is oppressive. It started making me paranoid."

"You never told me that!"

"I didn't exactly realize it," she said. "Anyway, I feel a lot better now."

Tina plucked an errant leaf off Erin's shoulder. "I'm not saying this is a bad thing. I'm just concerned."

"Thanks. It's nice to have people watching out for me." Tina had been wonderfully supportive these past few weeks.

"Tell him I'm sorry about my dad putting him on leave,"

she said. "I don't think it's fair. Rick's unhappy about it, too, but I can't say anything to my father. He'd only crack down harder."

"Thanks. I know you'd help if you could."

Joseph emerged. After greeting him warmly, Tina said, "Are you sure you don't want me to call Rick about his boat?"

"It's all arranged," Joseph explained. "Thanks for coming by."

"You're good for Erin." Tina patted his arm. "She's finally got some color in her cheeks."

They watched as she got into her car and crunched down the driveway. "I tried to watch what I said," Erin noted.

"I doubt she'll go telling tales. You know I've always thought highly of her." Joseph turned back to the house. "Now let's collect our stuff and get a move on."

"Yes, boss," Erin teased. In spite of the circumstances, the prospect of going out on the water lifted her spirits.

Whether or not they accomplished anything today, it felt almost like one of their old adventures.

A MODEST-SIZE BODY of water, Sundown Lake had been created by nature and improved by the local residents, who'd dredged a large part of it in the days before environmental restrictions. In addition to a small public marina on the eastern shore, there were a number of private tie-downs.

Erin and Joseph made a circuit of the northern shore, the noisy outboard motor adding nothing to the charm of the experience. If Erin had had any notions of a romantic interlude, she'd left them at the dock.

At this time of year, many of the vacation cottages sat empty and there were few people around. Joseph showed the picture she'd made to a couple, but they didn't recognize Todd. He got out at the point Jean had mentioned and traipsed along the shore watching for clues, without success.

Afterward, they sliced south across the lake. "Your moth-

er's accident was down this way. Luckily for her, some of the
neighbors heard her screaming. It was nearly dark, and the
boat had drifted toward the fishing zone."

The aged pier was posted off-limits. Erin had heard a de-
veloper was negotiating to buy the property but, while local
preservationists campaigned at length to save it, it lay weed-
choked and abandoned.

"Isn't the water fairly shallow?" It looked that way to
Erin, with trees trailing over marshy reeds. "She could have
waded out."

"This whole area can be treacherous." Joseph slowed the
put-put of the motor. "One drowning victim about a year
ago got tangled up in the vegetation. He was known to be
a strong swimmer, so we presume he couldn't reach the
surface."

She pictured her mother struggling in the water, losing her
way and going under. A cold chill rippled over Erin. "I can't
figure out why she'd go sailing alone at dusk. Is it possible
someone lured her here and rigged the boat to sink?"

"It didn't sink. She fell out, remember?" he said.

That brought Erin to the sticking point in every theory.
"And of course she'd have told you if she'd been tricked. At
least, I assume she would."

"She certainly stuck to her story."

The engine sputtered to a halt. In the sudden silence, background noises loomed like figures emerging from a fog. Erin
heard the lap of water against old pilings, the chirp of crick-
ets and the creak of branches. The overhang left the irregu-
lar shore in gloom.

She hugged herself. Although she'd worn a light jacket, it
was crisp on the water.

"We should head back," Joseph said reluctantly.

"I'm all right. You need to finish whatever you're doing."

Although this place gave her the creeps, she wanted to understand what had happened. At least it might help her grasp

why her mother had been so moody the past five-and-a-half months.

They passed the pier, which reeked of rotting vegetation. Moss grew around the pilings, and holes gaped in the rickety surface. Erin wondered how anyone could believe it was possible to preserve this old wreck.

On the shore, a squirrel paused atop a tree stump, regarding them without fear. In a flash of blue, a bird darted down to snatch a tidbit from the weeds. There was beauty here in spite of everything, she thought.

A whiff of sweetness reached her from a cluster of vines. A recollection tingled at the edge of her consciousness. A parking lot…a van…flowers…

Joseph's voice banished the fleeting vision. "Let's suppose Lance brought her out here, pushed her into the water and swam ashore. It occurs to me that she might have suffered traumatic amnesia like you did, but only for the period immediately preceding the event."

"I thought she swore she'd come out alone."

"She might not remember what happened and doesn't want to believe her husband did such a thing. Or perhaps she did sail out by herself and he waylaid her."

Erin understood how baffling amnesia could be. "If that's true, how do we prove it?"

"We'd need either a witness or evidence tying Lance to the scene, but that seems unlikely at this point," Joseph conceded. "I didn't find any footprints. No muddy shoes or wet clothing, either at home or in trash containers around the area, because I searched for those, too. Unless he had an accomplice waiting in another boat, I don't know how he did it."

"Maybe he didn't." Much as Erin disliked her stepfather, she had to keep an open mind. "He doesn't have a criminal history."

"That's true, but how did you know?"

"My mom had him investigated before they got married," Erin said. "She isn't a fool."

"Good for her." Joseph poked at a slimy object with a safety pole. It startled Erin by springing to life and splashing away among the reeds. Some kind of amphibian, she realized. "On the other hand, he might stand to inherit a huge amount of money, depending on her will. I assume she has one."

"My family uses Horner and Fitch." It was the attorneys' office where his mother, Suzanne, worked. "After Dad died, she told me she revised her will to leave everything to me. I don't know if she's changed it since then. Couldn't you check?"

"I can't violate attorney-client privilege," Joseph reminded her. "Besides, even before I was suspended, I had no grounds to subpoena evidence as long as your mother claimed there was no foul play."

"You think she's protecting someone?"

"If she's lying, she's doing a darn good job of it," Joseph said. "Amateurs usually get nervous or change details of their story. I think she's telling the truth as far as she knows it."

"I hope so." Maybe the two of them had simply fallen victim to accidents after all, Erin thought. What a relief that would be!

Their boat drifted around a bend. She wrinkled her nose. "Something smells awful. Is it always like this?"

"Not the last time I was here."

The stench made Erin's eyes water. "What *is* that?"

"It smells like a large animal fell in the water." Joseph stopped. "I don't like this. I'm getting you out of here."

"I see something." Erin pointed. "That's weird."

A rumpled blue growth sprouted from a clump of weeds along the waterline. It took a moment to recognize that it wasn't a plant or a fungus.

It was an item of clothing. A windbreaker.

Erin spotted a stringy brown clump beside it. That wasn't

"Don't look."

Too late. She couldn't tear her eyes look away as the brown strings stirred in the water like an old mop. Or a wig.

Erin gasped. To her dismay, the stench invaded her mouth. "It's a person," she choked out. "It's a dead person."

Shudders ran through her. She leaned over the side of the boat and threw up.

Chapter Nine

"There's one good thing," Joseph said on Sunday night as he and Erin finished off a pizza at Giorgio's Italian Deli. It was around the corner from the police station, where they'd undergone separate interviews about their disturbing discovery.

"You mean that I finally got my appetite back?" The color had returned to Erin's cheeks, he noted with satisfaction.

"No. That the chief can't close the investigation now," he said. "It's obvious we weren't chasing our tails."

At the station, several officers had given Joseph a surreptitious nod or thumbs-up. Although sensitive to the grimness of the situation, he'd been grateful for the validation.

"He ought to reinstate you." She went for a third slice of pepperoni.

"I have a bad attitude, remember? I violated his orders, even if his orders were misguided. At least we're sure Rick will do a thorough job."

The body in the lake, although badly bloated after an estimated two weeks in the water, had come accompanied by ID: a wallet belonging to Todd Wilde. What he'd been doing in Sundown Valley and who'd killed him remained to be determined, and of course the police would double-check his identity by other means. They had a good idea of the means, peared to be gunshot wounds, and Rick had recovered a bullet lodged in a nearby tree.

He'd also found a key to a motel room where Todd apparently had been staying. Nothing there gave any indication of the parolee's activities, however.

The probe had started fast. Alerted by Tina, Rick had arrived in his motorboat while Erin was still upchucking in the water. He'd come to make sure Joseph didn't get into any further trouble with the chief, he'd explained.

A short time later, Norris had arrived at the scene in a foul mood. For a minute, Joseph had wondered if he were going to be fired, despite the fact that he'd proved he was right to keep digging.

Luckily, Lynne Rickles, a reporter from the *Sundown Sentinel,* had shown up. Unable to reach the public information officer on a Sunday, the chief had been forced to field her questions himself. In Joseph's opinion, he'd been overly helpful, showing the woman around the crime scene and probably contaminating it in the process, but at least he'd been distracted from his rage.

The guy wasn't about to admit he'd been wrong. He hadn't said a word about lifting Joseph's suspension.

The atmosphere at the police station, however, was definitely on Joseph's side. Yesterday, he'd discounted Gene Norris's description of him as a popular guy. Yet today, his fellow workers had greeted him warmly, even though police departments were highly political, with promotions often dependent on the goodwill of higher-ups. In the face of Chief Norris's antagonism, the show of support meant a lot.

"Poor Aunt Marie." Erin left her slice of pizza unfinished. "I hope her disappearance doesn't have anything to do with Todd. I know he was in prison when she left, but I can't stop worrying."

"Let's not jump to conclusions. Your aunt's probably off sunning herself in Hawaii," Joseph said. "Now, if you don't mind, I'd like to take a couple of pizzas over to the Homework Center for the kids. I want to tell my mother what's been happening before she reads about it in the newspaper."

"Of course!" Erin was curious to see the center, which she knew only from newspaper accounts and the information gathered by the Friend of a Friend Foundation. Although she helped support it, both distance and a desire to remain anonymous had kept her from visiting personally.

It was less than half a mile to their destination in the midst of a blue-collar neighborhood. Although small, the stucco building, a former church, marked a step up from the Homework Center's origin in a two-car garage.

On a Sunday night, Erin had expected to find it half-empty. Instead, the central hall was jammed with students grouped around computers and brightly lit tables. Volunteer tutors of all ages and backgrounds worked intently with the youngsters.

"Joseph!" Suzanne Lowery excused herself from a group and hurried toward them. Despite the gray lacing her brown hair, she bristled with energy that seemed to infuse everyone she passed. "I'm so glad to see you." She beamed at Erin. "And you, too. It's been much too long."

"It's good to see you." She wished now that she'd visited sooner, but it hadn't occurred to her that Suzanne might enjoy seeing her.

"Hey, Mom." Joseph gave her a hug. "You've drawn quite a crowd tonight."

"You know how it is. The kids have all weekend to do their homework, but they leave it to the last minute. Why don't we adjourn to my office? It's much quieter."

"Great," he said.

Suzanne's office was scarcely big enough for the bookshelves and file cabinets crammed into it, not to mention the desk and laptop. To clear off a couple of chairs, she whisked

When they sat, Erin had to be careful where she placed her feet. There was a pile of textbooks a little to the right and a box of computer paper to the left.

"I wanted to tell you what's been happening," Joseph said. "I figure you must have read today's paper, so you already know part of it."

"About the wedding? Yes. Erin, are you feeling okay?"

"I'm fine." She didn't want to play for more sympathy than she deserved. "I didn't really have a relapse. But it's been a rough day."

"She's a trooper. I wish she hadn't had to witness what we came across." Joseph described their upsetting discovery at the lake.

Suzanne didn't seem surprised to learn that the chief hadn't reinstated her son, despite the evidence. "Some people have moved on from what happened all those years ago and others, like Edgar, haven't," she said. "He should take a leaf from Mrs. Nguyen. She volunteers at the center twice a week and we've become friends." Mrs. Nguyen's late husband was the man Lewis Lowery had been convicted of killing.

"This place brings people together," Erin said. "I always thought the Marshall Company should do more for services like this."

"Thanks," Suzanne said. "Without you, I don't know where I'd be." Since she worked at the law firm that handled Erin's private business, she was one of the few people who knew who was behind the Friend of a Friend Foundation.

When Erin had graduated from college with a degree in marketing, she'd sought to organize a community outreach office for the Marshall Company. Although her father had shown interest, he'd been persuaded against it by her mother and Chet's predecessor as CEO. They'd argued that sponsoring the annual Sundown Music Festival and underwriting new facilities at the hospital were sufficient for good public relations.

Technically, they might have been right, but Erin believed a company of this size ought to do more. She'd taken the job with Bea's firm not only to establish her independence, but also because the company handled many service-oriented clients.

"You're the one who deserves the credit," she told Joseph's mother. "Without volunteers working countless hours, my contribution wouldn't mean anything."

"I'm not sure I agree, but thank you." Suzanne regarded her son curiously. "Now that you've made your point, are you going to leave rest of the investigating to Rick?"

He grinned. "What do you think?"

"I think you're going to hang on to this like a dog with a bone." She smiled ruefully. "I don't know if what you're doing is wise or not, but I'm proud of you. Mind telling me what you've learned so far?"

Since Todd might have been involved in framing Suzanne's husband, Erin didn't mind sharing their secrets with her. Besides, someone who'd spent so many years in the community might have useful insights.

Suzanne listened with obvious concern. "I'm sorry to hear Marie may be in danger," she said when Joseph finished. "In school, she found it hard being in her sister's shadow. I was glad when she started landing parts on television, but she never got the big break actors dream about."

"I hope she's safe." Among other things, Erin wanted a chance to get to know her aunt as an adult. "I hope we all are."

"I'm glad my son's looking after you," Suzanne told her. "I know how worried your mother was after your accident. Your head injury really frightened her."

Joseph's eyebrows formed their familiar pucker. "It sounds as if you've been talking to her. I didn't realize you two had much of an acquaintance."

"She uses our law office, you know."

"No, that wasn't why—" Breaking off, Suzanne ducked her head in a gesture reminiscent of Joseph when he was disconcerted. "I didn't mean to discuss a client. Please forget I said anything."

"I'm sorry. I shouldn't have asked."

A tutor came in to request Suzanne's help. Erin and Joseph accompanied her to the main room, where they enjoyed observing the activities for a while before departing

"I'm proud of my mom," Joseph said as they got into his car.

"You should be. She's impressive."

He cupped his hand over hers before returning it to the wheel and steering north on Sundown Boulevard. "She always liked you."

"I always liked her, too." One point from their conversation nagged at Erin. "Why do you suppose my mother went to see her lawyer if it wasn't to change her will?"

"Might have been a business matter," he said.

"The Marshall Company employs its own legal staff," she pointed out.

"She could have added Lance to the title of the house."

That was a reasonable supposition. "I guess so. It's likely she changed her will at some point though, isn't it?"

"I'm sure Lance did his best to talk her into it."

Joseph turned left at Grove Street. They passed the Mercantile Building, where Binh Nguyen had been killed. Before that tragedy, Erin used to love to browse through the crafts shops, but since then the place made her uneasy.

It seemed haunted, both by the friendly Vietnamese jeweler and by the quiet, kind man who'd been Joseph's father. By the time she'd met him, he'd left drinking in the past. Despite the trace of sadness behind his eyes, he'd had a merry sense of humor that always made Erin feel like one of the family.

"At the risk of poking into something that's none of my business, I was wondering whether you have a will," Joseph said.

"Me? Yes." Two years ago, Abe Fitch, one of Suzanne's employers, had suggested after reading her father's will that, with such a large inheritance, she needed to make one out for herself. "I left my trust fund to Friend of a Friend Foundation and my interest in the Marshall Company to Mom."

"That would give her complete control of a company worth, what? At least a hundred million dollars?" he said.

"Something like that." She didn't like the obvious conclusion. "Which means that if she did leave her interest to Lance and both of us died, he'd get the whole thing."

"Not a happy prospect, is it?"

"If I revise it, I don't know who to name." Other than Marie, there were no close relatives. "Maybe I should leave the whole thing to the foundation. I don't know." She rubbed her temples, which had begun to pound.

"No hurry," Joseph said. "I just thought I'd mention it."

Erin's brain wouldn't drop the subject. Her not-for-profit foundation, which didn't require a full-time staff because of its limited scope, was run by an executive at the Bank of Sundown Valley. Her father had helped her set it up three years earlier, when she'd decided to turn over the generous annual allowance he gave her and live on her earnings. Only a year later, her income had skyrocketed after his death. Even so, the board remained small, consisting of a few of Erin's former teachers and friends of her parents who'd been sworn to secrecy about her sponsorship. They weren't prepared to run the Marshall Company, that was certain.

Fortunately, she didn't intend to die any time soon, she reminded herself, so the question of altering her will could wait.

Returning to Joseph's cabin felt like coming home. She hoped Todd's death meant the danger had passed, but there remained the question of who had killed him and why.

Inside, Joseph double-checked the window coverings before flicking the light switch. A warm glow filled the expansive room. "Care for some entertainment or are you ready to turn in?"

"I'm tired but wide awake." Erin's watch read eight o'clock.

"How about some music?"

"Sure." She settled onto the couch while he slid a CD into the player. She was wondering why he didn't give her a choice, when the familiar chords of a hit from their teen years began to play.

"Isn't that one of the songs we…" She stopped, hearing background chatter. Instead of the recording artist, her own voice began to sing, more or less on key. A moment later, Joseph's tenor joined in a duet. "I can't believe you saved that! My recorder ate my copy." The loss had nearly broken her heart all over again.

"I had it transferred to a CD for safekeeping." Easing onto the couch beside her, Joseph stretched his legs atop the parquet coffee table. "I can burn it for you if you'd like."

"I'd love it!" She closed her eyes, reveling in the music despite their vocal flaws. The night Joseph had taken her to the karaoke bar had been one of the happiest of her life.

Ironically, the previous night, her sixteenth birthday, her parents had hosted a country club dinner in her honor that had been tedious at best. Although Erin had requested a party, she'd pictured something casual at a local nightspot, not this stiff affair populated half by friends and associates of her parents.

Joseph and Tina and her other pals had been good sports, but she could tell they didn't feel at home. The Norrises hadn't been country club members then and neither had the Lowerys, so for them it must have seemed like alien territory. Even the dancing had been restrained.

The only gratifying part was the generous pile of gifts. The following week, she'd enjoyed donating many of them—not the ones from her close friends, though—to a women's shelter.

That had been on Friday night. On Saturday, Joseph had surprised her with a trip to a karaoke bar. In front of a room full of strangers, they'd recorded versions of their favorite songs. The good-natured clapping and cheering had buoyed Erin, and she'd left on a high.

That night, she'd nearly made love with Joseph. He'd had the maturity to hold back. He'd been protecting her even then.

"You were the best friend I ever had," she said. "I wish we could have stayed together."

He draped one arm over the back of the couch. "I'm sorry I cut you off so abruptly. I figured you'd reject me sooner or later, so I lashed out like a wounded animal."

"You should have accepted support from the people who cared about you." Erin rested her head against his forearm. "My heart ached for you. And for myself, too. I missed you a lot."

When he didn't respond, she wondered if she'd made a mistake by raising the subject. Then he said, "When I wasn't licking my wounds, I put all my energy into bucking up Mom and Dad. There wasn't room for anyone else. Not even you."

Erin did exactly what she'd wanted to do all those years ago when she hadn't had the chance. She reached out and pressed her palm against Joseph's cheek and gazed directly into his eyes.

"I hope someday there'll be room for me again," she said.

"There already is room for you. Right here." When he drew her onto his lap and encircled her in his arms, Erin buried her face in the curve of his neck.

She loved the gentleness with which he held her and the tension in his body that told her he wanted more. This was where she'd yearned to be for as long as she could remember, even when she hadn't allowed herself to acknowledge it.

As he stroked her hair, his lips came down on hers. The kiss lingered until he tightened his grip on her, but there was none of the rushed quality they'd experienced the night before.

They simply melted into each other as the heat rose slowly. This was both more intimate and more real, Erin thought. Toying with the buttons on his shirt, she began to remove the barrier between them.

To her disappointment, Joseph shifted her onto the couch. "Let's not get started," he said. "You don't need this, not after what you've been through today."

"If it feels good, why not?"

"In two days, while already suffering from post-traumatic stress, you've called off your wedding, had a couple of good scares and discovered a dead body. It's a wonder you're not a basket case," Joseph told her. "A man would have to be a real jerk to take advantage of those circumstances."

She sighed. "Why did I have to choose the world's most ethical male?"

He wrapped her in a bear hug and they rocked together for a long, wonderful moment. "Peace?" Joseph asked when he let her go.

"For now," Erin conceded with as much grace as she could muster.

On the CD player, Joseph's seventeen-year-old tenor voice was crooning a mournful ballad. After they broke up, she used to play this tape over and over, even though it made her sob, because while he was singing, she'd felt as if she could see directly into his soul.

Yes, there remained a bond between them. Yet she had to admit that she didn't know him as an adult. He'd gone to college, become a police officer and handled cases that must have affected him. Surely he'd had other involvements that had changed him as well.

And in some ways she didn't even know herself, Erin admitted. Away from her job, estranged from her mother, she wanted to crawl into a nest and stay here forever. Perhaps he was right. She might be clinging to Joseph because he represented security.

Maybe a few precious days were all they had. A part of her wanted to throw caution to the wind and make love so that she'd have wonderful memories to treasure forever. But they'd hurt each other deeply before and might again. Joseph had hit one thing right: Erin was in no condition to risk a broken heart.

He cleared his throat. "Maybe this wasn't the best choice of music."

She was about to ask why not when she registered the tears streaming down her cheeks. They accompanied this song so naturally that she'd hardly noticed them.

"Don't mind me," she said. "I'm sentimental."

They listened for a while longer, until the disk ended. Erin listened with regret to the faint whirr of the machine disconnecting.

"Want something to drink?" Joseph asked.

"Sure."

While he put on a Yanni CD and went into the kitchen, Erin picked up Jean's yearbook from the coffee table. She flipped back to the sophomore class and looked up Marie Flanders.

The family resemblance was unmistakable despite the dyed-black hair—or maybe that was her aunt's natural color—and the heavy 1970s makeup. Until now, Erin had thought she didn't have a clear memory of Marie, but the ironic twist of her mouth was surprisingly familiar.

She hoped Aunt Marie was, as Joseph had suggested, sunning herself in Hawaii. It was hard to fathom that a person could simply disappear without anyone knowing what had happened. She might be trapped somewhere, or lying comatose in a hospital bed, or in a shallow grave. What if the same fate was closing in on Erin and Alice?

She jumped when glasses clinked close to her ear. "Sorry," Joseph said. "I was wondering if you'd like some of this fruit juice blend. It's supposed to be soothing, but from your reaction I'd say it has the opposite effect."

She smiled apologetically. "Don't blame the juice. My imagination got the better of me."

"Good. Let's hope this stuff lives up to its reputation, then."

As he knelt beside the coffee table to pour from the carafe, Erin noticed that the yearbook had flipped to photos of students hanging out on campus. She was about to close it when several faces jumped out at her.

There was Aunt Marie with that long black hair. Todd Wilde, the boy whose picture she'd updated only yesterday and whose body lay in the morgue, perched beside her atop a picnic table. Behind them, wearing an expression of uncertainty, stood a chestnut-haired girl Erin recognized with a jolt.

Thirty years ago, she hadn't developed pouches under her eyes and she'd worn her hair loose instead of pulled into a bun. But the woman hanging around with Todd and Marie was unmistakably Brandy Schorr, Alice's new housekeeper.

Chapter Ten

In the middle of the night, Joseph arose and, on a large sheet of paper, set to work on a chart resembling a family tree. As long as he couldn't sleep, he might as well do something useful. Maybe, he reflected as he ran his hand through his disordered hair, a chart would help him identify more clearly the connections between these people.

After Erin's discovery in the yearbook, he'd gone to the database, where he'd learned that Brandy had had a few minor skirmishes with the law over the years for such offenses as substance abuse and petty theft. She'd also undergone rehab. Armed with the information, he'd called Rick to explain about Brandy and her link to the missing Marie.

"I'm more interested in her involvement with Wilde," Rick had said. "I'll interview her first thing tomorrow. We still don't know why he was snooping."

Despite knowing Rick would pursue the subject, Erin had been too upset to sleep. To calm her, Joseph had put on a CD of musical accompaniment for karaoke and persuaded her to sing with him. The ploy had worked. Soon they'd been enjoying old favorites, laughing at their slipups and inventing new words to the songs.

When she cut loose that way, Erin lit up his heart. That hadn't changed and probably never would, Joseph thought.

After she went to bed, he'd dozed on the couch and awakened two hours later with his mind abuzz. When sleep continued to elude him, he'd decided to draw this relationship tree.

Thirty years ago, Alice and Jean had been seniors in high school, Marie and Todd sophomores and Brandy a freshman. Not until Alice was in college had she met Erin's father, so Joseph drew a branch for him farther up the tree. His own father had grown up twenty miles away and Edgar Norris had moved to town as an adult, so their branches joined even higher.

Next came their children: himself, Erin, Gene and Tina. He omitted Jean's kids, since they didn't appear to figure into the puzzle. Toward the top he penciled in branches for Chet and Lance and, on impulse, Rick. Chet and Lance were from L.A., he noted, and Rick from San Diego.

If you looked at it one way, they were all tied to one another in various ways, which meant you could weave a theory pointing to almost anyone, Joseph thought wearily. The problem was, you could also shoot down those theories if you tried hard enough.

What was he missing?

Although Marie's disappearance might be unrelated, it troubled him. She'd left voluntarily, according to her roommate, but someone else might have enticed her away or caught up with her later.

He also wasn't comfortable with the idea that Chet had acquired enough money to loan a large amount to his campaign. A six-figure salary and a talent with stocks made a plausible explanation, and yet…and yet…

And yet I'm not seeing the whole picture. I guess I'm too tired. Or too absorbed in Erin to think straight.

Joseph went to the window and, between the blinds, stared into the night. When he bought this house, it had been a place of refuge, and he was glad it could provide shelter for Erin now. But in the long run, the only effective way to guard her was to figure out what was going on and who was behind it.

It would be easier if he didn't suspect this case might touch upon his father's wrongful conviction. His old wounds made it doubly hard to keep things in perspective.

There were so many possibilities. Old conspirators turning against one another. Todd, the absent Lorenz and someone else, smarter than those two. Someone who might still be living in Sundown Valley. Someone who had everything to lose if he—or she—were caught.

Perhaps Todd Wilde had been foolish or desperate enough to blackmail a former conspirator from the Nguyen murder, Joseph thought. But that was, of course, just another theory. And it didn't explain Todd's apparent interest in the Boldings.

There was, he realized, one person he hadn't talked to who might be able to shed light, at least on his father's case. Manuel Lima, who had hired Joseph, had been chief of police when Lewis Lowery was convicted.

Although he'd retired three years ago, he still lived in town. The police database probably contained his phone number and address.

If Joseph contacted Lima, he had no idea whether his former boss would agree to keep their discussion confidential from Norris. But even at the risk of putting his job in jeopardy, it all boiled down to the need to keep Erin safe. Whatever the cost, Joseph had to follow up on every lead and talk to every witness.

Tomorrow, he was going to give Lima a call.

ON MONDAY, the *Sundown Sentinel* hit painfully close to home. In addition to an old photo of Todd, the paper ran a picture of Erin in her wedding dress, complete with tiara and choker. It had obviously been shot by the photographer she'd hired for the event.

In the picture, she clasped her bouquet in front of her as if it were a shield. Despite the wistful smile on her face, to Erin her eyes appeared vulnerable and a little frightened.

She'd let down her guard and given the man a glimpse of her inner turmoil. Apparently he'd felt no compunctions about selling it.

Although the main story focused on the finding of Todd's body, a sidebar speculated about why the town's heiress, supposedly so incapacitated she'd called off her wedding, had gone boating with a suspended police detective who used to be her high school boyfriend. It was the kind of gossip readers would hash over during their coffee breaks. Remembering Gene's concern about the effects on Chet's campaign, she suspected this was what he'd been worrying about.

"There's nothing we can do about it," Joseph said when he noticed her staring at the photograph. They were finishing a late breakfast since, after yesterday's excitement, Erin had slept until nearly noon. "Besides, that picture makes you look gorgeous, which isn't difficult."

"I think I look wounded," she admitted.

"Then people should sympathize," he responded with maddening nonchalance. "Are you still planning to talk to that financial officer about your trust fund? I can come with you if you like."

"Thanks, but it's better if I go alone." Erin wasn't worried about being attacked within the walls of the Marshall Company's headquarters. "The less we're seen in public together, the better. This could hurt you, too, you know."

"The chief's already got it in for me, so what the heck?" Joseph didn't seem fazed by the glare of publicity. She realized he must have endured much worse during his father's trial. "If you don't need me, though, I'll drop you off and go visit Chief Lima."

"Great," she said. "I'll meet you afterward at the mall." She named their favorite ice cream shop.

"Not the arcade?" he teased.

Erin chuckled. "I miss the place, but I doubt it's still there, with all the competition from video games."

"You never know," he said. "But ice cream's fine with me. You're sure you don't want me tagging along this morning?"

"I can handle it." She put more bravado into the words than she felt.

After six weeks of convalescence, the prospect of marching into her father's company to ask for an advance on her quarterly payments gave Erin pause. She didn't look forward to facing people who, until now, had seemed so much older and wiser that she'd never even considered herself their boss.

But she had to get her hands on some of her money. And, with Alice under Lance's influence, she ought to take a closer look at the responsibilities that came with her father's legacy. Ready or not, she had to take the first step of simply walking in there and making it clear she was going to be around for a while.

She didn't have much of a choice. By now, Erin's notoriety had probably reached Orange County, so she could hardly go back to work as an anonymous assistant at Bea's firm. When the van struck her in the parking lot, it had effectively ended that phase of her life.

Whatever the future held, she could no longer pretend she wasn't Andrew Marshall's daughter. How ironic if, by trying to get rid of her, someone had catapulted her into assuming the mantle she'd long avoided.

Less than an hour later, as she ventured into the lobby of the Marshall building, Erin gripped her purse and reminded herself to breathe. The soaring two-story entryway, with its curved staircase and open mezzanine, dwarfed her. Once, she'd thought she might enjoy working in the public relations and promotions office, until she learned that its primary activities were assembling brochures and annual reports.

That's not the way Erin would run things if she were in charge. At the Homework Center, she'd learned that the local school libraries suffered from slashed budgets. Also, that a proposed central science high school had failed to get off the ground due to inadequate funding. There was so much this company could do.

She didn't recognize any of the people bustling by and, although surely some of them had seen her photograph plastered across the newspaper, none of them seemed to notice her. When she'd last come here eight months ago to attend the annual board meeting, Erin had barely said a word.

That naïve girl was gone. Smoothing down her blue, high-collared dress, Erin took a deep breath and gathered her courage.

The elevator doors opened. Out came Stanley Rogers, his hair a little grayer than she remembered but his smile as warm as ever. When she'd phoned him an hour ago, he'd immediately agreed to meet with her.

"Miss Marshall!" The chief financial officer, who'd worked for Erin's father for as long as she could remember, caught her hands in his. "You're looking well. I've been worried about you."

Her uncertainty eased. Stanley's familiar creased face and fatherly concern reminded her that she belonged here.

"I haven't entirely recovered," Erin admitted as he escorted her onto the elevator. "Sometimes I get headaches."

"I'm sorry to hear it." He pushed the button for the fifth floor, the location of the executive and board offices. "How's the memory?"

"The doctors say that may never come back," Erin admitted.

"The important thing is that you're healthy in every other way." Stanley stayed in good shape for a man in his sixties, she noticed. He and her father used to go hunting together, trekking up and down the hills, so perhaps that accounted for it. "We'll get you fixed up financially, don't worry about that."

They emerged into a plush, carpeted antechamber. At a broad reception desk, an unfamiliar woman looked up from her computer. "This is Elena Gabriel, the new board secretary," Stanley said.

"Welcome aboard," she said.

"It's a pleasure to meet you, Miss Marshall." The young woman ducked her head shyly.

Good heavens, Erin thought, *I intimidate her.* That was a new experience.

"What happened to Betsy Rydell?" she asked Stanley.

"We promoted her to assistant manager of the mall. She was thrilled."

As they passed into his outer office, Erin found she didn't recognize Stanley's secretary, either. Turnover had to be high, she supposed. Bea had complained about the same problem at her firm.

The wood-paneled inner office extended to include a conference table, bookcases, a massive desk and a computer stand. A large window overlooked the parklike grounds and the mall next door.

"Great view," Erin said.

"Thanks." The financial officer gestured her to a leather swivel chair and sat behind the desk. "On the phone, you mentioned an advance on your quarterly payment," he prompted.

"I already donated the last one to my foundation," Erin explained. "I know I'm not due for another payment until January but circumstances have changed."

"Don't think twice about it." The executive waved a hand. "How much do you need?"

"I don't know." It was hard to assess her expenses for the next few months because there were so many variables. "A few thousand, I guess."

"That's all?" Stanley rested his elbows on the desk. "Miss Marshall…"

"Erin," she corrected politely.

"All right, Erin," he said. "I don't see how you can pay your expenses for very long on so small an amount."

"I don't want to deplete my capital," she said. "The foundation relies on the income."

His forehead wrinkled. "You know, your trust fund contains more than thirty million dollars."

"What?" She blinked, scarcely believing she'd heard right. "I thought it was ten million."

"As half owner of the Marshall Company, you're also entitled to half the annual profits," he said. "You may recall that you instructed me two years ago to add that money to your trust fund."

"I'd forgotten." She hoped she didn't sound as ignorant as she felt. "I was in a daze after Dad died. I don't remember what I said."

"Those were your instructions," Stanley told her. "You also told me to roll over most of the investment profits because you feared the payouts would swamp your foundation. I offered to send you a full accounting quarterly, but you said you wouldn't understand it anyway."

Had she really said such a foolish thing? She must have, Erin mused. "You're telling me I could draw a check for millions if I wanted to?"

"It's not quite that simple," he admitted. "The money is in stocks, bonds and real estate, and you'd take a loss if you tried to liquidate it too quickly. However, I'm sure I can arrange for whatever you need."

Erin was embarrassed to realize that she could ask for a million dollars and this man would give it to her. It was ridiculous. Such an incredibly large amount of money that she'd done nothing to earn.

She glanced past him out the window at the mall her father had built. Andrew Marshall had been pleased that his daughter valued public service above personal luxuries. He'd be proud of her now—or would he?

She was worth thirty million dollars—actually, much more—and what was she doing with it? Making small grants here and there. With that kind of money, she could not only fund all the projects she'd learned about at the Homework Center but also buy the old fishing pier and build a nature preserve. And there had to be other projects that would benefit the whole community.

It was time to stop thinking small. She ought to ask for enough money to hire guards if Joseph went back to work and to find another place to live if she had to. She couldn't impose on him forever.

"A hundred thousand dollars." She tried not to gulp after she said it.

"No problem. We can transfer it directly to your bank account if you like."

"That would be fine." She could scarcely believe he'd agreed without blinking. Even though she'd grown up surrounded by wealth, Erin's father hadn't believed in spoiling her. She'd never even owned a car until college.

Over the intercom, Stanley instructed his secretary to take care of the matter. "If you require more, don't hesitate to ask," he told Erin afterward. "I'm not sure where you're staying, but if you need a place, I can help you there as well. As you know, this company owns a lot of property."

"A friend is putting me up," she said.

"Detective Lowery?" He might have read that in the newspaper, or perhaps Chet had mentioned it. "Your father thought highly of him."

"I know." She was glad to hear it confirmed by an objective party.

"Is there anything else I can do?"

On the verge of saying no, Erin remembered her decision to begin assuming more responsibilities. "I'm afraid I've shirked my duties as part-owner. I'd like to remedy that."

"You haven't done anything wrong," Stanley told her.

"Some people would say my behavior was immature, and

they'd be right," Erin told him. "I was so overwhelmed after Dad died that I didn't want to deal with all this money. But that's got to change."

He cleared his throat. "I understood from your mother that you were no longer concerned…that you'd withdrawn your request…"

"For what?" Erin asked.

"I'm sorry. I keep forgetting that your memory's been affected," he said. "We've got everything computerized. What kind of information would you like?"

"The whole thing," she said impulsively. "A complete accounting of where my money is, the rate of return, everything that's happened for the past two years." Seeing his startled expression, she added, "I don't mean right this minute. Obviously, it will take a week or so."

"You mean for the whole company?"

No wonder he'd been taken aback! "No, just my trust fund," she said. "I'm sure you do all that audit stuff on a regular basis anyway, right?"

"Of course. We'll put together an up-to-the minute picture for you," Stanley said. "Is there some reason for this request, or simply curiosity?"

"I'm going to be staying in Sundown Valley," Erin told him. "If Chet wins the election, he'll be leaving, and my mom's not in great shape, so I'm going to have to take a more active role with the company." No matter how little she relished the prospect, she had to do this. "If you don't mind, I'll rely on you to help educate me."

"It will be my pleasure." Stanley tapped his fingers on the desk. "I hope you'll consider—that is, should Chet leave us, I've been considering applying for his position. I realize you'll want to interview other candidates, but I trust my experience will count in my favor."

"I'm sure it will," Erin said. "My father always believed in promoting from within."

Looking relieved, Stanley got to his feet and escorted her to the outer office. His secretary greeted them with a sheaf of memos. "I've been holding your calls, Mr. Rogers," she explained apologetically.

"I'll have someone escort you downstairs," he told Erin.

"It's not necessary." People really did think of her as a little girl, she reflected. Until now, she supposed she'd given them reason to do so.

They shook hands. "I'll be in touch," Stanley said. "We'll get you that information you requested."

"Thank you."

That hadn't taken long, Erin thought as she passed the board secretary's desk, which was empty at the moment. Joseph's meeting with the retired chief would probably last for a while longer. That gave her time to pick up a few items she needed at the mall.

Smiling to herself at the prospect of shopping, she pressed the elevator button. A moment later, it opened to reveal a tall, blond man who raked her with a startled gaze.

"Chet," she said. "I was just…"

"Erin." Catching her arm, he steered her toward his office. "I've been wanting to talk to you."

She tried to think of a polite reason to refuse. Before she found one, he'd whisked her into his quarters and closed the door.

RAINBOW ACRES, where Manuel Lima and his wife lived, had been built about ten years ago. As with many Marshall developments, a greenbelt meandered around the perimeter, providing a path for joggers, cyclists and dog walkers. Inside, the main street curved past a tree-shaded community pool.

The Limas' home occupied the end of a cul-de-sac. All the houses, subject to homeowners' association rules, were painted in a bland assortment of earth tones. Each small yard sported a discreet mixture of grass, flowers and low-growing trees.

When Joseph used to patrol here, the manicured perfection of the place had reminded him of a trip to Disneyland. Each time he drove through, he half expected to see team members in funny costumes run out and sweep any stray litter from the sidewalks.

Although he'd never had occasion to visit the chief at home before, he'd known where the house was. If you were going to patrol near where your boss lived, you made sure you didn't miss any problems.

On the phone, Lima had said he'd be glad to talk to him. He hadn't mentioned that morning's newspaper account and neither had Joseph. All the same, he figured his former boss had to be wondering what the heck was going on.

He parked by the curb. Two houses down, a mother sat on a lawn chair, reading a novel and watching her toddlers at play. No danger of anyone breaking into his vehicle around here, he mused.

When the bell rang, Lourdes Lima, a stocky woman with salt-and-pepper hair, ushered him inside with an unexpected hug. A retired Spanish teacher at the high school, she'd shepherded Joseph through four years of the language. He'd always suspected that her behind-the-scenes recommendation hadn't hurt his quest to join the force.

"Whatever is going on, I know you're on the right side," she told him. "How about some coffee and *churros?*"

"You bet!" He hadn't eaten any of the Mexican treats since Mrs. Lima used to bring them to Spanish class.

"My husband is on the patio," she said. "Please go ahead." She pointed through the family room toward the rear sliding glass door.

In back, Joseph found the old chief working a crossword puzzle at a table beneath a beach-style umbrella. Behind him, an emerald patch of lawn and an exuberant burst of roses testified to the Limas' gardening talents.

"Lowery." The stocky man arose to shake hands. Although

he had to be nearly seventy, Lima's hair remained dark with a white crest in front. "You're looking well."

"So are you, Chief." As he sat, Joseph observed that his slacks and short-sleeved shirt looked almost formal compared to the chief's Hawaiian top and shorts.

"You've been a busy man," the chief said. "Busted up a society wedding and found a body, all in one weekend."

"I try not to let any grass grow under my feet," Joseph responded dryly.

"You said you wanted to talk about the Nguyen murder." As always, Lima went quickly to the point. "You see a connection to Erin Marshall's accident?"

"Todd Wilde was questioned about his whereabouts that night," he explained. "Now, shortly after he's seen spying on her mother's house, we find him dead. To top it off, his body was floating not far from where Alice Bolding nearly drowned. That's a lot of coincidences."

"The night of the Nguyen murder, he produced a witness who gave him an alibi we couldn't shake," the chief said. "I presume you read the report?"

"I figured requesting it from records would raise too many questions," Joseph admitted. "I used the computerized library at the newspaper instead."

"The editors didn't ask what you were after?"

"The paper makes its records available to the public for an hourly fee," he said.

"Very enterprising."

The scent of cinnamon ushered the arrival of Lourdes with a tray of *churros* and a pot of coffee. The fluted pastry sticks, which had been fried and rolled in cinnamon sugar, looked crisp and smelled irresistible.

"My wife only makes these once or twice a month," Lima said. "Your timing is impeccable."

Lourdes set the plate in front of them. "Lean forward, both

of you, so you won't spill sugar on your clothes," she cautioned as if they were kids.

"*Sí, Mamacita,*" Manuel teased.

Joseph lifted a pastry and savored the first mouthful, letting the flavors percolate through his senses. "This is as close to heaven as you can get without dying."

Mrs. Lima clucked her tongue in pretended disbelief. A smile betrayed her pleasure as she poured them each coffee.

"Wonderful," the chief added. "You've outdone yourself." Satisfied, his wife retreated into the house, and he returned his attention to Joseph. "I lost track of our conversation. What is it you want to know?"

"For starters, who gave Todd Wilde his alibi?" The news reports had been sketchy in that regard.

"Ever heard the name Marie Flanders?"

At Joseph's start, coffee slopped onto his saucer. "I didn't know she was involved in the case."

"She swore Wilde spent the night club-hopping with her in L.A.," he said. "Why are you so surprised?"

"She's missing." He outlined the circumstances.

"In light of what happened to Wilde, that worries me," Lima conceded. "She struck me as a troubled young woman, but it's been years since I've heard anything about her. I was hoping she'd straightened out her life."

"Did you believe her testimony?"

"It wasn't up to me," the chief said. "The D.A. decides who to prosecute. You know that."

"You didn't have an opinion?"

He shrugged. "It might have been true. On the other hand, she struck me as the type of woman who would lie if her boyfriend asked her to."

"What about Alfonso Lorenz?"

"His mother swore he got off work early that night and told her your father had sent him home," Lima said.

"Did you believe her?"

"Who knows? She was his mother." After a sip of coffee, he added, "We searched his house without finding the jewels, but that doesn't mean they weren't stashed somewhere. Later, when he left the country, the D.A. still didn't believe there was enough evidence to reopen the case."

The D.A., who'd died of cancer several years later, had been a politically ambitious man who, in Joseph's opinion, hadn't been willing to admit he might have made a mistake. Especially not after the man he sent to prison was killed there.

Joseph downed another *churro*. "What about Chief Norris?"

"What about him?"

"Any idea where he was that night?"

The question hung in the air. "That's quite an implication," Lima said quietly. "Do you have reason to suspect him?"

"Do you?" Joseph asked.

"I am not a hostile witness," the chief reminded him.

"I'm sorry." He took a long breath before asking rhetorically, "Do I have evidence linking him to the Nguyen murder? No. Just an uneasy sense that he might not be entirely innocent."

"I wondered about that myself," Lima said.

"You did?"

"Not that I had any evidence, but despite his past alcoholism, it seemed out of character for your father to commit a violent crime," he said. "Also, the explanation that he got so drunk he fell over backward and smacked his head didn't wash with me, especially since no one could say exactly what he fell against."

"What about the defense attorney? Was he incompetent?" Since the lawyer had retired to Costa Rica while Joseph was in college, he'd never had a chance to question him.

"He did a decent job but not a great one. Your family couldn't afford one of those elaborate defenses with experts giving demonstrations about the angle of the head injury and that sort of thing. He presented a reasonable case, I thought, but the jury didn't buy it."

"Let's get back to Chief Norris." As long as he'd raised the subject, Joseph might as well pursue it. "Were you satisfied with his investigation?"

"If not, I'd have put someone else on the case," Lima said.

"But you said you have doubts about him," he pointed out.

"They came after the fact," his host explained. "For one thing, he strongly opposed my hiring you. I don't understand why Edgar would hold your father's actions against you unless he had a guilty conscience."

"Thanks," Joseph said. "Anything else?"

"When I heard he'd been elected to the country club board of directors, it occurred to me that money meant a lot more to Edgar than it did to your father," Lima said. "Which meant he had a greater motive to go after those jewels. But I'm sure he wasn't directly involved in what happened that night."

"How?" he pressed.

Lima polished off another *churro* before replying. "He had an airtight alibi."

"No alibi is perfect," Joseph said. "Whoever testified for him might have a motive of his own. Where was he that night?"

"With me," the chief said.

Chapter Eleven

Tugging free from Chet's grasp, Erin moved away on the thick carpet. "If you're mad about the story in today's paper, I'm sorry. But when we decided to go boating, I had no idea we were going to stumble across a corpse."

"I'm not angry. That isn't what I wanted to talk to you about." Chet's eyes remained opaque. Being around him felt almost surreal. She'd nearly married a man she now realized she hardly knew. "How are you feeling, by the way?"

"A little woozy." A tremor of apprehension ran through her. Although he'd never been abusive, he had uttered what sounded like a threat on Saturday. "What did you want to talk about?"

Chet gestured her to a chair. Erin shook her head, and they stayed where they were, poised like two fencers waiting for the other to make the first move.

In his three years as CEO, Chet had made the space his own, she noticed. He'd not only remodeled but also enlarged it, expanding into the adjoining office that had once been her father's. In addition to an expanse of glass, a broad desk and what seemed like miles of carpeting, a massive array of black audiovisual equipment reminded her of something from a James Bond movie.

Until two years ago the CEO had kept a low profile, since much of the real power had remained in the hands of her father. After Andrew's death, Chet clearly hadn't hesitated to step into the breach.

"I have a message from your mother," he said.

"What is it?" It was more important than ever to make contact with her mother since the discovery of Todd Wilde's body had confirmed there was something evil afoot.

"She called this morning after reading the *Sentinel*," he said. "She's worried about you being out on the lake when you're not well."

"That sounds like her." Erin's mother *would* get more worked up about the possibility of her daughter catching a chill than about the fact that an old acquaintance was dead.

"By the way, why did you go boating?" Chet asked.

"Joseph thought the fresh air might be good for me." She kept her tone bland. The truth about their investigation was none of his business. "By the way, did you know him?"

"Who?"

"Todd Wilde." There was no reason they should have met. Still, she'd learned from Joseph that it was better to ask an unnecessary question than to risk omitting an important one.

When Chet shook his head, she saw no sign of guile on his face. "I'm afraid not, but it makes me uneasy for your mother."

"Me, too," Erin said. "Look, Lance told me not to call the house and I'd hate to tangle with him, but please ask Mom to phone me directly. She has my cell number."

"I don't think you realize what bad shape she's in," Chet said.

A knot of dread formed in Erin's chest. "Is there something she's not telling me?"

"It isn't my place to say so."

"Chet!"

He regarded her searchingly. "She doesn't want to upset you, but I think you have a right to hear it," he said. "Erin, your mother has cancer."

Cancer. The dreaded word hung in the air.

Erin didn't want to lose her mom. In all the concern about the near drowning, she hadn't suspected this furtive, deadly foe. "What kind of cancer? Is she getting good care?"

"It's breast cancer, so there's hope," he said. "She's being treated at the oncology center here in town. You know they're top-notch, and they've been very accommodating about her privacy. She didn't want people to see her while her hair was growing out."

"So that's why she was avoiding everyone." Erin tried to absorb what he'd said. "When did it start? Does this have anything to do with her accident?"

"She's been in treatment since before then," Chet told her. "She went out on the water to try to collect her thoughts. She said she was nauseated from her treatment and made the mistake of leaning over the edge, and that's when she fell."

"She should have told the police!"

"Do you have any idea how many people have access to that report? She refused to risk it."

"I understand. I wish she'd told me, though." Alice must have believed she was protecting her daughter, but that wasn't true. Secrecy had only made things worse. And they'd lost time they could have spent together.

"She'll be relieved when I tell her I've seen you, although not thrilled that I shot off my mouth," Chet said. "I'll ask her to call you."

"Please tell her it's important." Although this information put Lance in a less suspicious light, Erin still didn't trust him. The day of the wedding, his order that she leave her mother alone hadn't been related to the cancer.

Chet reached out as if to take her hands. She flinched, and he stopped. "I'm afraid I haven't acquitted myself very well in your eyes, have I?"

"I guess you haven't," she agreed.

"Surely there's some way we can make this up," Chet said.

"I'm sorry I lied. But at a time like this, with your mother ill, we should pull together."

Erin got another uneasy sensation. Part of her wanted to agree, to trust that he could make things right. Mostly, though, she knew better. "I'm never going to marry you. I don't love you."

"Everything was fine until that detective interfered." The words bristled with irritation. "He wants to clear his father's name and he'll use you to do it. You may trust him, but he's got his own ax to grind. "

"Don't underestimate me," Erin said. "I'm not clinging to Joseph or anyone else."

"Aren't you?" Chet took a step closer. "I've known you for a long time. I understand what you're like."

She resented the way he towered over her, forcing her to either step backward or tip her head back to look up at him. Erin chose the latter course rather than retreat. "You don't know me, you only know how I've behaved. Well, I'm changing, in case you hadn't noticed. Get with the picture, buster."

He stared at her. "You sound like your father."

"Good," she said. "I plan to do that a lot more."

To her surprise, he chuckled. "Good for you."

"Are you serious?"

"Maybe I did underestimate you," Chet said. "I always believed we were suited for each other. Now I'm sure of it."

That wasn't the reaction she'd expected. While Erin wanted them to continue on good terms, she preferred for those terms to be impersonal. "I'm glad you like the new me. You still need to take no for an answer."

"I promise to work on it."

"You can work on it by opening the door, for starters," she said.

With a mock courtly bow, Chet turned the knob and walked with her to the elevator. "I'll call your mother today. I'm sure she wants to see you."

"Thanks." She tried to hide her relief at getting away from him. How had she ever imagined she could live with that man?

When Erin reached the sidewalk in front of the building, she let the afternoon sunshine wash over her. The tang of autumn in the October day made her keenly aware of being alive and free.

Down the block, on the opposite side of the street, she caught sight of the Sundown Medical Center. Fifteen years ago, she'd attended the opening of the oncology unit that her parents had underwritten. Even after hearing all the statistics about cancer, Erin had never thought that someday a family member might be treated there.

Breast cancer had a fairly good cure rate, she remembered reading, but Alice didn't look well. Lost in thought, Erin scarcely noticed a van pulling out of the hospital parking lot.

It turned toward her beneath a row of trees. When leaves stippled the windshield, Erin's heart beat faster. She might not have a clear picture of what had happened that day six weeks before, but some part of her remembered. *A windshield. Glare. Someone at the wheel.*

The van tracked toward her, gaining speed. A sense of incredulity rooted her in place. This was her hometown. It was broad daylight and she was standing in front of the Marshall building.

Accelerating, the van veered toward her. Any minute, it would leave the road.

Erin started to run. On the sidewalk, her smooth-soled pumps skidded and she teetered, off balance.

She couldn't get out of the path. Not again. This couldn't happen twice.

The van swung away from her, straightening its course as it sped by. At the wheel sat a middle-aged woman, her gaze fixed in the distance. She didn't appear to have noticed Erin.

In the middle of the street loomed a pothole. The driver must have veered to avoid it.

The van cornered onto a side street and disappeared.

Adrenaline pumped through Erin. She hadn't been in danger, yet it felt like a close call.

Slowly, her breathing returned to normal. Determined to go about her business, she crossed the street and headed to a nearby branch of her bank. There should be plenty of time to pick up some cash from her newly fattened account.

All that money, she thought as she waited for the teller to confirm the balance and count out a couple of hundred dollars in tens and twenties. Millions and millions, and what would have happened to it if that van had killed her?

Alice might be dying. If Erin perished too, Lance Bolding would get everything. The opportunist who'd targeted her mother on a cruise could end up owning the company her father had spent his life building.

She refused to take that risk.

Beyond the bank stood the law office of Horner and Fitch, where Joseph's mother worked. By the time Erin emerged from the bank, she'd decided to take this chance to revise her will. If Joseph beat her to the ice cream parlor, he'd just have to wait.

At the front desk, Suzanne greeted her warmly. She became all business when Erin explained why she was there. "I'm sure Abe can find time for you," she said. "Just a sec."

In no time, the short, energetic attorney was ushering Erin into his chamber. Only thinning white hair hinted that he had to be around seventy.

Abe Fitch was, as always, warmly accommodating. Certainly, he agreed, she could change her will. Although usually it took several visits to create a new will, since the document had to be prepared for her signature, they could handle it today if she didn't want to wait.

Her anxiety about the beige van still haunting her, Erin agreed. Now that she'd made up her mind, she preferred to get the whole thing over with.

When she said she wanted to remove her mother's name from the will, Abe didn't ask for a reason, although he must have wondered about it. On the verge of telling him to leave it all to her trust, she stopped.

The Marshall Company was not only a vast corporation, it also wielded an incalculable power over the people of Sundown Valley by the nature of the projects it undertook and how it managed them. Her foundation, due to its mission, would use that influence only to enhance its own wealth. She couldn't expect a banker to exercise moral authority when he hadn't been charged with doing so.

She needed to leave her legacy to an individual she trusted. There was only one person in her heart.

"I want to leave my interest in the Marshall Company to my good friend Joseph Lowery," she told the attorney.

His hand jerked on his legal pad. She envisioned a black streak on the yellow paper. "Is he aware of this bequest?"

"No," Erin said. "Does he have to be?"

"Not necessarily," Abe said. "I just have to make sure there's no duress or undue influence, nothing that could give anyone grounds to challenge the will later."

"It's entirely my own idea," she said. "I trust Joseph to do the right thing with that kind of power. I know he'll use it well."

"I've always liked that young man." Abe asked a few more questions before saying, "I'll have Suzanne type this up. She understands that it's confidential. There are several people at the bank who sometimes witness documents for me when my client is in a hurry, if that suits you."

"Sure," Erin said.

They wrapped up the matter inside an hour. A will looked like such a simple document, Erin thought as she signed it, just a few pages of whereases and wherefores. The effect if she died, however, would shake this town to its roots.

Suzanne refrained from making any comment. She looked a bit stunned.

By the time Erin got to the ice cream parlor with the will tucked inside her purse, Joseph had dug into a banana split. "It's my lunch," he explained when she came in. "Sorry I didn't wait."

"I apologize for taking so long." Taking a seat, Erin ordered a two-scoop sundae. As he'd said, it was lunch.

WHILE THEY ATE, Joseph filled her in on his meeting with Manuel Lima. "He and his wife hosted a dinner party the night Binh Nguyen was killed," he told her after filling in about Edgar Norris's alibi. "Everyone stayed until at least 1:00 a.m."

The victim's watch, broken during his fatal beating, had stopped at 11:47 p.m. Although that didn't preclude the possibility of Norris's involvement in planning the crime, Joseph had to admit it weighed in the chief's favor.

"In a way, I'm glad," Erin said. "I'd hate to think Tina's father was involved in something so horrible."

"Someone framed my father," Joseph said doggedly. "If it wasn't him, I'm back to square one."

"Chief Lima didn't have any suggestions?" Erin asked.

"No. But he told me something interesting about Todd Wilde. Your Aunt Marie gave him his alibi for that night."

She demanded the details. When he finished, she said, "You're going to tell Rick, aren't you?"

"I already did." Joseph had made the call as soon as he left the old chief's house. "He said he's going to arrange for some divers to check the lake tomorrow near where we found Todd."

She paled. "Oh, my gosh. I hope they don't find another body."

"I hope not, either." Joseph appreciated the fact that Rick had shared details of his investigation as if the two men were working together. In a sense they were, even if it wasn't official. "He went to the Boldings' house to find out how your

mother came to hire Brandy. She says Brandy had trouble
finding a job when she got out of rehab, and she *had* been a
good friend to Marie."

"Did my aunt call and recommend her?"

"No. She says she hasn't heard from her sister in over a
year. She just decided to take a chance and it worked out."

"What was the timing exactly?" Erin asked.

"The previous housekeeper quit a few weeks before your
mother's accident." In investigating the near drowning, Joseph
had interviewed Mrs. Larosa. Other than the fact that she'd
found Lance so obnoxious she'd decided to leave, she'd had
nothing of value to contribute. "Your Mom hired Brandy a
week afterward."

"Do you suppose Todd was watching Brandy?" Erin asked.

"Might have been. Your mother had no idea." Honesty
forced him to add, "However, according to Brandy, she hadn't
heard from Todd in years and had no idea what he was doing
there."

Erin set down her ice cream spoon, although she hadn't finished her sundae. "You think he's killed Marie, don't you?"

Although it seemed likely, he preferred to dwell on more
cheerful alternatives. "If she saw him as a threat, she might
have gone into hiding." Since he had nothing more to add, he
tried a different tack. "It's your turn. What did you learn this
morning?"

"Not good news, I'm afraid." Erin wrapped her arms
around herself. "My mom's got breast cancer. She's been
keeping it secret."

"I'm sorry to hear that." He knew how upsetting that had
to be for Erin. "Is there anything we can do?"

"We've got to get her out of there," she said. "No wonder
she doesn't stand up to Lance. She's in no condition to fight
him while she's battling cancer."

"Any ideas how to accomplish that?" he asked.

"Chet's going to ask her to call me when Lance isn't around."

"Wait a minute." Joseph had been so startled to learn of Alice's illness that he hadn't questioned who'd told her about it. "I thought you were going to talk to the financial officer. How did Chet get involved?"

"I ran into him," she said. "He works on the same floor."

At the country club, Dever had alternately sweet-talked and bullied her. "Did he try his usual tricks?"

"He behaved decently." She chose her words with care, he could tell. "It was nothing I couldn't handle."

Darn it, he wanted to protect her. He didn't like her being alone with Chet, not even to discuss her mother. But she hadn't asked him to run her life.

It seemed safer to change the subject. "How about that financial guy? Did he provide what you asked for?"

"More," Erin said. "A hundred thousand dollars. Can you believe that? He acted as if it were pocket change."

A hundred thousand dollars. Joseph fought the temptation to whistle in amazement. It was a vast amount, although only a fraction of what Erin had inherited.

He didn't begrudge it to her. He knew she would use the money and the power that came with it well.

It was just that when a man considered a serious relationship, he wanted to take care of the woman he loved, or at least to share the responsibilities with her. Working together and helping each other created bonds that carried you through the hard times. He'd seen that with his parents.

For a woman as wealthy as Erin, a husband had to seem almost superfluous. Unless, of course, he brought a comparable measure of wealth or prominence to the union.

Husband? Whew, he'd made a wild mental leap. There was no point in getting worked up about something that would never happen anyway.

"Now that you're rolling in it, I'll let you pay for the groceries on the way home," he teased. "We can treat ourselves to lobster and caviar."

"I'd prefer spaghetti sauce and French bread, if that's okay with you."

"It's fine. I'm fresh out of lobster bibs anyway," he joked.

They stopped at the supermarket on Grove Street. Without making it explicit, Joseph realized, they'd agreed that Erin was going to stay with him for at least a few more days. Otherwise, why would they be conferring about what kind of steak to buy for tomorrow night and which kind of cereal they liked?

She had enough money to live anywhere she wanted with plenty of security, and she seemed to have recovered from her dazed state at the wedding. It might be selfish of him to keep her at his modest house, trying to protect her all by himself.

But how could a hired guard defend her when the enemy might be someone she knew? It took someone who knew the players to detect the undercurrents. It took a friend to understand which risks she had to take and which weren't worth it.

"Something else happened," Erin said as they drove home.

"What's that?"

"I don't think it's significant, but outside the Marshall Company a van headed toward me. It sped up and swerved, and I thought it was going to hit me." She shuddered.

He knew he should have been there. "What happened?"

"It went right by. It was just avoiding a pothole."

"Did you see the driver?" He switched from one winding road to another, drawing closer to home.

"A middle-aged woman."

"Familiar?"

"No, and I don't think she noticed me." She flipped a lock of chestnut hair off her neck. "The funny thing is I got a flash of memory, nothing substantial, just glare on a windshield. It might have been the van that hit me."

"That's a good sign."

"How come?"

"It means the memories are there," he said. "Sometimes

trauma victims don't have time to transfer what happens from short-term to long-term memory. In that case, whatever happened is truly gone and can't be recovered."

"You think my memories might still come back?" Erin asked dubiously.

"Possibly," Joseph said. "Willing to try an experiment?"

"Okay," she said.

"Relax and let your mind float. Don't focus on the crash." He swung onto Little Creek Lane. "Think about what you must have done that morning, driving to the carnival or talking to your boss. Things with no emotional load attached."

A sports car whizzed by in the opposite direction, hugging the sharp turns. Joseph recognized the driver as one of his neighbors.

Erin leaned her head against the seat rest. "I can almost taste this chocolate bar, and then I feel empty. Like I'm still hungry. It doesn't make sense."

"Did you think about eating one and deny it to yourself?"

"No. Wait!" A thin line creased her forehead. "There was a little boy…"

A sharp crack resounded from off to their right. "Get down!" Instinctively, Joseph swerved into a zigzag pattern.

Erin slid as low as her seat belt allowed. Another report echoed from the canyon walls.

A vibration shook the car. Whoever was shooting at them had hit the back of the car.

His aim wasn't great. But it might be good enough to kill.

Chapter Twelve

"Are you hurt?" Erin heard Joseph demand as he stepped on the gas.

"No." She tensed, huddled low and waited for the next shot. When it rang out, she shuddered. More shots. The car leaped forward.

"Joseph?" Her jaw trembled so hard she barely managed to say his name.

"I'm fine."

They zipped around a curve. The next bursts of sound were fainter. She hoped that meant they'd passed beyond the shooter's range.

"If you can reach your cell phone, dial 911," Joseph said.

She fumbled in her purse until she found the device. In her nervousness, she lost her grip several times getting it open, and it seemed to take forever before she managed to activate it and dial.

They were entering his driveway when the dispatcher said, "911 Emergency."

"Tell her there's a sniper on Little Creek Lane," Joseph said hoarsely. Gravel spun from beneath their wheels as they plunged upward.

Erin repeated the information and, as requested, gave the street number along with their names. "I'm sending someone right now," the dispatcher said. "Please stay on the line."

They crested the drive and lurched into the carport, barely stopping short of the far wall. "Stay here." Joseph opened his door. "I'm not going far."

The prospect of his getting shot terrified Erin. "Shouldn't we both lie low?"

"It's better this way." He drew his gun. "I'm not letting him sneak up and shoot us like sitting ducks."

As he exited in a crouch, blood roared in Erin's ears. *Please don't let anything happen to Joseph.* He was her safe harbor. She might possess reserves of strength herself, but right now she had no idea where they'd gone.

Against her ear, the dispatcher asked another question. Speaking softly, Erin described what was happening. "Joseph's taking a look around."

"Did you see anyone? Do you have a vehicle description?"

"I think he was shooting from the woods," she said. "We couldn't see him."

"I've got two cars responding," the dispatcher said. As if in confirmation, Erin heard the distant wail of a siren, followed by a second one.

"Thank you."

The driver's door opened. Erin's heart nearly stopped until she saw Joseph's ruffled hair and grim face. "He hit the car, right near the gas tank," he said. "We got lucky. A few more inches and we'd have gone up in flames."

She refused to focus on what might have been. "Any sign of him?"

He replied with a negative. "If he's smart, he'll melt into the woods before the cavalry arrives, but let's keep our heads down just in case."

Erin's palm brushed Joseph's cheek. "I'm glad you're here."

"Me, too." He kissed her hand. "Let's keep quiet in case he's still here. I don't want him to get the drop on us."

In silence, they listened for the warning crunch of gravel.

All she heard were birds twittering and the rising shrill of police sirens.

Finally a patrol car screamed up the driveway onto the gravel. Joseph holstered his gun. "Ask the dispatcher to tell the officer we're in the car and we're about to get out. We don't want to startle anyone."

Erin obeyed. When she finished, Joseph emerged slowly. She was relieved to hear the patrolman greet him by name.

While she was getting out, a second black-and-white appeared, and from overhead came the whir of the police rescue helicopter. Her family had paid for that, Erin recalled. Her father's idea of community service might not be exactly the same as hers, but she was grateful he'd chosen to fund this particular amenity.

Within minutes, more officers arrived and, with the aid of the copter, fanned out to search the woods. A couple of neighbors dropped by as well, full of curiosity and concerns. Each was questioned and checked for gunpowder residue.

"I guess you have to be suspicious of everybody, don't you?" she asked Joseph, who steered her into the house.

"You bet. Suspects often return to the scene of the crime. It fascinates them." He went to the front door. "Rick's here. I'd better go talk to him."

"I'll come too."

"No." He leveled her a quelling glance. "Stay inside. It's safe to assume you were the primary target. If this sniper's desperate enough, he might be sticking around to take another shot at you."

"Okay." Reluctantly, she hung back. He wedged the door shut, leaving her alone with her thoughts.

Who would be that desperate and why? Erin wondered. She couldn't imagine what kind of threat she posed to anyone.

Too nervous to sit still, she was pacing when another idea struck her. If people were trying to get rid of her, maybe they'd also made an attempt on Alice's life.

She called her mother's house. On the second ring, Lance's gruff voice said, "Bolding."

She cleared her throat. "It's me, Erin. I want to speak to my mother."

"I told you not to call." He sounded more irritable than angry.

"Someone just tried to shoot me and Joseph," she said.

"Anybody hurt?"

"No."

He let out a breath so harsh it hurt her ear. "Listen to me, Erin. You stay away from your mother. Got that?"

"Or what?" she challenged.

"Spare me the defiance crap. Messing with her is going to get you hurt. Do you understand me?"

"I'll talk to my mother if I want to. What's between her and me is none of your business."

The phone clicked off in her ear. Erin stood there steaming until the irony of the situation struck her. At least she knew Lance hadn't been today's shooter. In fact, she'd just given him an alibi.

Restlessly, she went into the kitchen and made a pot of coffee. Figuring the police searchers might get thirsty, she fixed a tray with foam cups and containers of cream and sugar and took them into the living room.

A short time later, Joseph and Rick came in. They made a beeline for the coffee.

"Thanks, Erin." As Detective Sergeant Ricardo Valdez poured himself a cup, his dark eyes surveyed her thoughtfully. In a way, his air of calm self-possession reminded her of Joseph. No wonder Tina liked the guy. "Are you feeling well enough to talk?"

"I think so," she said. "Any luck?"

Both men shook their heads. "Whoever he was, he's gone," Joseph said. "However, he left a little token in the trunk of my car."

"What kind of token?"

From inside his jacket, Rick lifted a small, clear evidence bag. It contained a bullet. "It went right through the car body and landed in the trunk."

"Could that help you catch him?" Erin asked.

"Only if we find a gun to compare it with." The detective's mouth twisted. "One thing I can say for sure. It didn't come from the same weapon as the bullet we found near Todd Wilde. Different caliber. Might be from a hunting rifle, which would make sense under the circumstances."

"Two different guns. That means more than one person is involved," she said. It was a scary thought.

"Or one guy who owns two guns," Joseph pointed out.

They reviewed with Rick everything they'd done that day. He let out a low whistle at the news that Joseph had interviewed Lima. "I'm going to keep this out of the report for now. It may not be relevant, and the chief will go postal if he hears it."

Erin hesitated when it came to her trip to the lawyer's office. But, she realized, she didn't have to reveal the contents of her new will, only the fact that she'd revised it.

"Good for you," Joseph said when she told them. He had to be assuming she'd left the money to Friend of a Friend.

"Did you happen to name any beneficiaries who might want to collect right away?" Rick asked.

She smiled. "There's no chance of that."

It was well after dark before the police finished. The gunman had escaped, leaving neither footprints nor snagged clothing behind—only the bullet.

When everyone had gone, the two of them fixed spaghetti and settled down for dinner. Erin felt as if they should try again to devise a theory about what had happened, but she was fresh out of ideas. Joseph, who seemed to feel the same way, launched into a description of Mrs. Lima's delicious *churros*. "One of these days I'd like to tour Mexico and see if anyone down there makes them as well as she does."

"Do they make *churros* in South America?" Erin would love to visit the archaeological sites she'd read about. Her father had often talked of traveling but, despite his wealth, never found time for it.

"I'd enjoy finding out. Whatever they cook, I'm sure it's delicious," Joseph said. "We could eat our way from Mexico City to Buenos Aires."

"By the time we get to Machu Picchu, they'll have to roll us up the mountain," she said.

Their gazes met across the table. Soft light from a chandelier bathed them in an intimate circle. Beneath the table, Erin became aware of his legs brushing hers.

"Of course, we could stay home and learn to make *churros* ourselves," Joseph said.

She sought a lighthearted response but failed. The silence lengthened. Much as she wanted to continue their banter, her spirits hung heavy.

"Is something bothering you?" he asked.

The answer came to her unexpectedly. "We could have died today. I don't mean to be morbid, but it's on my mind."

"We could die any day," he said. "That's the risk you run by being alive."

"Spoken like a cop!" She shook her head. "Doesn't what happened upset you at all?"

"Well, I'm glad we didn't die," he said drolly.

Erin wished she could take the matter as coolly as Joseph did. She might not be able to stop this mysterious attacker from coming after her, but she hated the power he had to fill her with dread. If only the prospect of death weren't so terrifying.

"How do you avoid being afraid?" she asked. "Today, when you got out of the car with your gun, you didn't hesitate."

"Things like that don't bother me," he said. "Living badly, wasting your life, getting soft and corrupt, those are things to be afraid of. Or getting framed and losing everything like my dad. But not death, especially if it's quick and clean."

An explanation came to her. "I guess that's because you know who you are." Seeing his puzzled expression, Erin explained, "You know what you're supposed to accomplish in life and you've set yourself on the right track. If you don't make it to the end, at least you'll know you went as far as you could."

"I'm not sure I follow the philosophy, but I'll take that as a compliment," Joseph said.

"It is." She planted her elbows on the table, something her mother would never have allowed even after they'd finished a meal. "That's why you have such inner serenity. Half the time, I feel frazzled and off-kilter. I've always sort of known what direction I need to go in, but I worry about what other people think and whether I'm making a mistake."

"Mistakes are part of the learning curve," he said. "The trick is not to keep repeating the same ones."

"You make it sound so simple!"

"It is simple," Joseph told her. "Figure out the next step and take it. Don't look too far ahead or you'll end up like the proverbial caterpillar, lying in a ditch because he couldn't figure out which foot to put in front of the other."

Studying him in the soothing light, Erin noticed a tiny twig that must have fallen into his hair earlier. She scooted around the table and plucked it off.

"Thanks." Joseph regarded it in amusement.

She didn't want to go back to her chair. Instead, Erin wiggled into his lap.

"What are you doing?" he asked as his body adjusted to support hers.

"Acting on impulse."

She thought at first that he might demur. Instead, he wrapped her in his arms and pulled her against him. Resting her cheek on his shoulder, she breathed his scent and wondered how and why they'd spent so many years apart.

Tilting her head, Erin kissed the corner of Joseph's mouth. She felt him holding back and wondered if she should stop. On the other hand, this might be a good time to stop burdening herself with useless inhibitions.

Tomorrow, someone might take another shot and aim better. Why not go after what she wanted tonight? It would give her one fewer thing to regret.

"Kiss me," she said.

"Are you sure?" His arms lay loose around her.

"No discussion." Erin smoothed one hand along the back of Joseph's head and guided him down.

His lips grazed hers. For a suspended moment, she thought he was going to pull away and then—slowly, tantalizingly— his thumbs played along her cheekbones and he kissed her again. His mouth lingered on hers, his tongue probing gently. Inside Erin, a response blossomed all the way to the taut buds of her breasts.

There was so much of him to explore. The rough line of his jaw. The tanned skin of his neck. The delicious masculine aroma of his shirt and, as she lifted it from his waistband, the texture of his bare chest beneath her hands.

Unzipping her dress, he lowered it over her shoulders. Cool air played along her bare skin until his warm breath replaced it. "If this is what you want, honey, I'm just the guy to give to you," he murmured close to her ear.

"Keep going," Erin said.

"No problem." The dress came down and her bra with it. Holding her from behind, Joseph cupped her breasts in his hands, flooding her with pleasure.

His hands slid to her stocking-clad legs and smoothed upward, stroking her until she could scarcely bear the heat. Erin released a breath that came all the way from her soul.

Beneath her on his lap, she felt his masculine hardness press against the fabric of his slacks and her wispy underwear. In her inexperience, Erin had imagined sex to be languorous and romantic, stoked by satin sheets and exotic perfumes, but she preferred this earthy spontaneity and Joseph's male eagerness.

Shifting position, she unworked his belt and felt him ease down the waistband of her panty hose. He caught her bottom tightly and before she knew it there was nothing between them.

"Just a minute, honey." He groped for something in his pants pocket. "Hang in there."

"Protection?" The other night, he'd said he didn't have any.

"Sometimes it pays to plan ahead." His lips brushed her earlobe.

Here she'd believed this was all her idea, yet Joseph had obviously made a stop at a store earlier. Erin didn't know whether to turn around and poke him or compliment his foresight. Under the circumstances, she decided, she ought to be grateful.

"Good for you," she said.

"Not that I was expecting anything," he noted.

"Sure you weren't." Since he seemed to be having trouble getting organized, Erin glanced down and saw the problem. "Let me help," she said.

"I didn't think you knew how," Joseph said.

"I can figure it out."

And she did. Holding him in her hands and hearing him groan in pleasure thrilled her. Wanting to excite him even more, Erin stroked his shaft until he shuddered. "Honey, you don't want to go any further with that."

"I don't?"

"Let's not waste it." Shifting her on his lap, he played one hand across her breasts, tantalizing them while, below, he caressed her body until it blazed white-hot.

When Joseph grasped her hips, Erin lifted herself and felt his thickness push into her. Something stopped him—her virginity, she realized—and then it was gone. She gave a little cry at the mingled sensations of joy and pain.

"Did I hurt you?" he asked hoarsely.

"Don't stop," she said. "Not ever."

He took her at her word.

Nothing about sex was the way she'd imagined it. Not this position, seated on his lap facing away; not this wild, rushing need; not the amazing way their bodies fit together. Especially, not the sensation of yielding herself completely.

From behind, his arms surrounded her and his cheek pressed hers as he moved in and out of her. Erin had never suspected she could merge so completely with a man or feel so complete.

The speed of Joseph's thrusting intensified. A spark jumped between them, ignited and burst into flame.

Erin couldn't distinguish his moans of pleasure from her own as waves of exquisite awareness rolled from her center to her fingertips. They sank back together, half-floating, for a span of time.

"I didn't know," she breathed at last. "I didn't know it was like that."

"I didn't, either."

"But…" Erin stopped. She didn't want to discuss his past. It was good to know, though, that he hadn't found such contentment with anyone else.

She never wanted to get this close to any other man. For her, there could only be Joseph.

At least she would always have this memory, for as long as she lived.

JOSEPH LAY NESTLED against Erin in the queen-size bed. He wanted to live exclusively in this moment when they belonged to each other.

He knew how easily circumstances could tear people apart, without warning and without recourse. He had to accept that it was going to happen and not let that worry him.

Above all, he hoped he hadn't done anything to hurt Erin.

Perhaps it was naïve in this day and age when people treated sex like a cheap commodity, but to him the connection they'd experienced meant they would always be a part of each other in some sense.

But he knew what his role was and where he belonged, even if it meant having to prove himself over and over again to a community that might never fully accept him. Erin, on the other hand, hadn't yet come to terms with her wealth or position. When she did, Joseph had to prepare himself for the fact that their paths were going to diverge.

Well, they had tonight, and maybe more good times before the end came. That was all he asked.

Joseph tightened his hold on Erin and let an unfamiliar happiness fill him. He fell asleep curled around her.

As Erin had expected, yesterday's shooting made the Tuesday morning newspaper. Lynn Rickles was scoring a lot of front-page bylines.

"I'm glad she doesn't pester us with phone calls," Erin said as she handed the newspaper to Joseph. They were eating breakfast at the small table in the kitchen after a lovely if turbulent night during which they'd awakened twice to make love.

He finished another bite of cereal before glancing at the paper. "That might be because I have an unlisted number."

"And here I thought she was treating us well because this is such a polite town!" she teased.

"Well, brace yourself," he said. "If this story hasn't already hit the big-city papers and TV stations, it should now. A sniper in the hills, a runaway bride and a corpse in the lake. Who could resist?"

"Do you think they'll send reporters all the way out here?" she asked.

"If they do, I'll chase them off the property," Joseph told her. "They'll have a hard time harassing us from the street."

That was reassuring, but of course the press was the least

of Erin's worries. Even though Lance obviously hadn't been the shooter yesterday, his gruff demand that she stay away from her mother only reinforced her concern for Alice.

Someone had to be either very afraid of them or very angry, she thought. Or else expected to gain something important from their deaths.

The fact that Lance hadn't fired the bullets didn't make him innocent. He could have hired an assassin.

Joseph turned the page. "Gene Norris is certainly doing his utmost to shield his candidate. He's announced that, on behalf of the Marshall Company, Chet's offering a reward for the person or persons who fired at you."

"Rick doesn't consider him a suspect, does he?" Erin supposed that her rejected suitor had an obvious motive to seek revenge. Nevertheless, she was convinced he hadn't been behind the attack six weeks ago, when he'd had reason to believe she might accept his proposal, and she suspected the same person was behind both assaults.

If only she could remember those crucial moments before she'd been hit! She'd been dredging up an image when the first shot rang out, Erin recalled. Something about a chocolate bar. Nope—whatever she'd been thinking, it was gone.

The phone rang. Setting aside the newspaper, Joseph picked it up. "Lowery."

His expression darkened as he listened. A vise clamped across Erin's chest. *Mom,* she thought. *Don't let anything be wrong with Mom.*

He hung up. "That was Rick."

"Is it my mother?" she asked.

"No, no." Joseph's expression remained clouded, however. "It's your aunt."

"What happened to Marie?"

"We were on the right trail," he said. "Unfortunately." From the regret on his face, she knew that whatever Rick had called about, it wasn't good news.

Chapter Thirteen

"Tell me," Erin said.

"Rick sent divers into the water first thing this morning." Coming to sit by her, Joseph enclosed her hands in his. "They found a woman's body."

She didn't want to ask, but she had to. "Is it her?"

"They're not sure, but she's the right size and they think about the right age," he said. "She's been in the water a long time. They're going to send for her dental records."

"Do they know what she died of?"

"There's no obvious sign of trauma, according to Rick," Joseph said. "It's possible she drowned."

Erin leaned against him, grateful for his warmth. The image of her aunt submerged in the lake chilled her. *Icy water closing over her. Impossible to breathe.*

"Erin?" He gave her a nudge. "What's going on?"

She started as if awakening from a bad dream. "I can't help identifying with her. After being out there in that creepy place, I feel like I know what she went through."

"We're not even sure it's Marie," Joseph reminded her. "Listen, Rick asked us to meet him for lunch to review what we know. It's strictly off-the-record. He's not mentioning it to anyone else, even Tina."

The implications weren't lost on Erin. "He believes the chief may be involved?"

"The possibility has to be considered." Shadows filled Joseph's dark blue eyes. "We're lucky to have Rick on our side."

"He's risking a lot," she pointed out. "His job, even his girlfriend."

"'I could not love thee, dear, so much, Lov'd I not honour more,'" Joseph quoted.

"I can't believe you remember that!" Erin had treasured the line from seventeenth century poet Richard Lovelace when she came across it in high school.

"It stuck in my mind when you read it to me," he said. "It's not a bad slogan to live by."

She'd been right when she concluded that Rick and Joseph had a lot in common, Erin thought. Both were men of integrity and courage.

"I wonder if anyone has considered comparing the caliber of either of those bullets to Chief Norris's gun," she said.

"We'd better save that one until we're ready to tip our hand," Joseph said.

ERIN'S COMMENT ECHOED in his mind a few hours later when they met Rick in the South of the Border Café. It was located in a blue-collar, largely immigrant section of town where they were unlikely to run into anyone they knew.

Keeping secrets kept getting harder, he thought. Just before they left the house, Tina had dropped by on her lunch break with a plate of lemon bars made by her students. "I hope you enjoy them," she'd told Erin. "The kids know you're a friend of mine and they made them specially for you. How are things going?"

There was no sign of guile on Tina's open face, only concern for her friend. Joseph had to remind himself that she lived with the enemy, or at least with a father who might be his foe. They didn't dare confide in her.

Erin had remembered that. For a woman who'd been amazingly naïve until a few days ago, she'd demonstrated with Tina that she'd learned how to give bland reassurances while playing her cards close to her chest.

Her chest. He'd better not think about that or any other part of her anatomy right now. After last night's incredible lovemaking, Joseph wished they could spend the day in bed.

But he had to prepare to let her go. Erin only belonged to him for a little while. She was growing stronger every day.

"A complicated case like this can take a long time to investigate," Rick told her after they ordered lunch. "Even though I've got other detectives assisting me, I need your help—both of you. I asked the chief to reinstate Joseph, but he refused. Without him, I feel like I'm working the case with one hand tied behind my back."

To be on the safe side, Joseph made sure the waitress wasn't near enough to overhear before murmuring, "Have you found anything that implicates the chief?"

"Not exactly. His actions concerning you seem indefensible, yet I can't figure any reason why he'd want to hurt Erin," Rick said. "Not unless she knows something, perhaps something she doesn't realize is important."

"What about Lance?" she asked. "He's got to be mixed up in this."

"I've subpoenaed his phone records," Rick told them. "I'm particularly interested in whether he's contacted Todd Wilde or Marie Flanders. One of my officers is going through them right now."

Joseph was grateful for Rick's thoroughness. "You wanted this meeting so we could compare notes, right?"

"Exactly. And maybe try a little brainstorming."

"Well, then, let's do it."

Over plates of Mexican food, they reviewed everything Chief Lima had said and what Erin had learned yesterday at the Marshall Company. "You know, there was one little detail that probably doesn't mean anything but I should mention it," she said. "The board secretary, Betsy Rydell, was recently promoted to assistant manager at the mall. Her replacement is a woman I've never met before. Stanley Rogers, the CFO, has a new secretary as well."

"What do you make of that?" Rick asked.

"I don't know," Erin admitted. "There've been so many personnel changes. My mother lost her old housekeeper as well. If someone wanted to keep secrets, wouldn't he remove anyone who might get suspicious?"

"Good point." Rick checked his tape recorder, which apparently was working fine. He'd explained earlier that he wanted to be able to concentrate on their discussion rather than on taking notes, which made sense to Joseph. "I'll talk to Ms. Rydell. Anything else you can think of?"

"My mom's near drowning happened very close to where Todd and Marie were found. Don't you think that's weird?"

"It could be due to the isolation," Rick explained. "Or simply a coincidence."

"Your mother insists what happened to her was an accident," Joseph reminded them. "But it troubled me right from the beginning." He shared with Rick his theory that someone might be blackmailing Alice into silence. "It can't be a threat to harm Erin. Someone has already tried twice to kill her, so why wouldn't her mother come forward? If it concerned Marie, that might change now that we know she's dead."

"Chet promised to arrange for me to see Mom," Erin said. "Maybe she'll open up to me."

"Going to the Bolding house could be dangerous." Rick's comment mirrored Joseph's concern.

"I don't care." Her chin came up. "I left Mom alone after Dad died, and that's why she turned to Lance. I won't abandon her again."

"Then keep Joseph with you," Rick told her. "I don't want to be fishing you out of the lake." Seeing her startled reaction, he added, "Sorry. We cops tend to put things bluntly."

She waved away the apology. "The important thing is,

you're not going to fish my mother out of the lake. Not if I can prevent it."

Joseph admired her loyalty and her nerve. At the same time, he vowed not to let her out of his sight until this case was resolved, no matter what she said.

IT WAS LATE AFTERNOON before Erin got the call she'd been hoping for. After greeting her, her mother's raspy voice said, "I'm sorry I didn't phone sooner. I've been worried about you. You weren't injured in that horrible shooting, were you?"

"No." She sank onto Joseph's couch. Across the room, he looked up from where he'd been trolling the Internet on his computer. "How about you? How do you feel?"

"A little weak," her mother said. "Chet told you about my illness, I understand. I'm glad he did."

"Me, too, " Erin said. "Listen, Mom, I don't like you staying by the lake. Weird things are going on."

"I know. I heard about…this morning." Apparently the possibility of her sister's death was too painful to discuss, or, more likely, Alice refused to acknowledge it until receiving confirmation. "I want to talk to you about, well, everything."

Excitement mingled with apprehension inside Erin. She hoped her mother meant to explain about the night of her accident, but her safety came first. "We'll pick you up in a few minutes. We can go stay somewhere away from all this trouble. How about a hotel in L.A.? I'd like you to see some cancer specialists there too."

"Honey, nobody's chasing me out of my home," Alice said. "Besides, I don't feel well enough for all that driving around. Listen, Lance went to play golf. He should be gone for a couple of hours. We'll have plenty of time to talk here."

Erin intended to pry her mother out of there one way or the other, but obviously the direct approach wasn't working. "Joseph and I will be right over."

"Lance is irrational on the subject of that young man," she

said. "He said that if he sees Joseph anywhere near the property, he'll tell Edgar Norris we're being harassed."

Erin hesitated. She needed Joseph's help, but they couldn't risk a showdown with the chief at this point. Not only might a harassment charge wreck Joseph's career, but further antagonizing Norris would make it doubly hard for Rick to investigate him on the sly.

"I'll take a cab," she said. Across the room, Joseph shook his head, but she ignored him.

"I've asked Chet to pick you up," her mother went on. "He should be there any minute."

"Chet?" she repeated uneasily.

Joseph's eyes blazed.

"I realize it's awkward, but he does work for us, you know," Alice said. "Or would you rather I sent Stanley Rogers? Oh, dear. Chet must be halfway there by now."

"I'd rather you sent Stanley," Erin said.

"I'm sorry I didn't think of it in time," her mother told her. "Honey, there's nothing to worry about. Do you think I'd let Chet drive my daughter if I didn't consider him completely trustworthy?"

Erin knew as an article of faith that her mother would do anything to keep her safe. "All right. But…" From outside, she heard a car murmuring up the street. "Oh, my gosh, I think that's him."

Clicking off the computer, Joseph checked out the window. As he watched, he took his holster from a table nearby and began strapping it on.

"I'll see you in a few minutes," Alice said. "I'm so glad you're coming. I love you."

"I love you, too, Mom." Erin waited until she heard a click, then hung up.

"I don't like it." Joseph glowered. "I'll take you myself."

Outside, the car made its way up the driveway. Erin marked its progress on the gravel.

"It's too great a risk if Lance sees you," she said. "Besides, Chet's already here."

"No."

Following Joseph's directions had become second nature. This time, she battled her instincts. "My priority is—what do they call it on those spy shows?—making an extraction. Getting her out of there."

"We'll do it together."

Inspiration dawned. "Follow us at a distance. If anything goes wrong, you'll be there."

"I don't want you alone with Dever."

"Joseph," Erin said, "this is my decision."

Their gazes locked. Finally, he gave a reluctant nod. "All right. On one condition. Just a minute." He hurried into the bedroom.

Outside, the car stopped and the smooth hum shut off. Joseph returned wearing a jacket over his holster and carrying her purse. "I put the other gun inside. If you need it, use it."

"All right." She wasn't sure she could, but at least he'd agreed to a compromise. The purse, when she took it, felt disturbingly heavy.

Erin dashed to the bathroom to brush her hair and straighten her slacks and sweater. When she returned, Chet waited stiffly on the front step while Joseph regarded him with open suspicion.

"Look, this wasn't my idea," Chet was saying. "Frankly, I wish I had your security skills, Lowery. If someone takes a shot at us, I'm not sure what I'll do."

"Hit the gas," Joseph advised.

"Thanks. I'll remember that." Chet started to run one hand through his hair but caught himself in time to avoid mussing its dark-blond perfection. "On the radio coming over, it said the police found another body in the lake. Any idea who it was?"

"A woman."

"Man, that's terrible." Chet was so agitated he barely smiled when he spotted her. "I don't know what's going on around here. Sundown Valley's always been such a quiet place."

"Not always," Joseph replied coolly. "You might recall that a jewelry store owner got killed some years ago."

"That's the case your father was involved with?" the CEO said. "I heard he didn't do it."

"Who told you that?" Skepticism colored Joseph's words. "Most people in this town had him convicted before he even went to trial."

"Well, if so, they've thought it over," Chet told him. "I've heard a couple of times that he got a raw deal. Maybe it's because they respect your mother so much. And you."

"Me?"

With a nod as if the matter were too obvious to discuss, the CEO turned his attention to Erin. "We'd better go. Your mother's anxious to see you."

"I know," she said. "I want to see her, too." She said a subdued goodbye to Joseph. When his eyes met hers, he gave a slight nod. She was glad he'd be following.

Chet ushered her into his luxury sedan. Acutely aware of the weight of her purse, Erin slid onto the seat.

Determination sustained her all the way down the hill and through town. As they headed west toward the lake, it began to fade.

She saw no sign of Joseph's battered car in the side-view mirror. If he was tailing them, he was being very discreet about it.

Worse, as soon as Sundown Lake came into view beneath the overcast sky, she couldn't help thinking about her aunt. Marie Flanders had lived on her own terms. She'd left Sundown Valley to become an actress, and Erin recalled as a child how scandalized the family had been about Marie's activities. She'd dated disreputable men, and there'd been rumors about occasional drug use.

But Erin also recalled their childhood jaunts to the movies and for ice cream or a hamburger afterward. Once, Marie had said she doubted she'd ever have children of her own. "I wish I had a little girl like you," she'd told Erin over French fries and soft drinks. "I'd be a good mom."

Erin wished her aunt had lived long enough for them to establish an adult relationship. Maybe they could have been friends. In any case, Marie deserved better than to die alone in the cold, reedy periphery of the lake.

At whose hand had she died, and why? Whoever it was, it might be someone Erin knew.

Not the man sitting next to her, she hoped. She studied Chet's profile. He'd been quiet so far, lost in thought. Perhaps he was worrying about the impact of this latest grim discovery on his campaign, thanks to the link the newspaper kept making between him and Erin's family.

"I appreciate your doing this," she told him.

"Doing what?"

"Chauffeuring me," she said. "That's hardly part of the job description of a CEO. I know it's made Mom feel easier these past months, being able to rely on you."

He turned north off the highway and skirted the lake without responding. Erin had never seen Chet so uncommunicative. Usually he was bursting with enough chitchat to fill any gap in the conversation.

He'd mentioned his fear that someone would take a potshot at them, she thought. Erin supposed she, too, ought to be watching the road, but she was more concerned about her mother than herself.

She checked the side mirror when they reached Aurora Avenue and, far back, glimpsed a familiar car. Although she couldn't see the driver, she relaxed. Joseph hadn't lost sight of her.

It seemed like weeks rather than days since they'd been reunited. So much had changed inside her during these few days. She'd lost her virginity without regret and, at least mentally, begun to move toward asserting herself as half owner of a major corporation.

Most of all, with Joseph she'd rediscovered what it meant to come home. Or perhaps she'd truly discovered it for the first time.

As much as her parents loved her, once she passed her early years they'd both been busy with their interests and adult friends. Often she'd eaten dinner with just the housekeeper or, later, by herself. As for talking things over, she'd never felt free to spill out whatever was on her mind without tailoring it to their expectations.

Joseph was different. In a way, Erin wished things could stay the way they were. Except, of course, that she wanted her mother to be healthy and safe, and right now she was neither.

When the Boldings' rambling house came into view, intense dislike filled her. How had she tolerated this place for a month? Reminded of what a depressing place it was for her mother to live while battling cancer, Erin resented Lance's influence all the more.

As soon as they pulled in, Brandy came out onto the porch. Her pulled-back chestnut hair, stark white blouse and black skirt gave her a severe air. The pouches beneath her eyes were even more pronounced than usual, Erin saw, and realized she must have been crying about Marie.

"I'm sorry," she told Brandy as she came up the steps.

"Why?" The housekeeper opened the screen door for her.

"I know my aunt was your friend," she said.

"Yes," Brandy said in a dull voice. "Yes, she was."

Inside, drawn curtains deepened the late-afternoon shadows. The cancer apparently had made her mother sensitive to light, Erin realized, but surely this stale air couldn't be good for her.

Although the glass front of the china cabinet appeared

clean, she noted a faint layer of dust on the bell collection inside. Her mother used to enjoy taking them out and using them to summon the family for dinner or simply explain to Erin where and under what circumstances each had been purchased.

She glanced toward the den where the wedding presents had been displayed. They were gone. At least Alice hadn't forgotten her attention to detail.

"I sent them back," Brandy reported. "Mrs. Bolding asked me to write notes as well, and I did that."

"Thank you." Erin knew that had been her own responsibility. "I shouldn't have left you that burden."

"It's nothing. I'll tell her you're here." The housekeeper vanished through the dining room. It was the only route to the bedroom wing, a layout flaw that in former times Erin's mother would have rejected out of hand.

She'd commented when they bought the place that she wanted a simpler lifestyle. She and Lance had planned to barbecue by the lake, to go sailing and to enjoy the breezy freedom they'd experienced on their cruise. Erin couldn't recall them barbecuing or going sailing even once during the month she'd spent here.

Brandy returned. "Mrs. Bolding's in the study. She'd like you to join her."

"Sure." Erin half turned toward Chet and excused herself.

"Don't mind me," he said. "I'll wait out here."

The study lay at the back of the house, with the bedroom wing jutting off to the left. Although dark paneling and closed curtains left it, too, in obscurity, Erin loved seeing her father's old leather couch and mahogany desk. She tried not to think about Lance using the gold fountain pen or the brass stapler.

"Erin!" Alice came to hug her daughter. "I'm so glad to see you."

"Not half as glad as I am to see you." Erin embraced her

carefully, sensitive to her thinness. "Mom, you should have told me about being sick! I'd have come right away."

"Lance was here," her mother responded. "I'm doing very well, honey. The treatments aren't my idea of fun, but my prognosis is good."

"Good?" That wasn't strong enough to suit Erin. "Did the doctor give you a percentage?"

"Ninety percent chance of recovery. He said they caught it in time."

Erin hoped her mother wasn't just saying that to avoid upsetting her. "I don't think this dampness is healthy."

"You might be right," her mother said.

"Really?" That was the first time she'd agreed with any criticisms of this place.

Alice gestured her to the couch and settled into a chair. "Tell me what you've been up to. I can't believe Joseph took you out on the lake in your condition, but I'm sure he had his reasons."

"We'd heard Todd Wilde was in the area, that he'd been seen spying on your house," Erin said.

Alice frowned. "Who told you that?"

"Jean," Erin said. "She happened to be out sailing with her husband."

"You've been talking to a lot of people." Her mother fiddled with her silver-and-turquoise bracelet. "He's still investigating, isn't he, your young man? I wouldn't be surprised if he's found out more than the police have. Does he think that van hit you on purpose?"

"We're still at a loss," Erin told her. "Mom, about your accident. Are you sure you're not holding anything back?"

Her mother interlaced her fingers in her lap. "I can't talk about it. Not here."

So she had been afraid to speak out! "Then let's discuss it somewhere else."

Alice gave her a wan smile. "You and I should go away for a few days."

"I'd like that." Erin mean to remove her for a lot longer than a few days, but she'd deal with that later. "Why don't you pack a suitcase? We can leave now, while Lance is gone."

"That wouldn't be right," her mother said. "I'm a Marshall. I don't have to sneak out of my own home."

"But…" In Erin's purse, the phone rang. She hesitated.

"Go ahead," her mother said. "I don't mind."

"Excuse me." Not daring to risk a conversation in front of Alice, Erin retreated to the hallway.

"Erin?" It was Joseph on the other end. "I lost sight of you in the house."

"Hold on." She scooted along to her former room and closed the door. "Mom and I were talking in the den."

"I got worried," he said. "Listen, do you have a pocket?"

She patted her slacks. "Yes."

"Leave the phone on and put it in your pocket," he said. "Unless the service gets cut off, I may be able to hear what's going on."

"Okay," she said. "Anything else?"

"Has she said anything?" he asked.

"No. She's considering coming with me, but not necessarily tonight."

"You know your mom," he said. "She does things her own way."

"That's for sure." Anxious as she was to get back to Alice, Erin relished Joseph's support. "I'm glad you're here."

"Count on it," he said. "I'll be listening."

She tucked the phone into her pocket, adjusted it to keep the lid open and pulled her sweater down to cover anything that might protrude. Feeling as if she were walking with eggs strapped to her hip, Erin strolled back to the den.

Alice greeted her with, "That must have been Joseph."

She couldn't deny it. "He likes to stay in touch."

"That's sweet. You two always were good together."

"I didn't think you were that crazy about him." Erin recalled numerous times when her mother had urged her to see other boys.

"Wasn't I?" Her mother tilted her head. "I was a bit of a snob, wasn't I?"

"I know better than to agree with that!" Erin joked.

Her mother managed a smile. By emphasizing the haggard lines of her face, the happy expression drove home how great a toll the cancer had taken. "I'll tell you what. I'm going to arrange for you and me to go on a little retreat, maybe to a spa. I don't want you to discuss it with anyone, though, not even Joseph."

"I don't keep secrets from him," Erin said.

"Really, does everything I say have to become common gossip?" Alice's sudden sharpness signaled one of her frequent mood changes.

Erin was trying to figure out how to placate her mother without making a promise she couldn't keep when she heard the side door in the kitchen slam open. Heavy footsteps crossed the linoleum, marched down the hallway and stopped outside the den.

Her stepfather's fleshy face stared at her with a distinct lack of welcome. Erin's heart got stuck in her throat. Her mother's house had just become enemy territory, and she was deep inside it.

Chapter Fourteen

In a thicket of trees, Joseph tensed as Lance's voice snapped out of the phone, "What the hell is she doing here?"

Although Joseph commanded a good view of the front porch and the lake side of the house, the man must have come in through the back door. Hearing that ugly tone made Joseph long to rush to Erin's side, but if he did, he might set a spark to an already explosive situation.

On the other hand, bodies had been turning up around here with frightening frequency. If he waited too long, he'd never forgive himself.

"Every time my back is turned, you're up to something," Lance snarled, presumably at his wife. "I want her out of here!"

Joseph weighed the value of drawing closer, perhaps finding a window through which he could observe what was happening. However, from what he remembered of the layout, the study was far from any exterior cover and it might well be curtained from view. Moreover, from such a position he'd never make it to his car in time to follow Chet when he and Erin left.

"I'm afraid you'd better leave now." Alice's calm words were, he guessed, intended for her daughter. "I'll call you later."

"Hello?" said a new, lighter male voice. Chet's, Joseph registered. "Lance! I didn't know you'd come in."

"I'll just bet you didn't," Erin's stepfather growled. "You brought her here, didn't you?"

"Do you—*crackle*—a problem with that?" Over the phone, Chet's response broke up a little.

Joseph shifted position to get a clearer signal. Something wet and sticky brushed his cheek.

"This stops here," Lance said. "You watch out, mister. Don't forget, I know enough to ruin you."

Ruin him with what? Joseph lifted his free hand to wipe the sticky thing from his neck. Turning, he came face to face with a huge reddish spider hanging in midair.

Astonished, he dropped the phone. Only his police training stopped him from uttering a string of curse words loud enough to carry to the far side of the lake.

Plummeting to the ground, the spider vanished among the leaves.

How annoying to run into an orb weaver that, on an overcast day, had decided to wait for prey. Joseph knew about spiders from a childhood spent tramping around the area, but he'd only seen this oversize variety on misty mornings.

Snatching the phone from the grass, he held it to his ear. What a relief to find the connection hadn't been severed.

Lance finished saying something Joseph didn't catch. Chet spoke again, angrily. "If we're tossing threats around, maybe it's time I told Erin the family secrets. She's entitled, don't you think?"

"I'm sure you wouldn't want to hurt my daughter," Alice said. "These things have nothing to do with her."

"They have everything to do with her," Chet answered. "Just remember one thing. I love my fiancée and I intend to take care of her."

His fiancée? The man apparently believed his own public relations fiction, Joseph reflected uneasily.

"What's going on?" Erin asked breathlessly. "Mom?"

"We've had some disagreements about running the company," Mrs. Bolding said. "They don't concern you."

"It's my company too."

"We all need to calm down." Lance ignored the irony that, as far as Joseph could tell, he was the one who'd come storming into the house threatening trouble.

"This has gone far enough," Chet said. "We're leaving."

"I want your promise," Alice told him.

"About what?"

"That you'll protect my daughter," she said.

"I already promised…"

"I won't have her upset. She's been through too much these past weeks."

"I agree," Chet said. "Erin, let's get out of here."

There was a moment's silence. Finally: "Mom, you'll call me?"

"You bet," Alice said.

Rustles and footsteps attested to their movements. Joseph debated whether to head for his car, which he'd parked on a path off the road, or wait until he saw for sure that Erin had exited the house.

Over the phone, he heard her say, "Oh! I left my purse in the study."

"I'll get it, Miss." That sounded like Brandy.

Joseph moved toward the street. If he didn't reach his car in time, he'd have trouble following Chet. But it bothered him that Erin had left the purse containing his gun out of her control even for a minute.

Neither she nor Chet spoke. It seemed like a long time before he heard her say, "Thank you, Brandy."

"My pleasure, Miss."

Joseph lengthened his stride, ducking tree branches while hanging on to the phone. He couldn't tell what was happening until he heard Chet's car start, in stereo—over the phone and in real life.

He sheltered behind a tree as the sedan purred by. Once it vanished, he broke into a run.

At his car, he started the engine and followed in the direction they'd taken. Only a faint buzzing came over the phone.

There was no sign of the car ahead. In a minute, Joseph knew he'd have to choose whether to head for the main highway back to town or swing onto Via Puesta del Sol, which took a meandering route toward the country club.

"Where are we going?" Erin's words crackled over the phone. Thank heaven! Joseph clamped it tighter to his ear.

"Let's stop by my place," Chet said. "We need to talk."

Tell him no! Whatever the CEO intended to reveal, it wasn't worth putting Erin at risk. Once they were alone at his house, there was no telling what might happen.

"I can't believe my mom would be involved in anything questionable." To his dismay, Erin didn't argue. He should have anticipated that her concern for her mother would override any distrust of Chet.

Joseph didn't have a clue where the man lived. He'd had no occasion to interview him, let alone check out his private quarters.

"Sometimes people…over their heads." Background noise overwhelmed part of Chet's comment.

Joseph reached the crossroads. Instinctively, he turned onto Via Puesta del Sol and hit the gas. It eventually led back to the highway, so if he didn't spot the sedan en route, he might pick them up later.

Or they might simply disappear. He wished he'd planted a locator on Erin, but he didn't own one of the high-tech devices.

He went by Rainbow Lane, which led to the pier near where the bodies had surfaced. A chill swept over Joseph. Night was falling fast, and he'd left Erin alone with a known liar entangled in questionable activities.

And he had no idea where they were.

"I love the way they named the streets around here after colors." If Erin was giving him a clue, she'd made a good start. As he recalled, streets called Azure, Emerald, Canary and Amber lay ahead. If only she'd tag on a more specific reference.

At least Erin hadn't sounded worried. He hoped that meant they really were en route to Chet's house, which she'd probably visited before.

"I didn't even know what carmine meant before I rented this place," Chet answered.

Carmine Way. From his years of patrolling, Joseph retained a mental map of the area. He knew the way to the winding street. That left the issue of picking out the right house.

And the disturbing fact that the road ended at the lakeshore. It came out less than half a mile from the pier.

ERIN PEEKED into the side mirror. Still no Joseph.

She'd heard a few noises on the cell phone, which she hoped meant they remained connected. Although Chet had accommodatingly mentioned the name of his street, however, she didn't remember the number. Once they arrived, she'd have to find an excuse for stating it aloud.

The streets here lacked lights, and only glimmers through windows and from porches pierced the thickening twilight. Although she'd visited Chet's house a few times before, Erin couldn't have found the place without directions, she realized when they reached it at last.

If there was a number affixed to the structure, it lay obscured behind fanlike palms. The number on the curb had faded too badly to read in the half light.

"What beautiful birds of paradise." She hoped the clumps of blue and orange flowers would help Joseph located the driveway.

"They're a bit overgrown," Chet replied. "The landlord needs to have the gardener trim things back."

The white wood-and-brick house structure, one story high except for a bedroom above the garage, had a boxy beach-cottage feel. Although she hadn't realized it was rented, Erin had assumed that, after their marriage, they'd either buy a larger place or live in Washington after Chet's election.

It was one of many things they'd never discussed. She wondered now how she could have been so immature.

She hadn't just been passive; she'd been out of touch with her own feelings. Maybe she'd feared at some level that if she let herself go, she would unleash more emotions than she could handle.

Instead, when she'd opened herself to Joseph, the opposite had happened. She'd discovered depths and resources that made her stronger.

They halted at the entryway. Leaving the car outside would help Joseph, Erin thought gratefully, assuming he managed to find her.

Maybe she shouldn't go inside. Once the door closed behind them, she had no idea what he might do.

But if she didn't, she might never find out what was going on. Undercurrents, hints and threats had underscored her mother and stepfather's conversation. Whatever lay hidden, it threatened her future.

Chet helped her out of the car and keyed the lock to the house. A sense of unreality dogged Erin as she stepped inside.

In the living room, the overhead light fell flatly across a beige sofa and a brown corduroy-covered armchair. On the coffee table perched a vase of artificial flowers that smelled suffocatingly dusty.

Erin sank into the chair, setting the heavy purse in her lap. She wasn't exactly afraid of Chet, but the knowledge that she had a gun bolstered her confidence. "What did you want to talk about?"

He moved restlessly to the couch and perched on the arm.

"There are some things…I mean, I wish I had…" The sentence trailed off. Until tonight, she'd never seen the usually self-possessed Chet so agitated.

"You wish you'd what?" Erin's hands had gone cold. His nervousness had to be contagious.

"To begin with, your stepfather thinks he can control me in Congress," Chet said. "That's why your parents backed me, for the power."

"Isn't that why people usually back politicians?" She didn't see why he'd expected otherwise. "People who can make big donations want a return on their investment, I imagine."

"It's not that simple," he said. "I knew… Well, things weren't entirely right. With your parents, I mean."

"Like what?" She wished he'd get to the point.

Chet fiddled with the TV remote control and then set it on a side table. "I guess I should start with a personal admission. I've done a few things I'm not proud of."

"Why are you telling me this?"

"Without the background, you can't understand the present."

She made a mental leap. "You mean someone's blackmailing you?"

He gave a reluctant nod. "More or less."

"What did you do?" When he didn't respond, she leaped to the next question on her mind. "Chet, you didn't actually break the law, did you?"

"Technically, I suppose I did." His jaw worked as he faced her. "I'm hoping you'll forgive me, Erin. I didn't think it mattered because we were going to be married."

"Forgive you for what?" She hoped Joseph could hear this. She hoped he was close by, in case…well, just in case.

"I borrowed money from your trust fund." He ran his hand through his full blond hair, for once not caring how badly he ruffled it.

Borrowed? He meant embezzled. She stared at him in dismay. "How could you do that?"

"That's a good question." Chet began pacing. "I don't know what I was thinking."

"How much?" Erin asked.

"I'm not sure."

"You're not sure?" she repeated. Not only had he helped himself, he hadn't even taken it seriously enough to keep track.

"Enough to pay for some TV commercials," he said. "I have to advertise on TV, Erin, or my campaign doesn't have a chance."

"Gene said you loaned yourself the money."

"Gene doesn't know," he told her. "He's not part of this. He believes in me. I hope you will, too."

"Who's blackmailing you?" She answered her own query. "It's Lance, isn't it?"

He nodded. "I'm sorry. I know it was wrong. I never meant for anyone to get hurt."

"Does this have anything to do with the bodies in the lake?" She hazarded a guess. "How about what happened to me and my mom, our so-called accidents?"

"Not directly," Chet said. "It's complicated."

"You can't just expect me to let the whole thing go!"

"I'll pay you back." He struggled with his words, as if the situation were too complex to explain.

What was so hard? Erin wondered. Lance had discovered the theft and apparently was trying to use the information to control Chet's political agenda. Her mom had to know about the embezzlement, too, she realized. Maybe she and Lance disagreed about whether to contact the police.

"I got caught up in something a lot bigger than I expected," Chet continued. "It keeps snowballing."

"Getting out of this mess won't be easy, but I'm sure we can do it." She used the inclusive pronoun not because she identified with this troubled man but because she wanted to reassure him.

He'd just disclosed damning facts about himself. Once he

had time to reflect, he might panic. Erin wondered how far he'd go to stop her from telling anyone else.

And how would he react if he discovered that Joseph was listening?

"I want to protect you," he said. "Stay away from Lance, Brandy, your mother—the whole lot."

"I can't stay away from Mom." Erin drew the line there. "I failed her once. This time, I'm taking her with me."

"You don't understand. You'll put yourself and me in terrible danger." Chet strode across the room. "I can't let you do that, Erin."

He reached into a drawer. She caught a flash of something metallic.

She couldn't afford to wait for Joseph. Desperately, Erin stuck her hand into her purse and groped for the cold, hard metal of the gun.

It didn't feel right. Too smooth, too solid. She opened her purse and looked inside.

The weight she'd felt was her father's brass stapler. Someone had taken the gun.

"Oh, no!" she blurted.

BIRDS OF PARADISE. A good clue, except that more than one house on Carmine Way grew the dramatic plants. Near the first clump Joseph spotted children's play equipment, so he ruled out that place, but he counted three more bunches of the flowers as he continued down the street.

All the while, he followed the conversation over the phone. Chet had embezzled from Erin's trust fund. That alone was enough to end the man's political career and send him to prison. Joseph's other hand clenched the steering wheel at the thought that this lying scoundrel had nearly conned her into marrying him to hide his crime.

"You'll put yourself and me in terrible danger. I can't let you do that, Erin."

The threat galvanized him. He hit the gas, searching for more birds of paradise and a clue to show him the right house. At the same time, he had to remain alert for children.

"Oh, no!" Erin's distress jolted him.

There it was. Chet's car. He nearly passed it. His brakes creaked as he stomped the pedal and immediately threw the car into reverse.

Joseph zipped into the driveway, leaving the door open so Chet wouldn't hear it slam. He'd missed part of the conversation, but he couldn't take any more chances.

"Get out!" he shouted into the phone as he drew his service revolver. "Get out of there!"

He ran at a crouch toward the house

"WHAT'S WRONG?" Chet asked as Erin stared dumbfounded into her purse.

"What?" Too shocked to think straight, she looked up to see him holding a photograph of himself with her parents in a silver frame. It must have been taken at one of the annual company dinner-dances.

"You said 'Oh, no' as if something were wrong."

Unable to invent a good story in a hurry, she decided to stick close to the truth. "I can't figure out how this got here." She showed him the stapler. "I felt something heavy and wondered what it was. I hope Lance isn't going to accuse me of stealing."

"That's bizarre. Maybe Brandy thought it was yours." Losing interest in the stapler, he indicated the picture. "I want to explain…"

"Get out! Get out of there!" Joseph's voice, blurred but unmistakable, issued from her pocket.

"What the hell?" Chet said.

Erin froze. She couldn't think of anything to say except the truth. "It's my phone." She took it out. "It was a precaution while I was at my mom's house."

His face flushed. "Joseph heard what I said?"

"I'm not sure," Erin admitted. "I didn't even know if it was still connected."

The door flew open. Chet flashed to his feet, clutching the framed photo, as Joseph dodged inside. Light reflected dully off the revolver in his hand.

"Put it down!" Joseph commanded. "Now! Hands in the air!" It had to be a police tactic to shout like that, she thought, to frighten and confuse his quarry. It certainly worked on her.

After a shocked pause, Chet set the picture on the coffee table. "Are you going to arrest me?"

"Erin, come over here." He didn't take his eyes from Chet as she crossed the room. "Are you all right?"

"He didn't do anything," she said. "I mean, apart from the embezzling." She couldn't explain about the missing gun in front of Chet.

"Turn around, Dever. Hands on the wall." Upon being obeyed, Joseph gave Erin the revolver. "Hold this." Only after he'd patted down Chet for weapons did he step back and reclaim the gun. "You can turn around. I'm not going to arrest you tonight. It's up to Erin whether she presses charges."

"So you're letting me go?" He straightened with a trace of his old swagger. "You barged into my house for nothing?"

Joseph's expression darkened. "I'll have to file a report about what I heard, of course." He had to be bluffing. As if he intended to inform the police that he'd been snooping!

Chet's hooded eyes assessed the lowered revolver and the two of them. "You set me up," he growled at Joseph. "You've been after me ever since you found out I was marrying your ex-girlfriend." His brain had finally clicked back into gear, Erin realized. "You knew she'd be in the car with me and you planned this to get something incriminating. I'd call it entrapment."

"Nobody trapped you," Joseph said. "Nobody induced you to steal Erin's money or to confess it."

"You're so full of yourself. The knight in shining armor!" Chet snarled. "You have no idea what you're dealing with."

Noticing the door standing open, Erin hoped the neighbors couldn't hear. She didn't want some gossipy type relaying this quarrel to the newspaper. Besides, they needed to leave so she could alert Joseph about the missing gun.

"We'd better go before the whole town hears us," she said.

That stopped them. "Erin," Chet said more quietly, "I'll repay the money. Please don't ruin my life over this. Believe me, I had nothing to do with the attack on you and I'm not sure who did." He'd called it an attack, not an accident, she noted.

"You must have some idea," Joseph said.

"If I knew, I'd tell you," Chet answered. "That's the truth. About the funds I borrowed…"

"I'll have to look into it." Erin couldn't commit herself without knowing how much he'd taken or what else he'd done. And didn't the voters have a right to learn as much as possible about a man they might be choosing to represent them in Congress?

"Fair enough." Chet's gaze fixed on the photo and he frowned.

Why had he started to show it to her? Erin wondered. "What did you mean to say about my parents?"

"Nothing."

Joseph caught her elbow. "Let's go."

Despite her curiosity, Erin went with him. She didn't want to risk another argument breaking out.

Halfway down the driveway, her knees started to shake. She barely made it into the car.

"You okay?" Joseph asked as they backed out.

"I think I'm having a delayed reaction."

"There's a blanket in the rear seat. I don't want you going into shock."

She hugged herself. "Just keep driving. I'll be fine when we get home."

In the yard, the headlights picked out the palm fronds. One of them swished, and she tried to see what had caused the movement. A raccoon or a possum?

The vehicle straightened and the yard fell into darkness. Her nerves were probably playing tricks on her, anyway, Erin thought.

"What made you say 'Oh, no'?" Joseph asked. "I got worried."

"The gun." Thank goodness he'd reminded her. "I looked in my purse and it's gone."

"Gone?"

"Someone must have stolen it while I was at my mother's and substituted a stapler. That's why I didn't notice the weight."

"You had it with you the whole time except at the end, right?"

Erin couldn't believe she'd made that mistake. "That's right." Before he could ask, she added, "It couldn't have been Chet. He was never alone with it."

"I know," he said. "You sent Brandy to fetch it."

"Lance could have taken it." She searched her memory to recreate the scene at the Boldings' house. "I think my mom was with him, though, so I doubt he'd have dared search my purse."

Joseph navigated toward the highway. "We have to report the theft, since the gun's registered to me, but first we should figure out what to say. As a peace officer, I'm entitled to carry a concealed weapon."

"But I'm not."

"You'd need a license," he agreed.

She hadn't meant to break the law. "What should we do?"

"This is my fault. Under the circumstances, I felt the most important thing was to guard your life. Now I have to figure out how to keep you out of trouble."

"You were nearby," she said. "Doesn't that count?"

"We'll figure something out. Meanwhile, we've got a bigger problem."

"What?"

"Finding out who took it and what they plan to do with it."

Erin hated to think what use someone might make of the weapon. "Let's hope they just wanted to disarm me."

"Yes, let's hope so." Joseph reached over and smoothed her hair. "I guess I made a fool of myself, bursting into Chet's house that way, but I'd make a fool of myself ten times over to protect you."

The warmth of his hand spread through Erin, relaxing the tightness in her shoulders and easing the dark cloud of dread in her heart. Despite everything that had happened, at least she was with Joseph.

At least she was with Joseph. She hoped she'd stay with him for a very long time.

Chapter Fifteen

At home, an urgency seized them both to seek refuge in each other. Erin began stripping off her clothes as soon as they got inside, and Joseph unsnapped his belt buckle while following her into the bedroom.

There was an extra measure of joy in the way skin whispered over skin. Their kisses were longer and sweeter than before, their closeness less self-conscious. When she welcomed Joseph inside her, Erin's spirits soared.

The world beyond this room ceased to exist as Joseph's caresses unleashed a torrent of desire. Fierce longing swept her higher and higher, until she could scarcely bear the tension, and then over a waterfall into a rainbow plunge. Shimmering with ecstasy, Erin clung to her man, exulting in their shared power and in the unsuspected depths of her passion.

She wished they could journey through time to retrieve the years they'd lost. At least, she thought gratefully, they'd come together now, united against the world. If only there were some way to guarantee she wouldn't lose him again.

After dozing, they ate a light supper. Then they made love again and slept all night in each other's arms.

TOWELING OFF her reddish-brown hair after they showered, Erin glowed in the morning light. With her heart-shaped face and delicate complexion, she reminded Joseph of a sprite too ethereal to capture. Well, he didn't want to capture or control her, only to be with her.

Pulling on a light jersey over his head, he lingered to watch Erin tuck her curves into a blouse and slacks. From a drawer, she removed a pendant and fastened it around her neck. Joseph was surprised to see a jagged half-heart of burnished gold settle into the hollow of her throat.

"You still have it," he marveled.

"I was wearing it the day I got hit." Erin regarded him through a curtain of hair. "I should have realized I'd never have done that if I'd intended to marry Chet." She peered into the drawer. "Gee, I'm glad I took my will out of my purse. Otherwise whoever stole the gun might have found it, too."

"If it was Lance, at least he'd have known you were leaving your money to charity and not to your mother," Joseph said.

"That's true." She wrapped her arms around herself. "So if he's trying to gain control of the company, he still has a motive to kill me. Maybe I should mail him a copy."

"You could simply let your mother know you've changed it. I'm sure she'd mention it to him." Joseph almost smiled, imagining Lance's fury at being outfoxed.

"On the other hand, she might take it as a sign that I expect her to die."

"That never occurred to me."

From below on the street a car rumbled. Then another. And a third.

"What on earth?" Erin said.

Joseph flicked open the blinds. At first, he caught only a blurry glimpse, and then a car exactly like Rick's came into view.

Ordinarily, he'd have been glad to see his friend, but behind it drove a black-and-white patrol car, trailed by Chief Norris's sedan. The chief and a uniformed patrolman hadn't accompanied Rick on a social visit.

Erin joined him at the window. "You don't think they're here with bad news about my mother, do you?"

"That many cops? No." An ugly sense of menace warned that it was bad news, all right, but not the kind she meant. "The only reason they'd bring that many officers is to arrest one or both of us."

"For what?"

He had a nasty suspicion. "My fingerprints were on the missing gun. If somebody used it carefully enough, mine might be the only prints."

"You're being framed?" A sick feeling twisted in the pit of her stomach. *Just like his father.* And it was her fault. She was the one who'd been stupid enough to leave her purse behind.

"Let's not jump to conclusions."

"I won't let this happen," she said.

"They may arrest you, too." If they took him into custody, they'd almost certainly hold Erin either as a suspect or a witness.

That raised a frightening possibility. Supposing that Norris was involved in the attacks on her. That would give him both the time and the opportunity to stage a deadly "accident."

Joseph made a split-second decision. Regardless of the impact on his defense, he couldn't let them get her. "Grab your purse and go out through the back before the patrolman circles around."

"You need me to vouch for your whereabouts!"

"We'll deal with that problem later. If Norris gets his hands on you, you might not survive."

She paled. "Oh, my gosh!"

"When you find a safe place, call a lawyer," he told her. "Don't phone me. They'll be listening. Now hurry!"

She grabbed her pocketbook. The drawn curtains of the main room prevented anyone from seeing as they sped to the rear door. "Go straight through the trees." The thick clump should provide cover. "Cut over the hill to the next road."

"What if someone stops me?" Her eyes were wide with fear.

"Insist on seeing a lawyer immediately. Say nothing until you talk to him, no matter what your instincts tell you," Joseph said. "At this point, I don't trust anyone except my mother."

"And mine."

In front of the house, car doors banged. Erin brushed a kiss across his cheek and whisked away, rubber-soled shoes carrying her noiselessly over the deck and into the grove.

The doorbell rang. Fetching his service revolver from the bedroom, Joseph set it openly on the coffee table. He didn't mean to provide an excuse for anyone to open fire.

The bell chimed three times, fast. When he answered, Rick stood on the step, regret coloring his face.

The chief waited to one side. The patrolman had to have gone around the house. If he'd noticed Erin fleeing, he'd have sounded the alarm, so Joseph hoped she'd avoided detection.

"What's going on?" he asked.

"May we come inside?"

Although he had no idea what had brought them here, he knew better than to give them a chance to snoop. Or to plant evidence. "Do you have a warrant?"

"Yes."

Bad news, Joseph thought. "Mind telling me what happened?"

From the side, Norris said, "Where were you yesterday evening?"

A flicker of Rick's eyes showed his dismay at the inappropriate question, although he didn't dare rebuke the chief openly. Instead, he began reciting the Miranda warning. "You have the right to remain silent…"

A chill ran through Joseph as he listened to the familiar advisory. He almost regretted that the chief hadn't kept questioning him, because without the warning, whatever he'd replied would have been inadmissible in court.

"I'm not waiving my rights," he told Rick when the detective produced a form for him to sign. "I don't even know what crime you're investigating."

His friend released a long breath. "I'm arresting you for the murder of Chet Dever."

"Someone killed Dever?" Stunned, Joseph tried to grasp the implications. At Chet's house last night, the two men had argued loudly enough to be heard by a passerby or neighbor. That might make him a suspect, but by itself the circumstance wasn't enough to justify a warrant.

I got caught up in something a lot bigger than I expected. Chet hadn't been kidding.

"Where's your service revolver?" Rick glanced past him. "Never mind. I see it."

"How'd it happen?" he asked, taking a long shot, since he didn't expect an answer.

"You should know," Norris said. "It was your gun that killed him."

"Oh, for…!" Although he left the sentence incomplete, Rick didn't bother to hide his annoyance. A basic rule of interrogation called for withholding facts in the hope that the suspect would implicate himself by accidentally revealing information. Apparently, the chief was too angry to care.

"It got stolen last night. I don't know for sure who took it but I have some idea." Surely they'd realize that, by targeting him, they gave the real slayer more time to cover his or her tracks. "You need to talk to Lance Bolding and Brandy Schorr." Of course either of them could have handed the gun over to a third party.

"Don't play games with me," the chief said. "Your fingerprints were the only ones on it."

It had required foresight, sophistication and cunning to lift the gun from Erin's purse without marring its surface and use it as a murder weapon. Brandy didn't strike Joseph as that conniving or that smart, but Lance did. "Bolding had an argument with Chet."

"So did…" The chief bit off his words. He hadn't entirely lost his senses.

So did I, Joseph finished sternly. Obviously they'd done their homework. Some of it, anyway.

After collecting the revolver, Rick patted him down for other weapons, set aside his wallet and took his cell phone. He undoubtedly intended to intercept any calls, as Joseph had anticipated.

"Where's Erin Marshall?" the chief demanded.

"In the bathroom." The longer he delayed them, the more chance she had of getting clear.

Ruefully, Rick produced a pair of handcuffs. When the metal snicked around Joseph's wrists, an impotent rage flared inside him.

Even though Joseph hadn't been present in the alley to see it, an imaginary vision of his father's arrest had haunted him for years. Lewis, confused and injured, being cuffed and dragged off like a criminal. Finding himself accused of a crime he hadn't committed and then, with sickening inevitability, being railroaded into prison while the town turned against his wife and son.

The chief called Erin's name, repeating it several times with increasing vehemence. "She'd better be safe," Norris growled. "If you've done anything to her…"

"You think I'd hurt her?" The idea was so preposterous Joseph hadn't even considered they might suspect it.

"After what you did to Chet, you're obviously capable of anything." Norris stalked off in search of Erin

Joseph forced himself to check a passionate defense of his actions. A prosecutor would tease and torment any statement he made and use it against him. Although he'd refused to waive his rights, that only precluded an interrogation. Anything he volunteered could be used in court.

The district attorney already had plenty to work with: motive, opportunity and means. And an easy way to discredit Joseph's only defense witness, on the grounds that she was his lover.

Whoever had stolen his gun yesterday had made quick and deadly use of it, he thought. Yet the slayer couldn't have known that Erin had never handled the gun. Perhaps it didn't matter who took the blame. Maybe the point was simply to get away with murder.

"Where *is* Erin?" Rick asked

"She's fine."

Norris stormed in from the bedroom. "She's gone! What've you done with her, Lowery?"

"Nothing."

"She witnessed the murder, didn't she?" the chief demanded. "So you killed her. You never belonged on the force. I knew you'd turn out bad, but not this bad."

Joseph was too distressed to answer. Erin, he thought, what have I done?

The chief, whether for ulterior motives or not, had already begun pinning the blame on Joseph for her possible murder. If the killer discovered he wasn't likely to be charged, he'd have no further reason for caution.

Especially if that killer was Edgar Norris.

SIX WEEKS of convalescence had left Erin out of shape. To make matters worse, she kept slipping on the steep slope. After she cut across several roads and a couple of rear yards, her heart thrummed and her shins were aching.

She pictured Joseph at the mercy of Chief Norris. What crime had been committed? Was someone dead?

Maybe it wasn't that serious. Chet might have filed a complaint against Joseph as payback for their quarrel, not to mention the canceled wedding. Then she remembered that the CEO depended on her goodwill to avoid ruin. It wasn't likely he'd create trouble for her.

Sinking onto a tree stump, Erin sucked into the autumn air.

How ridiculous, she thought, that an heiress worth millions had to flee through backyards like a fugitive. But if you couldn't trust the police, who could you trust?

Suzanne. Not only was she Joseph's mother, she worked for Abe Fitch. He could make a referral to a good criminal attorney.

Erin was reaching into her purse when the phone rang. Hoping it was Joseph with an all clear, she answered.

"Erin? Thank goodness you're okay." Alice's voice rang with relief.

"I'm fine. You're the one I've been concerned about," Erin said.

"I thought something terrible had happened!"

Surely her mother didn't know about the police showing up on Joseph's doorstep. "Why?"

"You haven't heard?" Alice asked. "It's all over the radio. Someone murdered Chet last night."

"He's dead?" Erin saw the tall blond man leaning over her bed at the hospital, tenderly taking charge of her. At the church, arrogant and threatening when she called it off. At his house last night, warning of danger.

She'd assumed he meant the risk of bringing his embezzlement to light. Why would anyone want to kill him?

"A neighbor reported suspicious noises," her mother went on. "The police don't release details on that kind of thing, I guess. Anyway, they found him in the house."

"How awful. Who could have done this?"

"According to the radio, there's a suspect. They've haven't released the name." Her mother sounded shaken. "It's horrible. Poor Chet. I don't know what we're going to do without him."

The missing gun. Was it the murder weapon? Was that why the police had come to Joseph's house?

What other reason could there be?

Whoever had done this had to be desperate. And since the only people with access to the gun had been Lance and Brandy, that put her mother in immediate peril.

"Mom, who's there with you?"

"Lance went to play golf again. He's such an aficionado," she said. "This whole business upsets me, but he doesn't seem to care. He made some crack about never liking Chet in the first place."

"That's disgusting." As she talked, Erin began making her way downhill in search of a street sign that would tell her where to direct a cab.

"Erin, when I first met Lance, we had such fun together. I resented it when you questioned my judgment." Her mother's voice broke. "Was I wrong? Did I bring this horror to the people I care about?"

"Let's not worry about that now." They both needed to think straight. "Where's Brandy?"

"She's about to head for the supermarket. I don't think she should leave me alone at a time like this."

If she'd trusted the housekeeper, Erin would have agreed. Given Brandy's old friendship with Todd Wilde, however, she was likely mixed up in wrongdoing up to her eyeballs.

"Let her go," she said.

"It scares me, being alone. Whoever did this to Chet is still out there. Would you come keep me company?"

"Mom, you have to leave as soon as Brandy's out of the house. Don't tell her anything." She braced for an argument.

"Maybe you're right. Honey, I'm really frightened."

Finally, Alice was listening! "I think Lance is trying to seize control of the Marshall Company. Brandy might be helping him. I think they may both be involved in Chet's murder. Let me call a taxi and come get you."

"Not a cab! Think of the implications," her mother said. "Some media outlet will offer that cabbie big bucks to smear everything we say and do across the tabloids. Chet's death is big news. A congressional candidate murdered, along with two bodies in the lake! You know how the media loves ugly stories about the wealthy."

At this point, Erin didn't care. Arguing with her mother, however, was likely to prove fruitless. "All right, you come pick me up."

"Brandy's car's in the shop," Alice said. "She has to take mine to the supermarket. I know—I'll ask Stanley Rogers to fetch you."

Despite the gravity of the situation, Erin smiled. How typical of her mother that, immediately after the death of their CEO, she shifted her sights and began bossing around the chief financial officer. Inappropriate though it might be to treat a top executive as a gofer, at least her mom had hit on someone reliable.

"Okay."

"Tell me where you are."

She reached a street sign. "At the corner of Far Oak and Pine. It's in the canyon near where Joseph lives."

"It won't take long if he's at the office," her mother said. "If he can't come, I'll call you back."

"Fine." Maybe it was better having Stanley with them, Erin thought. His good sense ought to help persuade her mother to use extreme caution.

Under other circumstances, it would have been Chet receiving the bossy call from the chairman of the board. Erin supposed she shouldn't feel so terrible about the death of a man who'd tricked and stolen from her, but she did. Despite his behavior, he deserved better than to be gunned down as part of somebody's power grab.

She recalled the photograph he'd produced of himself with her parents. What had been the significance of that? Chet had said it was nothing, but she didn't believe him.

Now, she supposed, she'd never find out.

AT THE STATION, the booking proceeded at its usual slow pace. Although Joseph understood the paperwork involved, he became increasingly restless. After Rick removed the cuffs, he signed the necessary forms so fast only an expert could have read his writing.

Finally the detective escorted him into an interrogation room and set up a video camera. He didn't turn it on yet, though. "Listen…"

"Is the chief watching?" Joseph indicated the two-way mirror on the wall.

Rick stepped out to check. When he came back, he shook his head. "He got called to a press conference."

"To tell the world about my arrest?"

"I presume so," Rick said. "Look, if you insist on a lawyer, that's your right, but it's going to delay things. You seem to have an idea who's behind this. I thought you might want to tell me before somebody else gets killed."

He had a point. Waiting for an attorney meant it could be hours before he was questioned. In the meantime, Rick would have to withhold any details of the investigation. And, of course, Joseph had no idea where Erin had landed and no way to contact her.

"I'll waive my right, but I want you to leave that thing off for a while." He indicated the video camera. "No audiotape, either. I want us both to be able to speak freely."

His friend ducked his head in assent. "Better start talking. The chief won't stay away any longer than he has to."

Joseph went to the point. "When we left Chet Dever's place last night, he was fine."

"The murder weapon has your prints on it."

"Someone stole it from Erin's purse yesterday at her mom's home. I didn't report it immediately because I'd put it there knowing she didn't have a license," he said. "Don't tell me the killer conveniently left the murder weapon at the scene."

The same thing had happened to his father eleven years ago.

Rick made notes on a pad. "We recovered it outside the house, under some bushes."

"Who found it?" Joseph asked.

The other man looked up from his writing. "The chief."

"You think that was a coincidence?"

"Where's Erin?" Rick asked, changing the subject.

"I sent her out the back door the minute you guys showed up," Joseph admitted. "I don't trust the chief. Somebody's tried to kill her a couple of times. It could be him."

The detective let out a low whistle. "Man, this is thorny."

"I've answered your questions. Tell me what you know that I don't."

His friend gathered his thoughts. Much depended on whether Rick accepted Joseph's story and believed him innocent. Confiding in a suspect was highly improper and would almost certainly compromise the investigation.

Finally, the detective said, "Remember I had an officer going over Bolding's cell phone records? I found a number of calls to Marie Flanders's number in L.A., beginning shortly after he married Alice Marshall and ending about six months ago."

Joseph supposed he should have expected as much. Lance's connection to Marie, along with Marie's connection to Todd Wilde, should make Alice's husband a suspect in both their slayings.

"He was one of the people who had access to Erin's purse when the gun disappeared," he said.

Rick made a frustrated noise. "Thanks to your sending her away, I can't substantiate your story about the gun or your whereabouts last night."

"Call her cell number." He provided it from memory.

Rick dialed. "Busy."

"She's probably on the line with her mother." Another possibility occurred to him. "What if Bolding uses his wife as bait to lure Erin?"

"I don't see what benefit he'd get from killing her," Rick said.

"As far as he knows, her death would leave everything to her mother. If Alice meets with another so-called accident or dies of natural causes, he'd control the Marshall Company lock, stock and barrel."

"I'll keep trying to reach her," Rick said. "Now I'm going to turn on the camera and you repeat the gist of what you told me. Otherwise our deal ends here."

Joseph gave a tight nod. It was a big risk, but he didn't see what choice he had.

Chapter Sixteen

While she waited for Stanley, Erin phoned Suzanne at the law office and explained about the stolen gun and that Joseph had apparently been arrested for murder. "Someone killed Chet Dever last night," she said.

"I'd heard he was dead, but I had no idea… I'll get the best lawyer I can." Suzanne's voice shook. "After what happened to my husband, I don't trust the police."

"Neither do I," Erin admitted.

"Tina told me about Chet when she called to cancel her tutoring this afternoon," Joseph's mother went on. "She's taking the day off school. Gene's so upset she's reluctant to leave him alone. Now I'm upset, too."

"I'm sorry," Erin said. "I didn't mean to drag him into this."

"Don't blame yourself. You're the best thing that ever happened to Joseph." A shuddering breath revealed how hard she was fighting to stay calm.

"He's a wonderful man." She had no right to say more than that, especially since she and Joseph had never really verbalized their feelings.

"All these years, I've told myself that what happened to Lewis was a fluke, that this town is safe and people are basically decent." Mrs. Lowery seemed to need a sympathetic ear, and Erin was happy to provide one. "I refused to believe that the person who murdered poor Mr. Nguyen and sent

Lewis to his death was still a free man. But in my heart I've always wondered about Edgar Norris, and now he's got my son."

"I'm suspicious of my stepfather as well," Erin said. "I have to focus on trying to get my mother to safety. I know you'll do what's necessary for Joseph."

"After I arrange for an attorney, I'll tell Tina what's happened," Suzanne responded. "She's a decent person and if her father won't listen to her, maybe Rick will. We've got to free my son."

"Please let Gene know that whoever killed his candidate, it wasn't Joseph," Erin added. "I can swear to that. Now I'm going to pick up my mother. Our CFO is giving me a lift."

"I guess we're each doing our best to protect our loved one," Suzanne said.

They're both my loved ones. Erin restricted herself to saying, "We can do this."

"Yes, we can."

She'd scarcely clicked off when a sports car swooped into view. Although she hadn't expected the sixtyish executive to drive such a racy vehicle, her eye flew to the star-shaped Marshall Company parking decal, right next to a VIP sticker from Las Vegas.

Stanley poked his graying head out the window and greeted her warmly. Grateful to have an ally, she slid inside and fastened her seat belt.

WHEN JOSEPH HEARD his phone's distinctive ring in Rick's pocket, he hoped at first that Erin had disobeyed his orders and called him. He realized it wasn't her, however, when Rick identified himself to the caller and asked, "Have you spoken with Erin Marshall lately?"

Apparently her answer satisfied him. After switching off the videotape, he said, "It's your mother," and gave Joseph the phone.

A frazzled Suzanne detailed her arrangements for a lawyer, who'd be arriving in a couple of hours, and related her conversation with Erin. "Maybe I shouldn't have, but after she hung up, I called and told Tina everything. She's worried about what's going on and so am I. She and her brother plan to drive over to the Boldings' house right now. I suppose they'll run into Erin."

"Why are Tina and Gene getting involved?" Joseph didn't want any member of the Norris family butting in. "Mom, they might tell the chief where they're going. I want him as far from Erin as possible."

"I'm sorry. I thought maybe she could help," his mother said. "There's more. I didn't think about it when I was talking to Erin but something's been bothering me about Alice Marshall—I mean, Bolding. The problem is, it's confidential. Attorney-client privilege."

"People's lives are at stake," Joseph said. "If you have information, you can't withhold it." He didn't normally believe in taking the law into one's own hands, but he refused to risk sacrificing Erin over a technicality.

"Give me the phone," Rick interjected. "If she has information, I want to hear it."

Although it violated his instincts, Joseph asked his mother to cooperate with the detective. Reluctantly, she agreed.

"What do you know?" Rick paid close attention to the answer, interrupting with a few terse questions. He listened solemnly for a while, then thanked Suzanne and ended the call.

"What is it?"

"Not long after Erin's accident, Mrs. Bolding went to the attorney's office and asked to be made her daughter's trustee," he said. "She sought to have Erin declared incompetent. The lawyer told her it wasn't appropriate for a short-term disability."

"She wanted to disenfranchise her daughter? That doesn't sound like her," Joseph said. "Was Lance involved?"

Rick frowned. "According to your mother, Mrs. Bolding insisted that he not be informed. Of course, he wouldn't have been anyway, but she didn't seem to realize that."

"I don't get it." These weren't the actions of a loving mother or a brainwashed wife, either. "I can't picture Mrs. Bolding pulling a power play behind her husband's back. She's got her hands full fighting cancer."

"Mrs. Bolding has cancer?" Rick asked.

"That's what she and Chet told Erin."

"I'm getting a strange feeling." The detective flipped through his notes.

"Talk to me!" Suzanne had said the financial officer from Marshall was driving Erin to Alice's house right now. It wouldn't take them long to get there.

"After we tracked Bolding's phone calls, I spoke with Marie's ex-roommate in L.A.," Rick said. "She told me Marie's suffered for years from hepatitis C, possibly due to drug use. You know it can lead to liver cancer? She said Marie lost a lot of weight but refused to go to a doctor. She insisted she was on the verge of making her dreams come true and nothing was going to stop her."

"So she might have planned some scam with Todd Wilde? Blackmail or threats, maybe?" That would certainly have given Lance a motive to kill them, but Joseph didn't see what it had to do with Alice trying to take her daughter's money.

"There's more. Your mother just told me something else," Rick went on. "When they were in high school, she said Alice and Marie looked so much alike people used to joke about them being twins. Finally, Marie dyed her hair black to put a stop to it."

At first, Joseph didn't see the relevance. Then his stomach lurched. "Did you ever make a definitive ID on the woman's body?"

"Not yet," Rick said.

Abruptly he understood what he'd missed about the near

drowning. Although he realized he couldn't have guessed before now, that proved small comfort.

If he was right, it might be too late. "We have to reach Erin."

"I'll put out a bulletin and send a car to the Boldings' house." As Rick turned to go, the door behind him smashed open.

"What the hell is going on?" the chief of police snarled. "I look in here through the mirror to find the two of you jabbering away like best buddies." He indicated the camera. "Why isn't that activated? Sergeant Valdez, you're relieved of duty pending an Internal Affairs investigation."

"I have reason to believe Erin Marshall is in immediate danger," Rick said. "Joseph and Suzanne Lowery have given me valuable information—"

"Do you want to be arrested too?" Norris snapped.

Rick hesitated. "I have to issue a bulletin."

"You don't have to do anything unless I tell you to." The chief kept his gaze fixed on Joseph. "Get out of here and keep your mouth shut, Valdez, or I'll have your badge. I'll see that you're charged with obstruction of justice, too."

"It isn't only Erin who's in danger," Joseph said. "Your kids…"

"You leave my family out of this!" The chief reached for his holster.

Rick was moving slowly backward. Maybe he would make the right decision and get help, Joseph thought, but he couldn't afford to wait and find out. Not with Erin's life and possibly his own hanging in the balance.

He pivoted and with one swift motion slammed his fist into Chief Norris's jaw.

"Isn't it a shock?" Stanley asked as they zipped along Old Lake Highway. "I can't believe Chet's gone. I always figured you two would get back together."

Erin didn't bother to correct his misguided notion. "I'm sorry about what happened, too."

"The whole office is in mourning. I gave them the day off, but I went in," he said. "Your mother asked me to hold down the fort until the board can consider new applicants for his position."

"Thank you." The business had to keep going, of course.

"His parents want to schedule a funeral as soon as the coroner releases the body," Stanley added. "I'm sure they'd like you to attend."

Erin hadn't considered anything so practical. "Of course, the Marshall Company will pay for everything. " She knew practically nothing about organizing funerals. "Do they need help choosing a mortuary?"

"I'll take care of it." After giving her a brief smile, Stanley lapsed into silence.

Erin felt a little guilty that she hadn't considered the impact of Chet's death on his parents or on the firm's employees. It had to be hard on Stanley, losing his closest colleague.

Concerns about Joseph and her mother came first, however. As they neared the lake, she replayed scenes from the previous evening: Lance storming into the house accusing Alice of playing games. Brandy retrieving Erin's purse. Chet admitting he'd embezzled her money.

So much had happened that she hadn't been able to consider many of the implications. Now an unnerving thought came to Erin.

Her father had once said that not a penny moved in or out of the Marshall Company without Stanley keeping track of it. Chet had had no direct access to her trust fund. He couldn't have stolen from it without Stanley's cooperation.

She stole a quick look at the man sitting next to her, sturdy and familiar as the town's main street. He'd worked for the Marshalls all of Erin's life. He and her father had become friends, although she doubted Andrew had been truly close to anyone outside his family.

Her dad had found the financial officer amusing. After one hunting trip, he'd told her, laughing, that it was a good thing their campfire card games were played for pennies. Stanley had a talent for losing every hand while remaining certain each time that his luck was about to change.

Good-natured Stanley hadn't minded the ribbing. Someday, he'd insisted, he would hit the jackpot in Las Vegas.

Erin caught her breath, remembering the VIP parking sticker on the windshield. The casinos reserved those for big gamblers, didn't they?

Her father had dismissed the signs and maybe, back then, Stanley had had the sense to hold himself in check. But there'd been no one looking over his shoulder these past two years.

She didn't dare reveal what had just occurred to her. If it were true, her mother's faith in Stanley might be badly misplaced.

Chet had come clean about his embezzling. How far would Stanley go to cover up his?

THE BACK of Norris's head thudded into the wall. He collapsed like a beanbag.

Breathing hard, Joseph assessed Rick's reaction. The detective hadn't drawn his gun. That was a good sign.

"If you like, I'll handcuff you and gag you," Joseph told him. "Otherwise, you'll have to shoot me, because I'm going after Erin."

"You'd never make it out." His friend knelt by the chief. "He's breathing okay. I'm guessing he'll have a doozy of a headache. We ought to call the paramedics, just in case."

"I'll call them from his car. Toss me the keys."

"I've got a better idea." Rick took out his cuffs. "Give me your wrists. You're going to have to trust me on this one."

"Rick…"

"You want to get out of the station or not?"

The detective had a point. Not only did every officer in Sundown Valley know about Joseph's arrest, he'd just given them an excuse to shoot him if they caught him escaping.

He held out his wrists. The cuffs snapped over them.

Rick whirled him about and shoved him into the corridor, closing the door after them. "Better hustle," he said close to Joseph's ear. "Any minute, the chief's going to start squawking like a wet hen."

Heads turned as they navigated toward the parking exit. The patrol captain, Mario Hernandez, regarded them dubiously as he emerged from the break room. "Where're you taking him?"

"To make an identification," Rick said.

"Yeah, well, I hope he identifies whoever shot Dever, because we all know it wasn't him." Hernandez met Joseph's eyes. "Your father was a good man. I always believed that."

"Thank you," Joseph said.

As soon as they reached the detective's car, Rick removed the cuffs and they roared out of the parking lot. On the point of ordering the nearest patrol car sent to Erin's aid, however, they heard the radio crackle with an All Points Bulletin.

It named the two of them.

"Guess the chief came out of it," Rick said dryly.

"I'll never forget this." Joseph knew he'd just wrecked his friend's career and probably much more unless they could prove that the chief's wrongdoing had forced them into it. Even then, Rick's relationship with Tina didn't stand much of a chance.

"Yeah, we can watch each other's backs in the pokey when they lock us up." He tossed over Joseph's cell phone. "Call Erin and warn her."

He dialed. Behind them, a siren blasted the morning peace. To Joseph's relief, Erin answered with a tentative, "Hello?"

"It's me," he said. "Don't…" Jumbled noises filled the phone, followed by a painful scrape and then nothing. "Erin? Erin?"

"What happened?" Rick veered west onto the highway.

"Somebody got her," he said grimly.

ERIN STARED at Stanley in disbelief. He'd just yanked the phone from her hand and heaved it out the window.

"I'm sorry." The executive made a vague gesture. "Cell phones interfere with my pacemaker. I guess I overreacted."

"We have to go back and get it," Erin said. "That call was important. I'll take it outside the car."

She hadn't known Stanley had heart problems. Come to think of it, wasn't that an urban legend about cell phones and pacemakers?

"I remember the spot," the CFO said. "I'll bring it to you later. Your mother's anxious to see you."

His clipped words and nervous manner alarmed her. She no longer doubted her suspicions about an embezzlement. And perhaps much more.

Two days ago, Erin had gone to his office and requested a full accounting of her trust fund. A few hours later, someone had fired at her and Joseph, possibly with a hunting rifle.

On the phone, Joseph had tried to warn her about something. It had to have been Stanley.

They turned onto Via Puesta del Sol too fast for Erin to risk jumping. Almost immediately, the sports car swerved again onto Rainbow Lane.

This wasn't the way to her mother's house. Rainbow Lane led to the old fishing pier.

"I ALWAYS KNEW the chief disliked you, but there's obviously more than that going on," Rick said.

Joseph managed to tear his thoughts away from Erin's imminent danger. "You've heard about my father's case. Norris must have been involved in the robbery, although he had an alibi for that night."

"The chief may not be my favorite person, but I never figured he'd do anything like that," Rick said. "Why plan a jewelry store robbery when he had everything to lose?"

"Two and a half million dollars can buy a lot of status. Maybe he figured his kids deserved the best."

The scream of their siren, which Rick had activated along with his emergency flashers, didn't quite drown out the shrieks of their pursuers. More than one car had joined the chase, judging from the sound of it. "They'd have been lucky to get ten percent from a fence. So, say, a quarter of a million. Split three ways, that's what? Math was never my subject."

"Roughly eighty thousand." A substantial sum but hardly vast wealth. Joseph had to admit, it seemed unlikely Norris would have risked his freedom and his position for that amount, let alone trusted to the discretion of a petty crook like Todd.

Ahead, a black-and-white pulled out from a side street, light bar blazing, and halted partially blocking the four-lane highway. Beyond it, traffic halted.

"Hang on," Rick said.

"Go for it."

The detective yanked the wheel. As they spun into an opposing lane, Joseph caught a grab bar to keep from sliding.

"You must've aced LED." That stood for Law Enforcement Driving.

"My favorite part of the police academy." They careened past the patrolman.

Under other circumstances, Joseph might have enjoyed the thrill. But the way someone—perhaps Stanley Rogers—had ripped the phone out of Erin's hand frightened him beyond measure.

He couldn't bear to lose her.

OVERGROWN TREES cast shadows on the windshield. Vague memories flickered through Erin's mind as she stared at the man's reflection.

Swinging to miss a pothole, Stanley scraped a flowering bush on the shoulder. The cloyingly sweet scent swept away the remaining confusion and Erin saw the past with painful clarity.

The van. The glare on the windshield. The glass clearing to show Stanley's face, revealing to her that people connected with the Marshall Company wanted her dead. That meant they most likely wanted her mother dead, too.

There was no time to figure out how Lance had become involved with Stanley or what role Chet had played. Ahead lay the dank, merciless lake. Whatever Erin did now, it was up to her to save her own life and Alice's as well.

Unsnapping her seat belt, she shoved open the door. Startled, Stanley grasped the thin fabric of her blouse, throwing her off balance. When Erin wrenched loose, she nearly tumbled headfirst onto the pavement rushing beneath them.

"What are you doing?" he demanded. "Stop that!"

She clutched the door handle and kicked with all her strength. Although her rubber sole barely grazed Stanley's shoulder, his arm jerked in response and the car skewed wildly.

Centrifugal force nearly flung Erin out the side. She was hanging on for dear life when, with a sickening crunch, they clipped a tree.

The impact hurled her shoulder-first into the driver. His head flew back and banged the side window as they jolted to a halt.

The sound of Erin's harsh breathing filled her ears. Stanley lay motionless. Reluctant to touch him, she turned off the engine and dragged herself away.

Trying to ignore shaky knees and an aching shoulder, she climbed out the passenger side and surveyed the damage. Although scrapes, large dents and a crumpled bumper marred the sports car, it looked driveable.

She had to get to Alice's house. Never mind that she wasn't supposed to drive. If the police stopped her, she would enlist their aid.

Rounding the car, she opened Stanley's door. He flopped partway out. Despite some blood on his temple, he seemed to be breathing normally.

According to a CPR class Erin had taken, she shouldn't move him. But she couldn't summon paramedics, she realized after a quick check of his coat pockets revealed no cell phone. Maybe he actually believed that business about the pacemaker, or maybe it was in his pants. She tried to force herself to search there and felt bile rise in her throat.

Giving up the attempt, she grasped him under the arms and hauled him backward until his legs cleared the vehicle. Moaning, he stirred. Shivers threatened Erin's composure. She had to get away before he regained consciousness. Even injured, he was larger and stronger than her.

She locked the doors, strapped herself into the car and turned the key in the ignition. It froze.

On the pavement, Stanley's eyelids fluttered open. He regarded her dully and then with growing alarm.

Erin wrenched at the key. It refused to turn. On the street, the man braced his arms, levered himself into a sitting position and, from his pants, took out a phone.

He had to be calling his accomplice. Telling him what—to kill Alice?

Erin looked down at the key, the ignition, the gearshift. It had slipped into neutral. Some cars didn't start unless they were in park, she remembered, and moved the lever.

The key turned. The engine purred to life.

She shot forward. It was too late to stop Stanley from making his call, and she quailed at the prospect of deliberately running over him. Better to get to Alice's house and grab her fast.

It was less than a mile away. Maybe she still had time.

Chapter Seventeen

To Joseph, the entire world seemed alive with sirens. The cruisers remained mercifully unseen, however, as Rick took a series of shortcuts.

"They must have figured out where we're going by now," Joseph said. "We might find Aurora Avenue blocked."

"If it comes to that, be prepared to bail. I'll do my best to hold them off," his friend said.

"Don't get yourself killed."

"I'll try not to."

Ahead, a car pulled out of a minimart, oblivious to their siren. Joseph hit the horn and the idiot halted, leaving them room to circumnavigate and pick up speed again. Fortunately, this part of town had light traffic on a weekday.

"While you were talking to your mother, you mentioned Tina," Rick said. "What was that about?"

The remark had been eclipsed by the news of Alice's visit to her lawyer, Joseph realized. "Apparently Tina's worried about Erin, so she and her brother are heading to the Boldings' house, too."

"What can she be thinking, putting herself in the middle of this situation?" Rick's jaw worked. "It would kill me if anything happened to her, even though she'll probably never talk to me again after she finds out we decked her father."

"I'm the one who decked her father."

"I let you," he said.

"I thought my lightning-fast reflexes caught you off guard."

"In your dreams."

Tina wasn't going to the Boldings' house alone, Joseph recalled. "You don't suppose Gene is mixed up in this, do you? He *was* working closely with Chet."

"At this point, I wouldn't be surprised if the whole town was involved except for you, me and Erin," Rick said. "And maybe Tina."

"Maybe?"

"The woman dotes on her family," he said. "I don't know what she'd do to protect them."

Joseph knew how far Erin would go to protect her mother. As far as necessary, even if it cost her own life.

The problem was, the woman waiting for her might not be her mother.

AS THE SPORTS CAR flew toward the Boldings' house, Erin registered the distant shrill of sirens, probably heading to a wreck on the highway. She hoped no one had been seriously injured.

Even beneath the midday sun, the house looked dark. She saw no cars in the turnaround. Maybe her luck had held.

Getting out, she ran up the front steps and was thankful to find the door unlocked. A breeze accompanied her inside, stirring the curtains and making shadows pulse in the living room.

"Mom! I'm…." Erin spotted someone sprawled on the couch. She stopped, tensing. It couldn't be her mother. *Please, no.*

Moving closer, she recognized Lance's chunky form. His jowly face had gone slack, and although he had to have heard her call his name, he barely rolled his head in response. In a weird way, he reminded her of Stanley lying on the road, except that her stepfather appeared to be conscious.

"What happened to you?" Erin asked.

"D-d-drug…." As if the effort exhausted him, his eyes shuttered.

"Oh, there you are." Her mother emerged from the bedroom wing. "I was so worried when Stanley called."

"Stanley called *you?*" She'd expected him to telephone his conspirator. "You mean he tried to phone Lance."

"I'm afraid my husband isn't taking calls right now." Alice didn't sound like herself. She had the same raspy tone, but the inflection had become flatter and colder. "He's a little under the weather."

"Do you feel okay?" Erin didn't know how to react. Something was terribly wrong.

"I'm a little thirsty," her mother said. "Let me fix you a glass of something."

"We can get a drink on the road."

"I made fresh lemonade, the way you like." Her mother gave her a stiff smile.

Brandy must have drugged her and Lance both, Erin thought. "No, Mom, we're leaving. Right now. Is Brandy still here?"

"She went to the store." Alice maintained that unnatural smile. "Honey, you shouldn't have pushed Stanley out of the car. He says he might have a concussion. We'll be lucky if he doesn't sue."

"Stanley tried to kill me," Erin said.

"Just now? I can't believe it!" The look of amazement didn't ring true. It reminded Erin of a B-grade actress feigning an emotion.

Everything looked different, even her mother. Had the scent of flowers not only restored her memories but also sharpened her perceptions?

Maybe her mother had been this way all along. When Erin arrived at the Boldings' house after being hospitalized, a lot of things had struck her as unreal, but she'd attributed the effect to her head injury. Now she felt as if something essential was missing from her mother's personality.

Around her, the house seemed airless and close. "Let's go outside."

"Why?"

"Because we're leaving. And because this place gives me the creeps."

"What's the matter?" demanded the woman in front of her. "Why won't you have a glass of lemonade with me? Aren't I good enough for you?"

The ugliness of Alice's expression took Erin aback. Her mother loved her, and there was no love in that face.

A BLACK-AND-WHITE cut them off on Shore Drive near the intersection with Aurora. When it lurched into their path, Rick had no choice but to hit the brakes.

Behind the wheel of the cruiser, Joseph recognized Bob Wheeler, a patrolman who'd been on the force less than two years. Shortly before making detective, Joseph had helped to field-train him.

"He's alone," Rick said. "I'll try to stall. Move!"

Keeping low, Joseph bolted for the trees. Rick got out on the other side, hands held high.

"Halt!" He ignored Bob's command and kept going, expecting the whine of a bullet at any second.

"Wait!" came Rick's voice. "Listen to me."

From behind drifted a few phrases—"the chief" and "Erin Marshall." The detective was obviously trying friendly persuasion.

At any rate, Bob must have realized he couldn't be in two places at once. Better to secure the prisoner at hand than risk losing both of them.

Funky cottages dotted the sloping terrain and a couple of children riding tricycles stopped to watch as Joseph dodged past. At least he no longer feared getting shot. No officer would fire with bystanders at risk.

Still, he expected the black-and-white to pick up the pursuit any second. How long could it take to handcuff Rick and stick him in the rear seat?

Unless, of course, the officer believed his story.

Less than a quarter of a mile left. Joseph's legs, muscular from workouts, chopped easily across the ground. He might just make it unhindered.

From the rear came the rumble of a car. Apparently Bob hadn't lingered, after all.

Joseph ducked behind a screen of branches. With a sinking sensation, he noted that it wasn't nearly thick enough to cover him.

Apparently his luck had run out.

"AUNT MARIE." Erin didn't know she'd spoken until she heard the name.

The woman's eyes narrowed menacingly. "Hello, Erin."

The boating accident. No wonder Joseph had suspected something was wrong even before they found the woman's body in the lake.

Her mother had to have drowned five and a half months ago. All this time, Alice Marshall Bolding had been gone, killed and replaced by her own sister.

Tears stung Erin's eyes. Alice had loved her daughter dearly, while Marie had twisted everything, manufacturing an estrangement to keep Erin at bay and making Alice appear temperamental and uncaring. Not only had she murdered her sister, she'd dishonored her memory.

Marie and Lance must have cooked up the whole scheme in L.A., how he would charm the rich widow and then help kill her. Judging by his present condition, however, he'd bitten off more than he could chew.

"How could you?" Erin asked. "How could you do this?"

"It wasn't easy, even for an actress." Her aunt acted as if the reproach were a compliment. "Too bad they don't give Oscars for real-life performances."

"That's not what I meant!"

"Think of all the people I had to bribe or blackmail or hide from," Marie went on with unnatural calm, as if they were having a conversation over lunch. "I thought I was rather clever about it. Of course, things got a little sticky after Todd spotted me and figured it all out. You'd think he'd have known better than to try to blackmail *me*."

"You shot him?"

"Oh, I didn't have to do it personally. I have friends in high places."

"What about me?" Erin knew she should run, but a morbid fascination held her in place. "Where did I fit in?"

"You were the biggest threat of all," Marie said. "And the richest prize. When you're dead, I'll have everything."

"No," she said. "I changed my will."

Her aunt's hands clenched. "Damn that Stanley. He should have done it right the first time. He's such an idiot! What is it about you, Erin? You're not that beautiful. Why did Chet care about you? He would have told you everything."

Last night when he produced the photo of her family, he must have intended to jog her memory of Alice. "You shot him and framed Joseph. Or did you have Stanley do your dirty work for you that time, too?"

"Of course," her aunt said. "I just hate shooting people. It's so messy. But I'll make an exception in your case." She took a small gun from her pocket.

A sense of unreality stole over Erin. She didn't even feel fear, at least not yet. "How could you turn two businessmen into killers?"

"You mean those two thieves?" Marie gave a mirthless laugh. "The same private eye I hired to track your mother's activities for Lance did a little corporate snooping, as well. A compulsive gambler and a politician who needed money. I knew they had to have their hands in the till."

Erin pretended to pace, trying to put a little distance between them. If she kept Marie talking, maybe she could get far enough to make a run for it. "You're the one who had the secretaries transferred."

"As it turned out, I might not have needed to," her aunt said. "You know, this would make an interesting scientific experiment. I couldn't fool Chet and Stanley, but you'd be amazed how many people simply accepted me as Alice. Well, no, I guess you wouldn't be surprised, since you're one of them."

Watching Marie's lizardlike eyes, Erin shuddered. She should have trusted her instincts. *I knew something was wrong, but I refused to believe it.*

She edged backward. A few more steps and she'd take the risk.

"Well, I'm afraid I don't have all day. Come on, little rich girl." The words dripped with venom. "I'll figure out how to get around your will later. Right now, we're taking a boat ride."

"Okay." Erin seized the excuse to start toward the front.

"Not that way!" Marie barked. "Through the back!"

The knob. She wrenched it and dodged onto the porch.

The gun roared with her aunt's fury.

A GREEN SEDAN SPED past Joseph. Inside, he saw Tina Norris in the passenger seat with Gene driving. Neither of them glanced his way.

Joseph let out a long breath. He still had a chance of reaching Erin, assuming that she'd made it to the Boldings' house. He didn't want to think about the possibility that she hadn't.

That financial officer had to be one of Marie's cohorts. Joseph could see now that he should have suspected anyone and everyone connected with the Marshall Company.

He loped along the shoulder, hearing the blare of sirens grow closer. One started up nearby, sharper than the others.

Bob's, he thought. Good intentions or bad, there was no way of telling.

Rounding a curve, Joseph saw the house hunkering ahead. There were two vehicles parked in front of it, Gene's and an empty sports car.

The front door slammed open. Erin! He barely had time to register her presence before a gunshot blasted from inside.

Joseph broke into a run.

HUGGING THE HOUSE, Erin scooted away from the door and past the front window. Across the parking area, Tina was exiting a sedan.

"Look out!" Erin screamed.

Marie lurched onto the porch. For one uncertain moment, she eyed Tina before swinging toward her niece. Erin ducked behind the glider, the only shelter at hand. It was far too small to cover her.

"No!" The cry came from Gene. What was he doing here? Erin wondered as he raced toward them.

Marie wavered. Apparently realizing he intended to take the gun, she pivoted and fired.

Less than twenty feet away, Gene staggered and went down. Tina screamed.

As a siren wailed up the road, someone else broke from the trees and pushed the frozen Tina to cover behind the sedan.

Joseph. Relief mingled with dread. Marie would shoot him down, too.

"Stay back!" Erin cried.

He emerged from behind the car, yelling, "Run, Erin! Get out!"

With a curse, Marie shot at him. Blasts rang out, one after the other. The car jounced on its springs as it took the hits.

"Go!" Joseph shouted.

Marie sighted him again. Committed to saving Joseph at any cost, Erin leaped up and flung her purse.

Her aunt's arm flew up for protection. Seizing on the break,

Joseph sprinted across the clearing and ducked behind the sports car beside the porch.

The barrel of the gun found its target again. Marie seemed fixated now on killing Joseph.

Yanking off one of her shoes, Erin threw it as hard as she could.

"Stop it!" Marie batted away the projectile.

Erin flung the other shoe. This time she scored a direct hit to her aunt's head just in time to send a bullet blasting skyward.

Scuttling around the car, Joseph made a flying leap. His timing was wrong. Recovering, Marie took point-blank aim.

"No! Not him!" Erin screamed. She scarcely noticed the black-and-white car hurtling into view.

As if in freeze-frame, she saw her aunt pull the trigger. Amid a deafening series of booms, Joseph jerked to one side and collapsed.

FIRE SEARED Joseph's leg as the bitter scent of gunpowder filled his nostrils. Firecrackers were detonating all over the place.

When he finished rolling aside, he saw blood splatter the doorway, the windows and the front of the house as if flung with a giant paintbrush. Marie, held upright by the force of the blasts, finally tumbled forward and slid halfway down the steps, the gun dropping to the ground.

The cavalry had arrived, he thought with grim humor.

"Nobody move!" Rick commanded. Behind him, Joseph heard Bob radioing for paramedics. "Who's in the house?"

Erin's voice, trembling but clear, replied, "Just Lance, as far as I know. He's been drugged. He's on the living room sofa."

Joseph reached down to his leg. Although it stung fiercely, his hand brought up only a trace of blood.

"Gene?" The wavering cry came from Tina, kneeling at her brother's side. "Gene, talk to me!"

More sirens. The chief had arrived, Joseph saw as he raised himself to a sitting position. There was going to be hell to pay.

He didn't care. Erin had survived, and that was all that counted.

TEARS STREAKED Erin's face. She wasn't sure who she was crying for—herself, her mother, Gene or Joseph. Probably all of them. And even for her aunt, who'd wasted her life and destroyed so many others.

As soon as Rick lowered his gun, she bolted off the porch to kneel beside Joseph. "How bad is it?" If she hadn't feared hurting him, she'd have gathered him in her arms.

"Just a flesh wound, I think. You?"

"Safe and sound. She wasn't my mom, you know."

"I figured that out."

He glanced uneasily toward the chief, who'd rushed out of his car and knelt beside his son a dozen feet away. "My mother hired an attorney. I'm afraid he's going to have a lot of charges to deal with when he gets here."

"You're damn right!" Norris's face contorted with fury as he looked up. "This is your doing, Lowery."

To the other officers, he shouted, "Where are the paramedics? Can't you see my son's bleeding here?"

Far off, more sirens approached. Help was on its way.

"Don't blame Joseph. Gene insisted on coming." Tina crouched beside the two men. "He kept saying he had to make things right. What did he mean, Dad?"

"Don't worry about it," Norris said. "We know who's the problem around here. The same jerk who's always been the problem."

Officers hurried past them into the house, fanning out and searching for occupants. There'd been no sign of Brandy, Erin remembered. Was she lying somewhere drugged, or had she simply gone to the supermarket?

She averted her face from her aunt's bloody, crumpled form. It was too painful to look at her.

"Dad, leave Joseph out of this," Gene wheezed. "You know Todd killed Mr. Nguyen. And I—"

"Shut up!"

Gene forced out the words. "You shouldn't have covered for me."

Erin's gaze met Tina's. What she saw there was shock and horror.

All along, the chief had been protecting his son. Erin wondered at what point he'd intervened, although it hardly mattered now. Obviously he had skewed the investigation to ignore any evidence clearing Joseph's father.

Since her aunt had provided Todd's alibi, she had to have known he'd committed the murder and that Gene was involved. After assuming the role of her sister, that must have given her ammunition with which to blackmail Chief Norris into closing Joseph's investigation, and doing who knew what else.

"What are you talking about?" Tina asked her brother.

"The robbery was my…" He groaned, pain halting his words.

"Shut up!" their father demanded. "Don't you have any brains?"

From the way Joseph stirred, Erin thought he was going to respond, but he held himself in check. "Let the other cops hear it for themselves," he murmured to Erin.

At one side, Rick had produced a pad and was quietly taking notes. Apparently he didn't need to advise Gene of his rights as long as the information was volunteered.

Gene pushed on, addressing his sister. "I thought it was easy money. But it all went wrong. Dad said he 'fixed it,' but it didn't stay fixed. I'm ashamed of what we did to Joseph's father." His voice weakened.

"Dad, is this true?" Tina demanded.

Her brother went limp. "Gene!" The chief bent over his son. "For God's sake, don't die!"

Sirens reverberated, coming closer. With a sigh, Gene opened his eyes. "Marie made you kill Todd, didn't she, Dad?"

"Shut up! Don't you have a grain of sense?" his father demanded.

"Who's Marie?" Tina asked.

A paramedic unit came into view, trailed by an ambulance and a fire truck. Erin turned away in time to see two officers assist a wobbly Lance out the front door.

Sandwiched between the emergency vehicles rode Alice's familiar car. In the windshield, Brandy's face had gone paste-white.

Norris pointed to the new arrival. "Take that woman into custody. Nobody talks to her but me." He indicated Lance. "Or to him, either. I don't want their testimony tainted."

"Disregard that order," Rick told the men. "Chief, I'm placing you under arrest for obstruction of justice. Give me your weapon. Now."

"You have no authority…"

Two other officers drew their weapons and faced the chief. Glaring, Norris reached for his holster.

"Stand aside, Tina!" Rick raised his gun.

"I'm not a damn fool." Angrily, the chief handed his revolver to one of the other officers. "When I get done with you, Valdez, you won't have a career left."

"You refused to put out an APB to protect Erin Marshall, and we can all see the results," Rick said. "Everyone here heard your son's statement. You're not above the law, Chief."

"You'll never see my daughter again, you scumbag."

"That's up to her," Rick said levelly, and took out his handcuffs.

There was no further chance to talk as rescue workers poured across the scene, more ambulances arrived and the police gathered their suspects. Chief Norris. Lance. Brandy.

Erin saw a cruiser arrive with Stanley Rogers inside. They'd rounded up the whole gang, or at least its surviving members.

A paramedic took Erin's blood pressure to make sure she wasn't in shock. In the confusion, she got separated from Joseph.

"Where is he?" she asked Rick.

"They're putting him in the ambulance."

Through the welter of emergency vehicles, she glimpsed a stretcher sliding into a white van. "I'll go with him."

Rick's hand on her arm halted her. "Erin, there's no room. Besides, you're one of our key witnesses. I need you at headquarters for questioning."

She ached to be with Joseph, but he would want her to help wrap up this case, wouldn't he?

"Believe me, we'll get updates on his condition as soon as they're available," Rick added.

"What about the charges?" she asked. "Is he still accused of murder?"

"I have a feeling we're going to dispense with that by the end of the day," the detective told her. "That's one of the areas you can help with. You're his alibi for last night, remember?"

She nodded. It distressed her, all the same, to let Joseph go.

There was no reason they couldn't continue being friends and lovers. But as the rear doors of the ambulance slammed and it pulled away, a lonely sense of distance grew inside Erin.

Years ago, she'd believed nothing could come between her and the man she loved, but she'd been wrong. She desperately hoped it wasn't going to happen again.

Chapter Eighteen

The days after Marie's death proved hectic. What Erin wanted most was to stay with Joseph, whose wound had developed an infection. But once he began recovering, she had to leave the role of guardian angel to Suzanne.

On Thursday, dental records identified the body from the lake as her mother. Although Erin had suspected as much, hearing the confirmation tore at her heart. She faced the sad prospect of arranging a funeral and saying goodbye.

On Friday, Abe Fitch read Alice Marshall Bolding's will, leaving everything to her daughter. Erin was now sole owner of a company worth more than a hundred million dollars, a company that had recently lost its chairman of the board, CEO and CFO, and which required an immediate audit to learn the extent of the embezzlement.

During the next few days, while she stayed by herself at Joseph's house, reporters and news vans dogged Erin's every move. Knowing he would need rest and quiet when he came home, she transferred her belongings to a vacant penthouse apartment in a Marshall-owned building adjacent to headquarters.

There, she was protected by strict security and had a car and driver at her disposal even after she regained her driver's license. Occupying her own place also permitted her to install the extra phone lines, fax machines and computers necessary to keep in touch with the experts whose assistance she required.

On Monday, a former Marshall CEO came out of retirement to help her locate an executive search service, a corporate consulting firm, an independent auditor and a top public relations agency to get her through this emergency. In addition, the company's lawyers and staff served at Erin's beck and call. Nonetheless, the responsibility for major decision-making rested on her shoulders.

Erin had to stretch beyond the hesitant, compliant self she'd accepted for so long. Without Joseph to lean on, she found the strength to make sure everybody knew that she—not the consultants, the lawyers or the staff—was in charge.

Although Marshall was primarily a property development and management organization, Erin also wanted it to foster a stronger community spirit and promote good works in Sundown Valley. As she began learning the ropes from the former CEO, she kept this long-term goal in mind.

Throughout the long workdays, welcome thoughts of Joseph frequently filled her heart. Erin wished she could lie in his arms every night. Soon the time would come, she told herself, and tried not to worry.

When he left the hospital, Suzanne requested that Erin avoid his house for fear of provoking a media circus. Her son still tired easily, she explained apologetically before putting him on the line.

Joseph sounded weary and a bit detached. He was glad he'd been cleared of all charges, he said. With Norris in jail, a captain named Mario Hernandez had been appointed acting chief. Erin gathered that the interim chief took a more favorable view of Joseph than his predecessor.

"It looks like there'll be some promotions," Joseph told her. "If you ask me, Rick deserves a medal."

"So do you." Erin wanted to talk about more personal issues, but not over the phone. "I hope I'll see you at

Mom's funeral on Friday." The coroner had finally released the body.

"Of course."

They talked for a while longer with a kind of wistful formality. This was only temporary, Erin told herself.

But, her mind warned, her newfound power and immense wealth weren't temporary. She could only hope they made as little difference to Joseph as they did to her.

ON THURSDAY EVENING, Joseph propped his sore leg on the coffee table, set his aluminum cane beside the couch and clicked on the TV. He'd deliberately avoided newscasts during the past week, but tomorrow at Alice's funeral he'd have to face the whole town. He might as well find out what people had been hearing.

Suzanne arrived from the kitchen with an aromatic bowl of popcorn. "I can't believe you're watching this."

"Armoring myself," he said.

"I tried to do that a long time ago, but it never helped." His mother settled beside him. "At least your father's been vindicated. I hope somewhere he knows that."

"I don't doubt it." Joseph glanced at her fondly. There was a little more gray in her brown hair, probably put there by worrying about him, but she looked as vibrant and down-to-earth as ever.

On screen, a man whose name was either Brad or Brent said, "Who would have believed that an over-the-hill actress could manipulate a congressional candidate, a chief of police and the financial head of a major corporation, and leave a trail of bodies in her wake? Stay with us as we review for you the incredible events that have unfolded in the sleepy town of Sundown Valley."

When a commercial came on, Joseph lowered the sound. "Sleepy town?" he repeated in amusement. "Isn't sleepy a synonym for boring?"

"Marie would hate being called an over-the-hill actress," Suzanne added. "Not that I care, after what she's done."

Joseph took a handful of popcorn. It was lightly salted, the way he liked it.

He wished Erin were here with them. Since he came home, he kept waiting for her to appear as if she'd simply stepped out of the room.

Her presence lingered in the scent of shampoo on her pillow. Once he'd imagined he saw her bright eyes peering around the edge of the shower door, and while reading last night he'd listened subconsciously for her light humming as she flipped through a book.

There she was on TV, head held high as she faced a news conference. That tailored suit looked new, he reflected as he raised the sound.

"We still don't know the full amount of the embezzlement, but it may be as high as a million dollars," she said. "Next question, please."

The woman who less than two weeks ago hadn't known where to go or how to protect herself now faced an armada of microphones with confidence. "I always knew she had it in her," Suzanne said as Erin discussed her plans for finding a new CEO.

"She's her father's daughter." Able to stand on her own two feet, he thought. Part of a different world now.

"In some ways, yes." His mother handed him a paper napkin. "That doesn't mean she doesn't need you."

"I know that."

"Do you?"

"Mom!"

"Sorry," she said. "You know I never interfere in your private life."

On screen, Erin's press conference yielded to a streaky photograph of Brandy Schorr. Heaven knew where they'd dug that up. The announcer cited the housekeeper's past attempts to overcome substance abuse and how she'd been grateful for the job offered her by Marie.

"Ms. Schorr and Lance Bolding, who are cooperating with prosecutors, provided much of the information used in this report," said Brad or Brent. "The housekeeper admits she recognized Marie Flanders right away but claims she didn't know what had happened to the real Mrs. Bolding. She contends that she quickly became terrified for her own safety."

The screen shifted to a shot of Lance in a tuxedo. "Bolding, a former video producer, says he was financially strapped when Marie came to him with a proposal. The actress, whom he'd worked with, suggested he romance her widowed sister and marry her. However, he insists he never intended to take part in a murder scheme."

"I don't buy it," Suzanne said.

"It's hard to tell." Several times when he'd believed Lance was threatening Marie, Joseph now realized, the man had probably been trying to rein her in. The D.A. would likely consider them both accessories to murder, although given her peripheral role, Brandy might be granted immunity in exchange for her testimony.

"Bolding apparently didn't suspect the depths of Marie's resentment or the extent of her greed." Over news footage of Alice and her late husband dedicating a wing of the medical center, Brad or Brent described her prominence in the community.

He reviewed what was known about Alice's drowning. Lance's alibi that he'd gone shopping had finally been verified, with two customers confirming that they'd seen him at the mall that evening. "It seems Marie arranged to see her sister, drugged her, took her out in a boat and dumped her overboard."

His mother shuddered. "How cold-blooded."

"Marie Flanders gave the performance of her life, posing as her sister," the newscaster continued. "Most people accepted that this had been a simple near drowning. The one man who refused to believe it was Detective Joseph Lowery."

"We can skip this part." He muted the volume and averted his gaze from the footage of him leaving the hospital in a wheelchair. How embarrassing to see himself portrayed as some kind of hero when he'd simply been doing the right thing.

"I like this part," his mom teased.

"I'm sure it will be repeated ad nauseum," he responded. "You can watch to your heart's content."

In the silence, they heard a car halt in the driveway. "That had better not be some reporter." Suzanne went to the window. Usually mild-mannered, she'd proved to be ferocious when it came to protecting her son. "It's Rick. Good. But I'm afraid I've got to leave for a tutoring session, if you don't mind."

"Of course not." Joseph lowered his leg and started to rise until his mother waved him back.

"I'll see you at the funeral tomorrow."

"You're taking off work?"

"The law office is closing for a half day. Mrs. Marshall was one of our biggest clients," she said. "I'll swing by and pick you up."

"Don't bother. I can handle it." Thank goodness Marie had had the consideration to shoot him in the left leg. Joseph had gone for a short drive earlier today and enjoyed the sense of freedom.

"Don't push yourself too hard."

"Spoken like a mother!"

"You bet." She opened the door, greeted Rick and let herself out.

Rick came inside. "Mmm. Popcorn." He lowered himself onto the couch. "You're living a hard life."

"I'm cooped up like a wild animal." He was only half joking.

"What're you watching?"

"What everybody else is watching, apparently."

Rick didn't object.

On TV, the narrator was speculating that Marie had persuaded Stanley Rogers to kill her niece to keep her from learning of the embezzlement or perhaps claiming she already suspected.

"Fortunately for Miss Marshall, she was an old friend of Joseph Lowery," the announcer said. "The reignited relationship between the heiress and the cop whose father had been disgraced—more on that later—probably saved her life."

Another commercial followed.

Rick dug into the popcorn. "Thank goodness they haven't found out about Tina and me. Just imagine what a fuss they'd make."

"How's that going?" Joseph asked.

"She's sick about this whole business," Rick said. "I think she's going to give me a chance. In fact, she said she hopes I'll give *her* a chance, as if I'd be stupid enough to let her go."

"How's Gene doing?"

"Recovering." Rick never wasted words on more details than necessary. "As soon as he's well enough, according to Tina, he's going to plead guilty to being an accessory to murder and testify against his father."

"Did Norris make bail?"

"On the initial charge, yes. Then ballistics matched the bullet we found in the Wilde case against the chief's gun. He's back in the slammer, stubborn as ever and blustering away."

"What about the shot that hit my car?"

"Stanley Rogers's hunting rifle."

"Marie practically enlisted an army." In retrospect, it was partly dumb luck that he and Erin had escaped death, Joseph thought. Plus the fact that Chet Dever, for all his many faults, really had cared about her.

"Too bad she didn't put her organizational talents to constructive use." Rick downed more popcorn. "Say, producing horror films."

"You call that constructive?"

"I like horror films."

They watched more of the report. It detailed the murder of Binh Nguyen, Gene's apparent role and his father's culpability in framing Lewis Lowery.

During the next break, Rick excused himself. "Some of us have to work tomorrow. Chief Hernandez has us all providing security for the funeral."

"What's it going to be like when I come back?" Joseph asked.

"In what way?"

"I brought the chief down," he said. "Heck, I violated orders from the get-go. Norris may not be the best-liked guy in the world, but cops don't appreciate a renegade."

"The truth is, you saved our butts," Rick said. "Imagine the heat we'd have taken when this case eventually broke and none of us had had a clue. You're the detective who never gave up."

"So I can expect a ticker tape parade?"

Rick clapped him on the shoulder. "You've always had a me-against-the-world attitude. It's due for a major adjustment."

"Excuse me?"

"You figure it out." Rick jostled the bowl as he rose, and only Joseph's quick grab stopped it from spilling. "Sorry."

"No harm done."

They parted amiably. On TV, the program was reviewing the short life and poor choices of Chet Dever. Thanks to a careless fingerprint left on the door frame of his house, police now suspected Stanley in his slaying.

Chet's perfect white smile flashed from a campaign commercial, no doubt paid for by Erin's trust fund. A golden boy, the narrator called him, but an amoral one.

Joseph remembered that, when he'd learned of Erin's engagement, he'd figured Chet was a good match for a woman in her position. If the man had possessed more integrity, it might have been true. He'd have known how to help her run the company, handle the press and assume her position in society.

But she didn't love Chet. And he couldn't have really loved her because he hadn't known her, not the way Joseph did. He hadn't experienced her glints of humor, her inner resolve or the way she'd tried to stick by an old friend when everyone else deserted him.

Still, nothing changed the fact that Joseph was a cop and planned to remain one. What would he do with millions of dollars and a leading position in town? The role of wealthy executive and patron might fit Erin, but never him.

The newscast showed her again, responding to a reporter's question with a quick jest that brought a round of laughter. The truth was, Joseph thought, she didn't need him anymore.

The problem was that he still needed her. And he didn't know what to do about it.

The telecast concluded with a photo of a gaunt Marie in her mother-of-the-bride dress. "Even without intervention, it's unlikely Marie Flanders would have enjoyed her wealth for long. Ironically, according to inside sources, the former actress suffered from advanced liver cancer.

"This is Brent Bartell reporting from Sundown Valley, California."

Joseph killed the picture. Beyond the circle of light cast by a lamp, evening shadows filled the house.

He'd felt at home in this place from the moment a realtor showed it to him three years ago, and yet tonight the spacious main room and wraparound vista failed to lift his spirits. The place echoed with Erin's absence.

Without her, it no longer felt like home. Besides, although a great site for Super Bowl parties, it was clearly too small for the family he hoped to have someday.

He'd outgrown his canyon hideaway. Maybe he'd outgrown a lot of things.

The phone rang. When Joseph answered, Manuel Lima identified himself. "Hope I'm not interrupting anything."

"Not at all. I'm glad to hear from you." He'd thought of the retired chief many times since their meeting. "What's up?"

"I owe you an apology," Lima said. "And it's long past due."

Joseph didn't have to ask for what. Although he held no grudges, the former chief was the one person who could have thrown a monkey wrench into Norris's scheme.

"When Edgar investigated your father, I should have followed my instincts, even though I knew he had an alibi for that night," Lima said. "If I'd pushed harder, I might have discovered he was covering for someone."

"You had no reason to second-guess him." Joseph didn't hold any grudges against Lima. "Gene was only seventeen. Nobody suspected him."

"A man's responsible for what happens on his watch," his caller said. "Even if it hadn't been Norris's son, he could have been helping a fellow officer. I should have been more suspicious. I'm sorry."

"Apology accepted," Joseph said.

"I'm going to call your mother and tell her the same thing." Lima took a deep breath. "There's one more thing. It's probably not important, but I'd like you to know."

His curiosity piqued, Joseph asked, "What's that?"

"When you applied to the force, Norris opposed my hiring you, as you've probably figured. He also implied that Andrew Marshall opposed it. I got the impression they'd had a conversation about you on the golf course."

"So I understand." By way of explanation, Joseph added, "One of the other officers overheard."

The chief clicked his tongue. "Then I wish I'd said something sooner. All this time, you've labored under the wrong impression. Andrew Marshall was an important man and he'd known you for years, so I checked it out."

"You called him?"

"I did," Lima confirmed. "He told me he considered you an honorable young man who deserved to be judged on your own merits. He had no idea why Edgar thought otherwise. In hindsight, I believe the man invented it."

Marshall had called Joseph an honorable young man. Given his well-known tendency for understatement, that had been high praise.

"Thanks for telling me," Joseph said. "It means a lot."

"I only wish I'd done it sooner."

After hanging up, Joseph sat staring into the semidarkness as bits and pieces of memory assailed him: Gene's comment, in this same room, about Joseph being popular. The way the patrol captain—now the acting chief—had spoken highly of his father. Rick telling him it was time to lose his me-against-the-world attitude. Now, the news that Andrew Marshall had spoken highly of him.

The rejections during his teen years had stung so badly, he'd built a wall between himself and anyone who might hurt him, including Erin. Joseph knew he'd been unfair to her. Maybe he'd been unfair to a lot of people.

Sometimes during an investigation, a slow accumulation of seemingly insignificant evidence would suddenly rearrange itself in his mind. Seeing a pattern take shape, he would wonder how he could have missed it all along.

He felt that way now.

Eleven years ago, he'd pushed Erin away. He didn't intend to repeat that mistake, but events were happening fast. He'd better move even faster.

Joseph thought of something he'd kept in a drawer all this time without understanding why. Abruptly it, too, made sense.

He might regret this, Joseph thought as he reached for his cane, but tomorrow he was going to take the biggest chance of his life. If he made a fool of himself, at least he'd go down trying.

Chapter Nineteen

Mourners packed the Sundown Valley Community Church to say farewell to Alice Marshall. Although she'd been wed to Lance Bolding, the minister—following Erin's suggestion—omitted his name in view of the discovery that he had entered into the marriage for fraudulent reasons.

She was certain her mother would have approved.

At the conclusion of the service, tears sprang to Erin's eyes as a soprano's voice filled the sanctuary. Flooding through the high windows, sunlight bathed the banks of flowers and the brass-appointed coffin. What a welcome change from the darkness that had swathed the lakeside home, Erin thought.

To her right sat Suzanne, with Joseph just beyond his mother. They'd decided on the discreet arrangement to stem gossip, but Erin kept wishing she could reach for the comfort of his hand. To her left, she'd placed the Van Fleets.

The previous day, a talk with the minister had helped lay to rest Erin's sense of guilt for returning to her job after her father's death. Alice Marshall had been a strong-willed woman capable of making her own decisions, he'd told her. Furthermore, no one could have foreseen that the enmity between her mother and her aunt, which had begun long before she was born, would take such a violent turn.

Each person was responsible only for doing his or her best, he'd told her. And he knew her parents, in their love, would have wanted Erin to release the past and focus on the future.

That was what she intended to do, if she could only figure out how.

The problem was, she discovered after the service, a seemingly endless number of people wanted to talk to her. Although she'd decided to skip a formal receiving line, the crowd that formed around her blocked any possibility of finding a moment alone with Joseph.

She followed his movements from the corner of her eye as she stood on the church's broad front lawn. Strikingly handsome in his dark suit, he moved with the aid of a cane, not that he could have made rapid progress through the throng in any case. Well-wishers kept approaching to shake his hand or clap him lightly on the shoulder.

She would have loved to dart away, take his arm and haul him through the churchyard until they vanished from sight. Unthinkable, of course. She hadn't needed the public relations consultant's warnings or the sight of TV cameras on the edge of the property to remind her that the world was watching.

At last the crowd began to thin. The news vans left quickly, no doubt seeking fresher sensations. Only the local reporter, Lynn Rickles, stayed behind for a few final questions.

Since Lynn, a woman in her fifties, had interviewed Alice many times over the years, Erin relaxed with her while a staff photographer clicked away.

They'd nearly finished talking when Lynn indicated the gold chain at Erin's throat. "I wondered if your pendant had some special significance."

She fished the jagged pendant from the collar of her blouse, where it had slipped out of sight. "It's something I've owned for many years."

"That's an unusual design."

Erin knew she shouldn't volunteer anything further. The

last thing a woman in her position ought to do was to announce that she loved a man who didn't belong to her.

But if she didn't take a risk, Joseph might drift away, literally and physically. Hoping he was still within earshot, she blurted, "Someone gave it to me a long time ago, someone who has the other half of my heart."

The reporter blinked in surprise. The photographer adjusted his lens for a better shot.

Movement near her elbow startled her. Joseph appeared at her side, a breeze tousling his light brown hair as he drew something glittering from his shirt.

It was her pendant's mirror image.

"Erin thinks I lost this a long time ago," he told the reporter. "But the truth is, I love her too." Instead of trying to duck the camera, he slipped his arm around Erin's waist and drew her close.

The church's old-fashioned bell began to peal, sending joyous chimes echoing from the hills.

"What's going on?" Lynn asked. Normally the bell was activated only for weddings and christenings.

A prickly sensation came over Erin, and suddenly she understood. It was Alice, ringing a bell just as she'd loved to do in life.

Wherever Alice Marshall had gone, her daughter knew now that she was happy.

JOSEPH WHISKED HER AWAY to the rose garden her father had planted at their former home. Moments earlier, he'd secured the Van Fleets' permission to visit the property.

"It's the most beautiful place I could think of for us to talk," he explained.

"And full of wonderful memories." Erin inhaled the fragrance of a Double Delight even before she spotted its cream-on-pink blossoms. It had been one of her father's favorites.

They sat on a stone bench. Set into a hillside, the garden

overlooked Sundown Valley: the white towers of the medical center, the mall, the Mercantile building, the curving tracts of homes. It formed a testament to Andrew Marshall's decades of work.

In this direction, the hill shielded them from the sight of the lake. Erin had to admit, she was glad.

Joseph's presence beside her seemed the most natural thing in the world. She longed to treasure this moment for as long as possible without worrying about where it might lead. Or not lead.

"I thought I should explain about what I said to the reporter. I hadn't exactly planned it." He spoke with gentle resonance. "I kind of seized the moment."

Her chest squeezed. Was he backing away from his impetuous statement of affection?

"We all do things without thinking sometimes." If he wanted to be let off the hook, she wasn't going to try to tie him down.

"I apologize," he said.

"There's no need…."

"It wasn't an appropriate thing to say right after your mother's funeral."

"I'm to blame for that." She strove for a casual tone. "I shouldn't have blurted out what I did about the necklace."

Joseph stared over the valley. "You know I'm committed to police work. Cops don't exactly fit in with the country club set."

"You don't have to explain." Blinking away a sheen of tears, she rested her head on his shoulder. She felt the supporting strength through his suit jacket.

Erin ached to tell him that they ought to enjoy their time together because love was too precious to waste. Nothing in the world meant more to her, or ever would, than him.

But she couldn't force him to move outside his comfort zone. She couldn't force him to love her enough to take that kind of risk.

"I hope my line of work doesn't bother you," Joseph said. "I have to go on being who I am."

"I would never ask you to change." A lump nearly blocked the words.

"Of course, that doesn't mean we have to live in my house. It really is too small." When she failed to respond, Joseph added, "I realize we'll have a lot of adjusting to do. I figure you have your career and I have mine, but what we'd bring to a marriage is equal, because money doesn't outweigh things like courage and integrity. And certainly not love."

"Marriage?" Erin scarcely believed she'd heard right.

For what felt like an eternity, he didn't respond. Then he said, "I think I skipped something."

"What would that be?" Tears threatened to flow again, but this time not from sadness.

"The proposal."

Joy welled inside her. He hadn't been backing away; he'd been working up his nerve.

"I love you," she burst out.

"I was supposed to say that first." Joseph rubbed his thumb tenderly across her cheek. "So I'll say it now. I love you, Erin. I've always loved you, even when I was too bullheaded to admit it. I'd like to do the kneeling thing, but I'm not sure I could get up again even with the cane."

"That's all right." Remembering that they were sitting in full view of the town, she added, "And don't forget, someone might have a telephoto trained on us."

"There's a daunting thought."

"We don't want to leave a newspaper picture to embarrass our children," she teased.

"Before we have children, I really think we ought to walk down the aisle. Wait, let me do this right." All sign of teasing vanished as he took her hands in his. "Erin Marshall, will you marry me?"

She could hardly breathe. "Absolutely."

In the afternoon sunshine, Joseph's deep blue eyes sparkled at her. "You know, I think we should pose for that photograph after all."

"Is someone…" She was starting to look around when he cupped her chin in his palm and brushed a kiss across her lips.

Suddenly Erin didn't care if the whole world took their picture. Flinging her arms around Joseph, she made him kiss her again. This time, it lasted for a wonderful long while.

As they leaned forward, she felt something tickling her throat and realized it had to be the pendant. No, she thought, both of the half hearts were dangling together, making a complete whole.

In that moment, she knew the scars of the past were finally healing. She and Joseph had come home at last, to each other.

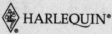

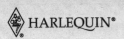

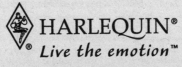

If you enjoyed what you just read,
then we've got an offer you can't resist!

Take 2 bestselling
love stories FREE!

Plus get a FREE surprise gift!